THE CHILDREN OF ZAGREB

LELITA BALDOCK

Storm
PUBLISHING

To request permissions, contact the publisher at rights@stormpublishing.co

Ebook ISBN: 978-1-80508-839-4
Paperback ISBN: 978-1-80508-841-7

Cover design: Eileen Carey
Cover images: Shutterstock, iStock, Trevillion

Published by Storm Publishing.
For further information, visit:
www.stormpublishing.co

ALSO BY LELITA BALDOCK

The Baker's Secret

The Girl Who Crossed Mountains

The Keeper of Lost Art

AUTHOR'S NOTE

The history of Yugoslavia and the Balkan States is rich, complex and often painful. Ethnic and religious tensions within Croatia between Croats and Serbs form the complex background to the events contained herein. The nuances of these conflicts go far beyond the scope of a Historical Fiction novel.

In this novel, I have not sought to side with one side or the other.

War crimes were committed on both sides of the conflict during World War Two and the Croatian War of Independence in the 1990s.

My aim in this novel is to share the experiences of everyday people living their lives through a tumultuous period of history that was full of fear and trauma. And to honour the bravery of Diana Budisavljević and the Red Cross nurses who stood up against the brutality of the Ustaše to save the lives of innocent children.

PART ONE

PROLOGUE

Croatia, Yugoslavia 1945

"Mama!" the girl cries. She sits up straight in her small bed, one hand gripping her blankets, the other pressed against the rough stone wall of her bedroom. Sweat laces her brow, and spots across her chest. Her breathing labours as she stares wide-eyed into the gloom of the pre-dawn light. Footsteps sound on the landing outside her room, light but swift. The door creaks open, the golden light of a lamp floods in, pressing back the darkness. Her tata comes first, eyes fierce in the glowing candlelight, mouth set in a grim line. He stands poised, as if ready to fight or run. Then releases a long, slow breath. Pity washes over his features, replacing the alert tension with sadness, and he steps aside, allowing her mama to enter. As she passes her tata, their eyes meet briefly, before the girl's mama hurries across the floor, her bare feet slapping on the cold wooden planks.

"Shh, there, there, my dear one," she croons, settling herself on the bedside and pulling the girl into her lap. "You are safe." She holds the girl tightly, smoothing her hair from her face with a gentle palm, her skin soft and warm. The girl buries her head into her mama's neck and gives into the sobs of terror that have awakened within her.

"Shhh," her mama whispers.

"I'll warm some milk," her tata says, placing the lamp on the bedside table before slipping from her room. The girl locks her hands around her mama, gripping her wildly.

Her mama rocks her, gently, gently, a soft song of comfort humming from her throat. Slowly, the girl's pounding heart begins to slow; her muscles loosen, and her trembling goes still. Gently, her mama draws her back and looks into her face.

"It was the dream again?" she asks. The girl nods, though she doesn't need to. Her mama knows about the dream. The warm, sunny afternoon, the smell of walnut bread, the taste of fear.

"Did anything new happen?"

The girl shakes her head. The dream never changes.

She is skipping through rows of grape vines, the purple fruit, juice-fat and glistening in the sunshine. A woman's voice calls from beyond the rows of grapes. The girl can hear it, but she cannot make out the words. Somehow, she knows it calls for her. She turns, her cheeks flushed red with exertion, her eyes shining with joy. A giggle rides her breath as she skips towards the voice, knees high, steps confident.

A woman comes into view. She is shorter than most, with wide hips and strong arms. Her brown hair is fixed beneath a shawl patterned in pale pink. Her nose is sharp but her smile is warm. The girl knows her and doesn't know her. But she is not afraid.

She opens her arms to the girl who springs up high, sure in the knowledge that she will be caught. The woman's arms come around her, gathering her to her chest. The girl wraps pudgy hands around her neck and snuggles close. She breathes deeply, lungs working from her run. The scent of freshly baked walnut bread is laced through the cotton of the woman's dress. The taste of grape on her tongue, the scent of bread in her nose, the warmth of love on her skin, the girl smiles.

She always wakes when the truck engine sounds. The woman

turns, sharply, clutching the girl tightly. A loud boom blasts through the sky. The woman screams, falling to her knees, the girl still pressed to her chest. As the girl falls the sky bleeds colour, greys, smokes then, just before the ground rushes up to meet her, black...

She doesn't know what comes next. She never sees anything to be afraid of. But every time the dream comes, she wakes in a pall of terror, her mind skittering away in red panic. There is something more, beyond the dream. The girl knows it, she can feel it, cold like snow reaching for her across the frozen earth. It is waiting. It can be patient. An involuntary shiver runs up her spine. Her mama's eyebrows knit. Her mouth opens in question and then her tata appears, a steaming cup of milk in his hand.

"Here," he says softly as he passes the cup to the girl. "Drink up, it will help you to rest."

She takes the cup and sips, as she does every night when the dream comes.

"Lay back," her mama says, taking the cup and settling it on the bedside table.

The girl obeys, sliding back down into her sheets. Her tata takes a seat by the window, pulling back the curtain and glancing outside absent-mindedly. Her mama stretches out beside her on the bed, wrapping her in an embrace. The warmth of her mama's body seeps through the cool cotton of her nightdress. Stomach full of milk, her eyelids grow heavy. Soon she cannot fight the need for sleep that tugs against her fear, and she drifts off to sleep.

The girl wakes to the pale light of early dawn, alone but warm within her blanket cocoon. Blinking herself awake she lays still and silent in the cool of morning. The shadow of fear from her dream that night has dissipated; only a faint echo of panic remains, tracing her nerves. Breathing deeply and rubbing the sleep from her eyes she rolls her legs over the bed's edge and pads to the window. Outside is dusted in snow. A light covering must have fallen overnight, the first of the season to stick to the browning grasses of her tata's farm.

No vineyards here.

Taking up the jug of water at her dressing table she pours a measure into a ceramic bowl and splashes her face clean. Dressing quickly, she makes her way out into the farmhouse, along the landing and down the stairs towards the kitchen. Warm light floods from the kitchen door and the soft sounds of her mama already up and preparing breakfast echo from within. The scent of fruit bread, not walnut, emanates from the oven. The low rumble of her tata's voice reaches her ears and the girl pauses. That is unusual; normally, Tata is already in the fields before the girl is up. Subconsciously, she slows her pace; her ears pricked, listening as she approaches the open kitchen door and, obscured by the fall of light, peers within.

Her mama stands by the stove stirring a pot of bubbling porridge. Her tata is sitting at the table, twirling something between his fingers. A glint of silver catches the light.

"It is time to tell her," her tata says. "The dreams are getting worse. Her memory is trying to return."

"But she doesn't remember," her mama says, her voice tight and anxious. "Why bring that horror back into her life?"

"Because then she can heal from it."

"We agreed we would shield her from the truth. She doesn't need to remember that place."

"But she does. On some level, deep in her mind, she already remembers. It will be better if we help her through it. So she doesn't have to face it alone."

"Face what?" she says, stepping into the room.

Both her parents look up at once. Shock lights in her mama's soft hazel eyes, but her tata merely smiles, his shoulders relaxing.

"How long were you listening, dear one?" he asks, but the words are not angry.

"Only a little. I didn't mean to, I was coming for breakfast."

"Hush, it is all right. We were talking about you after all."

"My love," her mama says, her voice pleading. But her tata doesn't turn away from the girl. "Come," he gestures, patting his knee. The girl crosses the room and climbs up into his lap. She is almost too big for this, almost. Her tata tucks her against his side. She leans into his strength and feels the calm rise and fall of his chest as he takes a deep steadying breath.

"Do you recognise this?" her tata asks, as he opens his palm out flat before her.

The girl looks down at his hand. There resting in the centre of his grasp is a small square token. Silver. She narrows her eyes as she stares at the object. Etched in the centre of the top surface are four numbers: 1834. The girl mouths the numbers, her small fingers reaching out to touch the metal. It feels cold. Across the room, her mama releases a heavy breath. The girl looks up. Shaking her head she says, "No, I don't recognise it. Should I?"

"No, sweetling," her tata says. Her mama gives her a wobbly smile. "It is natural that you don't remember, you were so very little when you wore this."

"Wore it? Is it mine?" The girl looks again at the token.

"In a manner of speaking," her tata says, voice suddenly husky, deeper. The girl looks up at him. Tears sparkle in his lashes. "Tata, what is wrong? What did I say?" the girl says, placing a hand on his cheek, the rough stubble scratchy against her palm.

He swallows audibly. "No, dear one," he whispers. "You didn't say anything. It is just a difficult story to explain."

The girl twitches nervously, her eyes seeking her mama, looking for comfort, for stability in the face of her tata's tears. But Mama's cheeks are also glistening. Suddenly, her mama strides across the room and bends over, wrapping both the girl and her tata in a firm embrace. Pulling back, she kneels before the girl, and wipes away the water that has gathered in her eyes. "We are going to explain everything to you, dear one," she says. "So that you understand. It is not an easy story. But you must remember. You are safe. Now, you are safe and, dearest," she grips the girl's hand tightly and presses it to her chest above her heart, "I swear to you, you will never be in danger again. Never."

The girl stares at her mama as a slow and terrifying realisation begins to descend over her. Her tata's overheard words, her night-mares. She gulps. Looking down she whispers, "It isn't just a dream, is it?"

"No," her mama says, voice shaking with emotion. "It is your beginning."

ONE
NADICA

Novska 1991

The wheel of Nadica's bike bounces over a stone, but her balance is steady as she makes her way along the edge of Novska. Small white-walled houses line the roadside, green lawns stretching between them. She sees a man and woman loading a car with suitcases and cooking utensils, their children standing in the doorway, eyes wide, hands clutched together. Another family is leaving for the border. Her next-door neighbours went the week before. Nadica doesn't know how many will stay. The Serb population of Croatia is scared. A vote to separate from Yugoslavia and be an Independent Croatia passed in May, igniting a wave of barely suppressed ethnic and religious tensions.

A temporary pause to negotiate terms has been put in place, but it is an uneasy truce. Skirmishes have broken out across Croatia, and the Yugoslav Army has reached the border with Serbia. Her country is at war, Nadica knows, but her mind skids away from that truth. The fighting has been to the east. It seems distant from her central village, even though the divisions reach right into her home. Her baba is a Croat, her deda is a Serb.

Relja thinks the Serbs are right to fight. Nadica is afraid.

Shaking her head, she banishes his haunting stare from her mind. Passing the last post box of her village, the long track to her grandparents' small farm opens before her, dotted with the occasional home. Around her, the beech trees rise from the earth, their branches, covered in the turning colours of autumn, swaying in the gentle breeze. Briefly, Nadica closes her eyes, lifting her face to the sun. It is soft and warm on her skin. Opening her eyes, her grandparent's drive splits the treelined road. She turns in.

At the end of the dirt track sits a small wooden cottage, a curl of smoke rising from the chimney. Deda must be keeping the fire stoked, despite the mild day. It makes sense. He's always looked after those he loves, passionately. As she approaches the house she spies the man himself. Tall and broad, he swings his axe one-handed, splitting the wood in a clean strike. Nadica jumps from her bike, dropping it onto the soft grass. Pulling a hair tie from her jeans she secures her long dark hair in a ponytail and heads towards him.

He looks up, his face brightening into a wide grin as he raises the axe in a wave. As Nadica advances, he turns to the small shed adjacent to the house and secures the axe. Nadica bends to gather up the split wood. Shutting the shed door, her deda comes to her and wraps his good arm around her shoulders, tugging her into a hug. His limp arm remains at his side. An old injury from the war, Nadica knows. Somehow, he is still stronger than most men. One-handed and at over seventy years old, his height and bulk make Nadica feel even smaller. She was always short. Together, they make their way into the cottage.

The central room is bracketed by a kitchen and two rooms; upstairs are three bedrooms. Her baba is by the oven. Hands covered by bright yellow mittens, she lifts a tray of krofna donuts from the oven. The scent of baked dough fills the air, and Nadica smiles. Baba always makes her favourites. She breaks away from her deda and walks to the fireplace, adding the freshly cut wood to the basket beside it, ready for use. The basket is already full. Her lips twist in amusement. Her deda is always over-prepared. You have to be in rural Croatia.

Wood deposited she heads to the kitchen. "How is she today?" she asks her baba as she sneaks a steaming krofna from the tray.

"Let it cool, Nadica!" her baba chastises, shaking her head. A wisp of grey has escaped her firm bun, but there is a light in her eyes.

Nadica blows on the krofna and then sinks her teeth in. Hot and sweet and buttery, plum jam oozes from the inside and melts on her tongue.

"She is sleeping," her baba answers Nadica's question. "But it's fitful. It will do her good to see you."

Nodding, Nadica hugs her baba, rubbing her back in reassurance. She feels the tightness in her baba's muscles, the tension, the worry.

Misa is dying.

There is no denying it any more. The cancer has come back to finish the job. All they can do is keep her comfortable and make sure she is not alone.

It is different from her tata's death five years before. That was sudden and a shock. The heart within his powerful body just stopped. With Misa it is slow. Nadica and her mama take it in turns to visit and help. Today is Nadica's day. They would come together, but one of them needs to open the small corner store they run in town. They still need to eat, even if a family member is dying.

They aren't truly related, Nadica and Misa, but Nadica loves her just the same. The old woman is like a second baba to her. Family comes in many guises, and Nadica has never known life without Misa in it. It is hard to watch her strength fade.

It is worse for her baba. Misa is her oldest friend.

Releasing her baba she glances toward the room that is set off from the kitchen. Misa's room. "I will go say hello."

The air in the room is warm but stale and there is the scent of sour breath in the air. Wrinkling her nose, Nadica goes to the window, cracking it open a little to allow some fresh air to circulate from the forests beyond. Misa lays on the bed; a thick patchwork quilt engulfs her tiny frame. Her eyes are closed, her breathing laboured. Nadica looks her over. She's barely there. Once Misa's energy could fill a market square. Now...

Nadica firms her emotions. Her family held her through the loss of her tata, Davor. This time she will be strong for everyone. Especially her baba.

She moves to the chair by the bed. The book is there. Nadica picks it up and settles in the chair, flicking through the pages to the bookmark. It has moved since yesterday. Misa must have had a tough night. Baba doesn't like to read, but she will if Misa needs her. Nadica leans back in the chair and the wood creaks. Misa stirs, her eyes fluttering open as her head slowly turns. Dark eyes blink and focus; deep bruises rest along the sockets, blue and purple with sickness. Pity floods Nadica's chest, but she forces it down. Misa doesn't need her pity. She needs her strength.

"Hi, Aunty Misa," she says, leaning forward to smooth the hair from Misa's head. She is hot to the touch and sweaty. "Do you want some water?"

Nadica takes up the pitcher that rests on the bedside and pours a glass, holding it to Misa's lips. The old woman drinks, her lips flaky and dry. Nadica replaces the glass on the table and picks up the small pot of lip balm. Dabbing a small amount on her finger she smooths it gently over Misa's raw lips.

"There, all better."

"Thank you," Misa croaks, her voice thick and tight.

"Shall I read to you?" Nadica asks.

Misa's head snaps to her, eyes suddenly wild. "You found her?" she says.

Nadica frowns. "Found who? Aunty Misa?"

But Misa isn't listening. Movements jerky and stiff she is

pressing her hands into the soft mattress, trying to sit up. But the quilt is too tightly tucked around her and her body too frail.

She releases a cry of frustration, edged with fear.

"Aunty, calm," Nadica says, standing quickly. "Let me help you."

"Where is she? Where is she?" Misa is saying, the pitch of her voice rising and rising. "You promised you would find her. I never should have stayed. I never should have listened to you!"

Nadica's baba and deda appear in the doorway, twin expressions of sorrow on their faces. No, not sorrow, guilt. Nadica frowns deeply as her baba comes to the bedside and sits down beside Misa's thrashing body. Her hands grip Misa's with an unexpected firmness and press them to her heart. "Misa, you are safe. You are home. Misa. I am here. Ilona is here. Jovan is here. And Nadica. You are safe. You are home."

Misa's glazed gaze swings between Nadica and her baba, and her breathing begins to slow. Then her eyes clear, sharpening back into the piercing stare Nadica knows as her Aunty Misa, and her head snaps to Nadica. "Why are you still here? You have to go!"

The words are as sharp as a slap and Nadica recoils on instinct, her stomach dropping in shock.

"Misa," her baba soothes. "You are safe."

Nadica cannot believe how calm her baba is. She is taking it in her stride like this isn't the first time she's seen Misa react this way.

Nadica feels a touch on her shoulder and looks up. Her deda nods his head towards the door, Nadica rises and follows, leaving her baba and Misa alone.

In the kitchen, she turns to him, questions on her lips, but her deda heads outside; soon, she hears the rhythmic chopping of wood echo from the side hut. Clearly, he doesn't want to talk about it. But Nadica is confused and worried. She's never seen Misa so agitated, so frantic. She'd looked at Nadica with eyes full of hate. *I should never have listened to you!*

Feeling shaky and unsettled, she busies herself in the kitchen, filling the sink and washing the dishes made dirty when her baba baked krofna for her. Best to keep busy.

Who did she think Nadica was? And telling her to go? What had she meant? Why would Misa want her to leave? Setting her discomfort aside, Nadica takes up a tea towel and starts to dry. Movement catches the corner of her eye, and she turns to watch her baba slip from Misa's room, shutting the door with a soft click.

Their eyes meet across the space of the kitchen. Tears wet the creases of her baba's cheeks.

"Thank you for tidying up."

Nadica's mouth opens and closes. She doesn't know what to say. She's too bewildered.

"Do you want to talk about it?" her baba asks. "I imagine you have questions."

Nadica puts down the cup measure she's been drying and nods. "If you are okay to talk?"

Her baba sighs heavily as she turns to look out the window, her gaze resting on her husband as he stacks more wood outside. Her lips twist in irritation, but the grimace is gone almost as soon as it appears. "I am not," she says. "But it is time. Come."

She leads Nadica into the lounge and they settle on the sofa by the open fire. Her baba takes hold of Nadica's hands, her skin soft and loose.

"She was angry at me," Nadica says, the shock, still too fresh to contain, welling up within her and threatening to make her cry.

"No, darling, not at you."

Nadica searches her baba's face and sees the tension that lines her brow. "Then at who?"

Her baba's shoulders droop, her eyes staring at the fire, unfocused, unseeing, as if she has disconnected and drifted far away.

"At me."

Nadica blinks in surprise. "At you? No, Baba, surely not. You two have been best friends forever."

"Since we were your age. Twenty-one going on forty, with no idea of the real world." Her baba smiles sadly. "Since Zagreb."

"Zagreb? What happened in Zagreb?"

"We studied to be nurses. And Misa introduced me to your deda."

"You were a nurse?"

"Da. Before the war. A lot changed after that."

"Tell me."

Her sad old eyes meet Nadica's. "Da," she says. "It is overdue."

TWO

ILONA

Zagreb 1939

"The dressing is loose," head nurse Dragica Habazin said. "Yes it is important to allow for blood flow, but you also must compress the wound to aid the stitches. And the bed is poorly done. Again."

"Yes, Matron," Ilona said, bobbing her head in deference.

Around her, the shuffling sounds of the Sisters of Charity Hospital echoed along the pristine white halls. It was her second week on hospital rotation. As one of only six lay women chosen from the nursing school at The Hospital for Infectious Diseases, Ilona had felt pride beyond her wildest imagination. To go to the Charity Hospital and train to work with the real doctors, rather than just administering typhoid vaccines and patching up scraped knees at a gymnasium: it was what she had longed for from the moment she was accepted into nursing school.

There was still a long way to go. Most nurses in Croatia were nuns, and jobs for secular women were few and competition intense. Ilona had to do well.

So far things had not gone to plan. The Matron Habazin was exacting and blunt, and held no qualms about correcting mistakes publicly.

Ilona swallowed, eyes flitting side to side, noting the small smile of satisfaction on her fellow student and childhood friend Radmila's face, the nervous twitch of Petra beside her, a wall of training nuns behind them.

Dragica squinted at her for a moment, her stern wide face pinching as she assessed her student. Ilona kept her expression perfectly plain with no trace of the frustration she felt inside at being corrected in front of the whole group.

Finally, Dragica nodded. "Shadow Misa for the rest of the rounds. Dismissed."

Ilona turned to Misa, the short, dark-haired girl from the country who was Dragica's leading pupil.

Misa smiled, though her eyes remained tight, and turned. Ilona followed.

"Serb," Radmila whispered derisively beneath her breath as they passed her. The young nun at her side gasped in shock.

Misa didn't even flinch, her face remaining impassive as she gilded past Radmila, Ilona behind her.

"Something to say, Radmila?" Dragica asked sharply.

"No, Matron," Radmila said.

"I thought not. On with your rounds, girls. We've many patients to attend and never enough hours."

"Da, Matron, yes," the gathered students chorused and dispersed through the ward.

Ilona continued down the corridor with Misa. When they turned the far corner heading for the adjacent ward, she stepped up beside the young woman.

"I am sorry," she said softly. "Radmila, she doesn't mean it. She's just... competitive."

She had known Radmila since they were small. They'd attended the same gymnasium on the outskirts of the city, and their tatas worked in the same factory, processing steel. She felt responsible for her friend's unnecessary rudeness.

"No," Misa said simply. "She means it."

Ilona glanced at her fellow student and saw the red that had crept up Misa's neck, spotting her cheeks and burning her ears. She didn't press. What did she know about it really, anyway? She knew how it felt to be looked down on. Had seen the way the wealthy men of the city sniffed when her tata passed. She hated it. It fuelled her drive to make something more of herself. To be a nurse, to work in the hospital. But to be judged for how you worshipped God, like Misa was? How could you overcome that?

They spent the rest of the afternoon doing their rounds, checking on their allotted patients, supervised by the nuns who had completed their training. The patients were mostly older men and women suffering from various conditions ranging from broken bones to breathing difficulties. As Ilona watched Misa moving through the wards, her small frame graceful yet unbending beneath the pale-blue nursing uniform, her respect only grew. Misa was good at this. Really good. The only way to know she was training and not yet an employed nurse was the small pin on her white apron. Beside her, Ilona felt clumsy and unsure, like her long limbs were disconnected and uncoordinated. But she would not let that stop her. Matron Habazin had given her this chance to learn from their leading pupil. Ilona was going to take it.

At the end of their shift, the two women walked out onto the streets of Zagreb together. The night was cold and still, the buildings of Zagreb upper town rising towards the star-littered sky. It was silent and calm, the people of the city having already retreated to the surrounding lower town suburbs where their homes sat, separate and still. Ilona pulled her coat tight around her neck against the bitter wind that whipped along from the city centre, channelled by the tall buildings that made up the old town. Her light-brown hair caught the light of the street lamp, glowing with a warmth she did not feel.

"You will get there," Misa said. They were the first words she had spoken to Ilona since they started their afternoon rounds together.

Ilona eyed her and shrugged deeper into her coat. "I don't know. Watching you... you are just so natural with everyone. The patients light up when they see you. When I take over, they frown."

Misa's laugh shocked Ilona. She'd never heard the woman laugh. "They don't," she said, voice still light from mirth. "You imagine it because you are nervous. But you have skill. Matron Habazin sees your potential. It's why she is so hard on you."

Subconsciously, Ilona shuffled her feet. "Do you think so? Truly?"

Misa faced her, looking directly at her in the deepening dusk. "I am good because this is not new to me," she began. "My mama nursed at the local primary school and gymnasium in Petrinja. Before the laws were changed, I helped."

Ilona cocked her head in thought. "You have already done nursing work?"

Misa shrugged. "I was about thirteen years old, but da. No one needed official qualifications then, so I just learnt from my mama. When that changed, I returned to school, like everyone else. But Mama kept up my training at home. I have a head start on you."

Misa smiled; it seemed more genuine somehow than before.

Pursing her lips in determination, Ilona nodded firmly. "I can do it."

"Da."

"Will you help me? Teach me?"

"Da. Shadow me again tomorrow; we can do our rounds together. You will see. You will make a wonderful nurse."

Joy, unexpected and bright, flowed through Ilona. "Thank you," she said.

"It is what friends do," Misa said.

Ilona lifted her chin slightly, a sense of realisation washing over her. They'd been studying alongside each other for months, sharing the same government-supplied accommodation on the edge of the upper town. Yet Ilona had never considered their connection. "Friends. Da, friends help each other."

Misa's eyes shone and Ilona laughed. Curling her arm through Misa's, bent slightly to accommodate their height difference, she turned them towards the streets of the city, heading for the nursing boarding house where they stayed.

Friends, she thought to herself. *I guess we are.*

Ilona continued to shadow Misa again the next day and then the next. The two found themselves sharing their break time in the nurses' lounge, a pair of women in nursing blue in a sea of black nun's habits and sleeves. Misa would continue her instruction on the tasks they were learning. Ilona felt her confidence slowly begin to grow. Soon enough their conversations began to expand outside of the hospital and into their personal lives.

"My town, Petrinja, is south of here. My fiancé, Radič, works in the steel factory. It is good work," Misa shared over a warming cup of coffee.

Ilona felt herself sigh. "It must be hard to be so far away from him."

"It is hard. In truth, he didn't want me to go. But we agreed that this was important. My town needs an experienced nurse. And it was always my dream to come to the city." Her gaze turned inward, her lips firming in determination. It mattered to her, Ilona saw. Misa wanted this just as much as she did, perhaps even more.

"My family live on the outskirts of Zagreb," Ilona said. "We were originally farmers in Novska, but tata wanted more for me and my brother Ivica, so he moved us to the city, supported me to study so I can support myself, at least until I am wed. You did it all by yourself." Ilona was impressed. How could she not be?

Misa shrugged. "Radič has always supported me. I am lucky."

The door to the break room banged open and Radmila waltzed in, Petra and the others in her wake. It was astonishing how Radmila had gathered the other students to her. Ilona suppressed a sigh. She really wasn't in the mood for Radmila's attitude at that moment. But Radmila had other ideas.

"Ilona," the angular woman called, crossing the room. "I have great news for your brother."

Ilona looked up at her and waited. "David has secured him work at the timber factory on the eastern side of the city."

Her frustration with Radmila washed away. "Oh, that's wonderful!" Ilona stood and hugged her friend in thanks. She might be rude and difficult, but they were still friends. When her brother Ivica lost his job at the steelworks, Radmila had promised to speak with her fiancé David who was a foreman at the timber factory. It had turned out well.

"I am home next weekend to visit," Ilona continued. "I will return with my family's thanks for all you and David have done for Ivica."

"Nonsense," Radmila chided. "It's what we do. Croats stick together." Her sharp eyes flicked at Misa and Ilona sighed, the swell of goodwill for her childhood friend receding.

Misa stood. Gathering her cup and notes she moved to the sink, deposited her cup and left the room.

"You really don't need to be like that," Ilona said to Radmila. "She is helping me."

"You don't need her help," Radmila said, her eyes still boring into the doorway Misa had passed through. "You have me."

"Hmmm," Ilona grunted. She was ready to retort, to defend Misa, but Radmila cut her off. "So, next weekend, shall we travel out to Dubrava together? It has been too long since I saw my parents too."

"Da," Ilona said, letting it go. She could be friends with both women.

THREE
ILONA

A month later Ilona sat in her parents' home. Her mama, Ivana, placed a steaming plate of Pašticada beef stew before her and Ilona breathed deeply. Her body ached from the balls of her feet seemingly to the ends of her hair. The long days at the hospital under the scrutinising eye of Dragica Habazin and the study each evening were taking their toll. Closing her eyes, Ilona took a moment to thank God for her good fortune to be able to visit her parents and brother Ivica on weekends. It was a time-consuming journey to visit as they lived on the opposite side of Zagreb on the edge of the city, so she only made the trip sporadically, but at least it was doable. Unlike poor Misa, whose fiancé and family lived miles away in the countryside.

"So what have the weeks brought since we last saw you?" her tata Bojan asked, his bushy grey-peppered eyebrows lowering and obscuring his eyes as he blew across his stew.

Ilona fiddled with her spoon, gaze flitting between her tata and her brother, unsure of how much to share. But her pause gave her away. Her mama said, "It can't have been that bad." Ilona looked up at her mama and tried to smile.

The burst of confidence she felt every time Misa praised her potential always faded almost as quickly as it had come. That evening, when Ilona had left their shared accommodation to take the bus across town to her childhood home, nothing but self-doubt had clouded her mind. The bus bounced to the thoughts in a beat: Did Misa mean what she had said? Did Matron see something in Ilona? Or was Misa just being nice? The other students weren't nice... She'd been glad to travel alone for this visit, Radmila's nattering last time had set her nerves firmly on edge.

"Ilona?" Her mama prompted, her neatly set curls bobbing as she shook her head at her daughter.

Ilona forced herself to smile. "It has been fine, Tata, Mama." She nodded to both parents. "Matron wants me to work on my wrapping. But Misa says that I am coming along well."

"Misa?" her tata enquired. "Is she one of the nurse nuns?"

"No, Misa is a fellow student and a good friend. We are in opposite rooms in the accommodation block. We often study together."

"I hope that helps you, not just her," her mama said firmly, her full mouth pursing in derision.

"It helps me more, I think," Ilona answered, honestly. "She is very good. And she already worked as a nurse when she was younger. In Petrinja."

From the opposite side of the table, her brother Ivica gave a loud snort. "Serb," he grumbled, then pushed his chair back from the table, the wooden legs scraping over the floor in a harsh shriek. Ilona looked up at him in shock. His dusty brown hair fell across his pale eyes as he hunched over himself. Two years her junior, Ilona had grown up in a household that expected her to care for her little brother. She knew him well. The twitch below his eye, the shift of his feet to the left, the puckering of his thin lips. He was uncomfortable. He'd reacted to her words, but part of him now regretted it. She swallowed the lump in her throat as her focus swung to their tata.

"Where do you think you are going?" Bojan asked, voice deceptively calm.

"I am tired. I do honest work," he answered, voice pitched at Ilona.

Ilona bristled. "As do I. I work with the sick, Ivica!"

Her brother shrugged his wide shoulders, his eyes darting side to side. "With a Serb."

"Misa is just another student, I don't know why—"

"Petrinja is a Serb town. Everyone knows it. You know it."

"Misa is my friend," she said, the words out before she considered them.

Ivica picked at something in his teeth and then glared down at her. "Then I am leaving the table because I will not eat with fools." He collected his bowl and turned for the sink.

"Ivica!" Ivana exclaimed.

"Enough!" Bojan's loud voice silenced the table. "Ivica, sit. Your mama has made you dinner. You will have the respect to eat it."

"And what of her respect?" Ivica flung a finger out, pointing directly at Ilona. "She speaks of a Serb as a friend. When we know, better than most, how corrupt they are."

Ilona stared at her brother in shock. "Ivica, what are you talking about?"

Her mama sighed heavily. "Ivica was not promoted at the timber factory."

"No," Ivica took up the tale. "Bogdan was. Because the boss is a Serb."

Ilona could not keep the tone from her voice. "Ivica, you only recently started at the factory. Why would you get the promotion over another worker who has been there longer?"

"David didn't get it either," Ivica spat. "And he has been there for years."

"And he got you a job. Because you are a Croat and *my* brother. Don't forget that Radmila vouched for you. So what is the difference?"

Ivica's scrutiny landed on her, full of malice. "We are Croats. That is the difference."

"Misa is from Petrinja, which is in the State of Croatia. Not Serbia," Ilona tried.

Ivica rolled his eyes. "And that makes a difference?"

"I said enough." Bojan had risen. Large hands placed palm down on the tabletop, her tata leaned menacingly across the table. "You two bicker like children," he said, voice low and gruff, eyes piercing his son's gaze. "Are you so eager to make this mistake?"

Ivica glared at Bojan, father and son locked eye to eye, silent anger prickling through the air between them.

"We live in a tense time. The balance within Yugoslavia is being tested."

"This is Croatia," Ivica threw at their tata. "Not Serbia."

"We are not in Belgrade. We are here in Zagreb," Bojan said.

"I will eat later," Ivica said, stepping away.

"You will not leave this table," Bojan said.

Ivica paused, hovering between choices, then slowly lowered himself into his chair.

"Now, we can eat in peace."

Silently the family ate their stew. As the now-cold liquid trickled down Ilona's throat, her mind pitched and bounced in confusion.

After the last sip of his stew was finished, Ivica excused himself to his room, her tata following suit and retreating to the couch, leaving Ilona and her mama to wash up.

"Mama," she said, unsure of how to begin. "What has gotten into Ivica?"

Hands scrubbing at a piece of onion on the edge of a bowl her mama sighed. "It is the times," she answered. "It is tough, you know this."

"Da. But Ivica has work. We are doing all right?"

Her mama gave a heavy sigh. "Don't let on that you know," she said. "But your tata was let go at the plant last week."

The air whooshed from Ilona's lungs in shock. She chanced a glance at her tata sitting in the next room listening to his radio.

"Why?"

Ivana shrugged. "Money. He was not the only worker they fired."

"So Ivica is worried..."

"He is our income now."

"Let me help," Ilona said. She had so little time around her training, but she could get work on the side. She would do whatever was needed for her family.

Ivana reached over and patted her arm, leaving a patch of water on her blouse. "Let it go," she said softly. "Your tata will find work again. And Ivica will settle. He is just a young man, pushing into adulthood. He is a good boy at heart."

Ilona's forehead tightened. "But mama—"

"Enough now," she interrupted. "We will be all right. We always get by."

As Ilona wished her tata goodbye, she watched the emotions playing over his face and saw the glimmer of shame she'd overlooked earlier. She longed to pull her tata into her arms and comfort him, but knew his pride would not allow it.

Walking through the darkened streets of the suburb to her bus, Ilona contemplated her brother's words. She knew there were problems with the structure of their society; everyone in Zagreb knew that. It was in the poverty on the streets, the gaunt faces of farmers on the land, the rich suits of the visiting politicians from Belgrade.

Power was too centralised, Ilona believed that.

But it wasn't the fault of everyday people like Misa.

Ivica was just angry and trying to find fairness.

It was a worthy fight. One she supported.

But not so far as to turn her back on Misa. The woman had been kind to her. More, Ilona needed her help. There was no threat from a woman from Petrinja. Ivica would come to see that when his passions cooled.

Until then Ilona would be careful not to mention Misa in front of him again.

FOUR

ILONA

"No, it's a moisture wrap, soaked to be wet," Misa was saying.

Ilona kept pace beside her, head bent down to bring her ear closer to her friend's instruction. Around them the seasons were changing, marking the passage of time. The trees were full of blossom, the gentle white and pink petals turned up to the warming spring sun.

"You are thinking of a wound wrap."

Ilona felt the irritation buzzing through her. How could she still not understand the basic differences between medical wrapping and when to apply what?

Controlling her frustration, she pressed her eyes closed and breathed in through her nose.

"All right, I think I might need to revisit those details. What about salves..."

She caught the small glance that Misa gave her, the furtive flick of her eyes. The frustration flared again, but she pushed it down. Misa was only trying to help, she knew.

And Ilona appreciated every bit of help Misa offered her in her studies. Yet the difference in their skill and knowledge grated. No matter how Ilona tried, Misa continued to broaden the gap between them.

She shook her head, a slight movement, and forced her mind to engage. Thoughts like that weren't useful. She had worked too hard to get into the nursing course at the Sisters of Charity Hospital. She wasn't going to stop now.

"So, if the wound is weeping–"

"Oh my God," Misa exclaimed, cutting Ilona off.

Ilona frowned, turning to her friend. But Misa wasn't paying attention to her. Suddenly, Misa pressed the textbook she had been using to quiz Ilona into Ilona's arms. Ilona barely had time to take the heavy book before Misa was racing along the street, heels clacking loudly on the cobbles.

Completely bemused, Ilona watched her run, her light spring coat flaring out behind her.

As her friend ran, the focus of her excitement registered with Ilona. Down the street stood a young man. He was dressed in a dark suit, his light-brown hair pressed to his head with grease. Hearing Misa's call, he looked up, his face brightening, lips spreading into an impossibly broad grin. He turned towards her, arms coming out wide at his sides, opening himself up fully. Misa did not slow her step, careering into him, her own arms wrapped around him tight. A small laugh of delight escaped his lips, carried on the gentle breeze to Ilona's ears. A beautiful, joyful sound.

She continued down the street towards them. Two people entwined in the tightest embrace of love. A ball of emotion formed in her gut. To feel such love...

As she approached, the young man looked up at her, an open smile forming on his lips. Loosening his grip on Misa, he nodded at Ilona and said, "Hello, apologies for the overt display. It has been a long time since we have seen each other."

Still within his embrace, Misa turned to Ilona. One arm remained around the man. There were tears in her eyes.

Wiping them away quickly, she explained in a flurry. "Sorry, Ilona. This is my fiancé, Radič." Her attention returned to him. "I wasn't expecting you."

He pressed a kiss to her forehead. "I like to surprise you. And I have one more." He turned, gesturing behind him. Another man waited, leaning casually back against the wall, his leg bent, foot pressed to the brickwork, a case at his feet.

Misa exclaimed in delight again, stepping from her fiancé's arms to embrace the second man. He unfolded from the wall, tall, lean and dark-haired, his eyes a dusky grey. His smile was like a firelight.

Turning back to Ilona, Misa introduced the man. "This is Jovan. He is from my village. Or was. He's been in Belgrade since we were teenagers. But we see each other every year, except this year and, oh..."

Jovan huffed a laugh, eyes twinkling as he regarded Ilona. "It is nice to meet you, Ilona. Excuse Misa, though as her friend, I am sure you know how emotional she can get."

Not really, Ilona thought, utterly stunned. She'd never seen anything like this display of feeling from her friend. In her experience, Misa was aloof and removed. Helpful and polite, but never warm. And never affectionate. Ilona was rapidly reassessing everything she thought she knew about the woman.

Gathering herself together, Misa regarded her fiancé. "Are you here long?"

"Just the weekend."

"Where are you staying?"

"With Jovan."

"Really?" Surprise lit Misa's face as she eyed Jovan. "You are staying here in Zagreb for a time?"

"Actually, I have great news," Jovan said. "I am here for a long time."

The two women snuck Radič and Jovan into their nursing accommodation. There was a 'no male company' policy, but the students found ways around that. Ilona measured coffee grounds into the džezva pot then set it to boil on the communal stove as Misa, Radič and Jovan gathered together at the table, chatting excitedly. Coffee prepared and poured, she went to join them. As she sat down, Jovan looked over. Misa didn't seem to notice.

"So," Misa pressed. "What is your news?"

Jovan took a sip of his coffee. "It's very good, thank you, Ilona."

Ilona nodded.

"Jovan," Misa whined. "Your news!"

"All right, all right," his mouth quirked up in a brotherly grin as he answered Misa. "I have been accepted into the Zagreb School of Music."

Misa covered her mouth in excited joy then moved to hug her friend. Ilona could only stare in surprise. "Your dream. Your tata has agreed to this?"

"Yes, yes," Jovan said, patting her back as he threw an apologetic grimace at Ilona. The expression made her giggle under her breath. It really was bemusing meeting this side of Misa. Misa calmed and resumed her seat next to Radič who could not wipe the smile from his face. Jovan continued. "Tata has agreed to two years. If I show him I am dedicated and succeeding, he will allow it."

"He should never have held you back," Radič interjected, punctuating his statement by draining the last of his coffee. "We all know how well you play. Every year you are the star performer at Petrinja's Christmas celebrations."

A shy twitch of the lips, a nervous shrug and Jovan's eyes flickered to Ilona. "Music is my passion, but it isn't a secure future."

"But you are so talented," Misa insisted.

"Thank you. So, I am here to study. I have taken rooms near the School of Music, on the edge of the upper town, and start Monday."

"What do you play?"

Misa's head whipped around at Ilona's words, surprised, as if her friend and roommate had completely forgotten she was even there.

Jovan's soft grey eyes met hers. "Violin."

"Beautiful. I love the violin."

"You play?"

"No, no." Ilona raised her hands in a subconscious gesture of denial as the skin of her face warmed with embarrassment. "I wouldn't have the talent. I just enjoy music."

"Everyone has the talent, given the opportunity."

Ilona's lips twitched in an insincere smile, and she looked away. That cut too close. Her tata had done all he could to support her education, but that could never extend to music lessons.

"I never played," Misa said, finding Ilona's stare. For the first time since she'd raced down the street to Jovan, something of the Misa Ilona was used to swam in her friend's expression. "Our family couldn't have that. Not on a market gardener's income. Music is for politician's sons."

Jovan shifted on his chair. He laughed at the friendly jibe, but his hand raked through his hair.

"Careful, my wife-to-be," Radič grinned. "Jovan was born in Petrinja, just like you and me. Our tatas were best friends."

"Da, but his tata moved to Belgrade to work for the parliament and the King."

"And ours remained."

"Different choices," Ilona whispered.

The table fell silent, all eyes turning to her. She blinked in surprise. She hadn't thought the joking friends had heard her.

"Yes." She met Jovan's eyes across the table, and read the gentle curiosity there.

"But your tata never forgot Petrinja," Misa said. "And you always visited, every January for Christmas..."

Ilona was only half listening. Eyes still locked with Jovan, the sound in the room had suddenly dimmed, and the air stilled. It was as if a bubble had formed around her thoughts, filling her senses with nothing but him.

"... Don't we, Ilona?"

"I am sorry? Don't we what?"

Misa cocked her head at Ilona, eyelids narrowing. Ilona fidgeted nervously. She truly had been miles away. "We have assessments next week. Matron Habazin is a tyrant! I don't know how any of us will pass."

"My brilliant Misa," Radič said. "How I wish you would fail, so I could make you my wife. But I know you would be angry—"

Misa swatted his arm playfully, returning her attention to Jovan. "After that, we will have time to be social, all together." Her gaze focusing on Radič. "You will visit again soon?"

"That would be nice," Radič said.

"Ilona is very nervous about her assessment," Misa continued, turning from Radič's hesitation and changing the subject as she stood up and collected the now-empty coffee cups. "But we are putting in the time."

"You were always excellent at our schooling," Radič said to Misa.

"Ilona is just as capable. We will both succeed." Her usual manner, focused and calm, had returned.

"I don't doubt it." Jovan smiled softly at Ilona.

Feeling suddenly jittery and unable to sit still, Ilona stood. "Well, it has been wonderful meeting you, Jovan, Radič. Please excuse me. I have so much extra reading to complete before the night is through. I will leave you to enjoy your time with Misa."

"I must be going too," Jovan interjected, pushing out his chair.

"So soon?" Misa said. "You are welcome to stay for supper. I am making stew."

"I will stay," Radič said, eyeing Misa, heat in his gaze. "As long as I can." The words held a deeper meaning that burned Ilona's cheeks and she glanced away, giving her friend and her fiancé a moment for privacy.

"I thank you, Misa. But I really must be going," Jovan said. "I only arrived this morning, and I have to return and properly settle in my rooms. I had to see you first, and tell you my great news."

"And I am so glad you did. We will see you again soon, I trust?"

"Of course, we are neighbours again."

Jovan bent down and collected up his violin case then made for the door, Misa on his heels.

"Good luck with your studies," he said over his shoulder to Ilona. "We need skilled nurses in this world."

"Thank you," Ilona said.

"Radič, you know where I am, come when you are ready."

As he disappeared through the front door Ilona headed for her room. What she'd said was true. She had many studies to complete, more concepts to commit to memory and formulas and procedures to reflect on. But that was not what had really driven her from the joyful companionship of the kitchen.

When Jovan had met her eyes, his handsome face open and calm, she'd been sucked in to his aura. He'd filled her senses, distracted her mind. She'd never experienced anything like that before in her life.

She didn't know what to make of it. Only that it made her breathless, made her heart race. She'd known she had to get away, to collect herself before... before what?

She didn't know.

But she hoped she would see Jovan again.

FIVE
ILONA

She saw him again, sooner than she'd dared hope.

Returning from her training shift at the hospital, her mind was full of explanations and details. As she walked, she worked to summarise all that Matron Habazin had taken them through that day. So lost was she in her day of learning she didn't notice him. Not until she'd almost walked into him.

Hand in her purse, rummaging for her apartment keys, brain repeating hospital formulas; they were much harder than the simple administration of vaccines in the Infectious Diseases Hospital... She caught movement before her.

Head snapping up she registered the figure of a man in the dimming evening light. Her hands flew up in surprise, her step faltering as she worked to halt her forward momentum. Giving a sharp cry of shock her foot slipped and she tilted forward, falling towards the cobbled road.

Strong hands caught her upper arms, stopping her fall and helping her to right herself.

Shaking from the surprise, Ilona straightened, apologies on her lips.

"I'm sorry, I'm sorry, I was in a world of my own. I simply didn't see you—"

"It is all right, Ilona."

That caught her attention, and finally she looked up into the face of the stranger on the street. Who was not a stranger at all.

"Oh." Her breath came out in a rush as her body tensed subconsciously. Jovan stood before her in the warm glow of early evening. His eyes were shining. Gosh he was beautiful.

"Jovan," she managed to croak, then subtly cleared her throat. "I wasn't expecting you."

Pausing a moment, his hands still holding her arms, Jovan smiled then dropped his grip. "I was not expected. I simply thought it was a beautiful evening and perhaps you might like to join me for a stroll through the upper town."

"I am sorry, Jovan. Misa is on the late shift tonight. But I am sure she would have loved to walk with you. Perhaps another night. She finishes earlier next week—"

"I didn't come to ask Misa."

"Me?"

"If you would do me the honour?"

His eyes had dipped lower, looking up at her through long dark lashes. Ilona felt her body heat rise as her heart began to thud in her chest. He wanted to take her out for a walk? This striking and accomplished man wanted to pass the evening with her?

He continued. "I have been strolling aimlessly around Zagreb these past few days and thought it was time I asked a local for a tour."

Ah, Ilona felt herself deflate. He was not here for her, not really. He was here to ask a local. Nodding to herself she shoved down the burst of disappointment that had hit her stomach. Of course, he was here for a tour. Why else would this handsome man and friend of her classmate have come to her? Silly girl to have ever considered an alternative.

Ilona forced herself to smile. "I am sure there are many locals at the music school."

Jovan shrugged. "Maybe. But I was rather hoping you would indulge me."

Something in his tone set her skin on fire, a warm prickling travelling over her neck and face. She glanced away, collecting herself and her thoughts. She couldn't spare the time, she had so much study to do. And what would Misa think?

He seemed to sense her hesitation and offered, "Just an hour. Around the old town. I'll have you home before Misa has finished her shift."

Ilona glanced at him, saw the honesty in his eyes and her heart knew her answer. "I'd be delighted."

They caught a bus up the rise to the upper town that circled the hill, then strolled through the lengthening dusk as the sun continued its slow descent over Zagreb. The rows of pastel-painted buildings in the old town were gilded in dusk, the red-tiled roofs as bright as fire against the deepening blue sky. At the Zagreb Cathedral, its white stone facade blazing in the sun, Ilona crossed herself and sent a prayer to her God above. Jovan averted his eyes, hands clasped behind his back. Ilona walked on. Around them, the people of the city were ending their days. Store owners were locking doors, pulling shutters closed; school children raced along the lanes, chasing each other, shoes and knees scuffed from a day of play; men in suits strolled for buses, suitcases dangling from their hands; women, arms ladened with brown bags of produce, led smaller children with golden curls bobbing about cherub faces as they headed home to cook. They turned off the market square onto a quieter street lined with spruce trees winding their way down from the old town. Jovan took Ilona's hand. His palm was warm, his skin soft and plump. Ilona glanced at him and saw the shy smile on his lips. She felt her own mouth curve with joy. An excited thrill raced from their clasped hands up her arm and through her whole being.

She didn't let go.

Hand in hand, they strolled as the city quieted and darkened. And slowly, slowly, peace descended over Ilona. Her mind emptied. Her world contracted down to this moment, the cooling breeze that gusted gently along the alleyways, the scent of blossom and sun-warm stone, the feel of Jovan's smooth palm against hers. For the first time since she'd begun her studies at the hospital, no anxiety tugged at her nerves. She felt calm, at ease. And in no rush to return to her dorm.

But as the sun dipped below the roofs of the city homes, she knew they had to turn back. It would not be right to walk the darkened streets with a man she barely knew. And Misa would be home soon.

She opened her mouth to say so to Jovan, but again he seemed to know her thoughts before she spoke. He gave her hand a gentle squeeze and turned them down a side street, heading directly back for the apartment block she shared with Misa and the trainee nurses. He clearly knew these streets better than he had suggested.

At the entrance to her building, they faced each other, still holding hands.

"Thank you," Jovan said. "That was the most beautiful evening I have enjoyed in Zagreb, or anywhere."

A blush crept up Ilona's cheek and she looked down shyly.

"Can we walk again tomorrow?"

Happiness burst through her at hearing that, and she met his stare. "I'd like that very much."

He was waiting for her the very next afternoon, his lean frame bent against the walls of her apartment building, one foot resting against the stone. His mouth curved in a warm smile as she approached, and he held out his hand to her.

She took it without hesitation.

They returned to the upper town and the grandeur of the Cathedral, but this time Jovan them led around the edge of the old city wall that braced the church to the neat park that hugged the back of the cathedral: Ribnjak Park. The warm afternoon sun shone through the burgeoning blossoms. Above them a small bird flittered, gathering twigs for a nest. Its small body disturbed a magnolia flower, loosing the fat purple-tinged petals and sending them falling in a cascade from the branch down to where they walked. Ilona leaned forward, her hands held out before her to catch the falling petals, soft and sweet as they kissed her palm. She laughed in delight.

"I like it when you laugh."

Ilona turned to Jovan. His eyes shone as he watched her. She felt the moment shift, his gaze becoming more intense, her heartbeat fluttering.

Uncomfortable, she broke the tension. Eyebrow arching teasingly, she said, "Is that why you pretended not to know Zagreb?"

Jovan burst out in an open, jovial laugh. Still grinning he asked, "What gave me away?"

"Not what, but who."

"Ah, Misa. You told her we went walking then?"

"I did," Ilona answered. She walked on, rounding the nearest tree, and trailed her fingers over the rough bark, remembering Misa's wry grin the evening before as Ilona explained she had been showing Jovan around the city.

"Jovan was born in Petrinja, like me, but his tata soon moved to Zagreb for his political work."

"So Jovan knows the city?"

"Oh yes, very well."

His ruse to spend time with Ilona had been revealed, and the realisation had fluttered in Ilona's belly all night. "We tell each other of our days," she continued.

Jovan stepped up to the opposite side of the tree, his hands bracing the trunk as his head peered around the wood to see her. "And I was a noteworthy part of your day?"

"It was a slow day."

A huffed laugh. "Or you wanted to know more about me."

"Perhaps." Ilona turned away, eyes raised to the treetops. Dappled sunlight glinted through the budding leaves, warming her skin. "It is only sensible to check up on strange boys who ask you out for walks in the dusk."

The scrape of his foot on the pebbled pathway told her he had followed. Tingles ran up her spine as her senses recognised the scent of his Brylcreem, his soap. "Only sensible." His voice was a whisper at her ear. She went to step away and put distance between them, but his hand caught hers.

Gently, he turned her around. They stood face to face under a fall of mellowing light, a canopy of rebirth framing them on the pathway. He was so close she could feel the warmth of his breath on her cheek, see the flecks of blue in his grey eyes.

"And what did Misa say of me?" The question washed over her, the timbre of his voice fitting against her heart and setting her stomach to bubble. She knew he wasn't really asking.

She nodded to the violin case strapped to his back. "Do you take it everywhere?"

"We moved around a lot when I was young," he began, swinging the case from his back. "Tata's work for the Parliament. Music was one thing I always had with me."

Ilona stepped forward and touched the violin case with gentle fingers. "Would you play for me?"

"I would be honoured to."

Kneeling, he placed the violin case on the ground and flicked the clasps, one, two. He drew the instrument from the case and stood, nestling it against his chin and setting his long fingers along the strings. "Any requests?" His eyes sparkled.

Ilona suppressed the rush of nerves that quickened her heartbeat. She knew nothing of music, of songs, only the lullabies of her tata and mama, not the music of study and art and performance halls. She shook her head stiffly, hoping that she hadn't exposed her ignorance. She couldn't bear it if he thought her a peasant.

"Then I will choose something just for you."

His eyes closed and he paused a moment, breathing deeply, his face going slack, as if his thoughts had drifted far away. Ilona felt her body go still, her whole attention focusing on Jovan and his violin, her breathing slowing in anticipation, as if she didn't want to make a single sound to interrupt.

Then he played.

An elegant, quavering sound whispered from the violin, Jovan's fingers vibrating on the strings. The note continued, its volume building and expanding out into the gardens around them. And Ilona moved. It wasn't conscious, it simply was. Her hand came out before her and twirled in the sunlight. Her body swayed, her eyes closing and her senses opening. She turned on the spot, her arms waving through the air. As she moved the notes of the melody grew louder, stronger, more insistent. She dipped her shoulder and pivoted, a smile breaking out over her face.

A bird on the tree branch above her shot up for the sky, the pumping of its wings releasing a fresh fall of blossom.

A hand took hers, warm and soft. Another wrapped around her waist.

"You have a beautiful smile."

Beautiful. Ilona had never considered herself beautiful. She thought herself too plain, too thin. But hearing that word from Jovan, she felt it. Still floating, Ilona allowed Jovan to draw her into him, moving them as one, swaying to the music... that had stopped. She blinked in surprise. Jovan stood pressed against her under the falling blossoms, his hips swaying with hers, their arms entwined. When had he stopped playing?

"You play beautifully," she whispered.

"You dance like an angel."

"I've never danced before. Not like this."

"I would like to dance like this with you, for a very long time."

"Hmm."

Ilona knew he had stopped playing, that the strains of the violin had silenced. That she was dancing in the gardens of Zagreb in Jovan's arms. Cheek to cheek, for anyone to see. But her mind was still full of the music. Her body moving to the lyric she'd never known before. And the warmth of his closeness. She needed it.

She looked up and their eyes met. His face was full of light.

His fingers traced the line of her jaw.

When his lips met hers, everything continued to flow. The music in her mind, the swaying of her limbs, the petals surrounding them. And Ilona knew she had met the love of her life.

SIX

ILONA

As the intensity of the summer heat escalated across the streets of Zagreb, so too did the passions of the people. The rise of Nationalist politics across Europe had increased the reach of a small but radical political group within the State of Croatia, the Ustaše.

Coming into the break room after a long shift, Ilona wiped her hand over her brow to clear the beading sweat. The sun was high overhead and strong, leaving the wards stuffy and warm. Radmila was sitting at a table, sipping coffee. She looked up and raised an eyebrow at Ilona. Standing slowly she tapped the table before her. No, not the table, a newspaper.

"They try to silence our voices. But we will not be stopped."

"What are you talking about?" Ilona asked, genuinely confused.

"You should read it. It is important."

Ilona crossed the room and glanced down at the newspaper: Hrvatski narod, Croatian People. Shock rattled through her, and her eyes snapped to Radmila.

"Radmila, this is the Ustaše. They are a terrorist organisation!"

They had been involved in the assassination of King Alexander I. It had been years ago, but it was still true.

Radmila smirked. "That's what Yugoslavia says. It's just propaganda to control us," she said. "David has been going to their meetings. They stand for us. For our independence. And now the government seeks to silence them."

Ilona scanned the page. A litany of proclamations about religion and race flooded her vision. She turned away. "I don't want to read this."

"Strange how one sibling can be so smart and the other..." Radmila left the sentence unfinished.

Ilona turned to her, eyes narrowing. "What do you mean?"

Radmila shrugged. "Ivica and David, they attend Slavko's meetings together."

Her stomach clenched. She didn't know much about politics, but she knew the Ustaše were dangerous. It was in the anger she saw in her brother's sneer. While there had been no repeat of his outburst months ago over dinner, every time she'd visited she saw the barely contained rage and hurt.

She still hadn't told her family about Jovan. She didn't expect a welcoming response.

"Times are tough in the city," Ilona began. "But we are all just trying to get through, no?"

Radmila gave a dismissive shrug. "We are not the problem."

Ilona stared at her in shock. She knew there was tension between Misa and Radmila, but this was deeper than competitiveness and dislike. Even bigger than religion. This was bitter and angry, like her brother. It was something she did not understand.

That evening she met Jovan in a small cafe on the corner of the park where they'd first kissed. As she approached he stood, his long frame unfolding from the neat cafe chair, his eyes igniting. Ilona forced herself to smile, but, her mind still full of Radmila's words, could not feel the happiness she saw reflected on his face. Still, she did not wish to worry him. She allowed him to kiss her cheek then settled down at the table. The night around them was warm and tranquil, the sky a shade of cobalt blue that only the long balmy nights of summer brought. It was usually her favourite time of the day. The extra hours of light as the sun argued with the moon over rest. But tonight she could not enjoy it.

Jovan ordered juices and leaned back, regarding her face.

"What is it?" he asked.

Shaking her head quickly, Ilona protested. "Nothing at all, just a big day."

She tried a smile, but instantly saw he was not reassured. He waited in silence, his question hovering between them. Finally Ilona relented. Sighing heavily she explained about Radmila and the Hrvatski narod newspaper, about her brother and the Ustaše.

Jovan listened as she spoke, face passive and calm. When her words ran out he leaned forward, cupped her chin and kissed her full on the mouth. Startled at the public display of affection Ilona sat up straighter.

"What was that for?"

The waiter arrived, a tray of juices in hand. They paused their conversation as he handed out their order. Then Jovan answered. "For being you."

Ilona snorted. "I am always me."

"Exactly."

"Jovan, you are going to have to explain. I have just rambled at you about my concerns regarding my friend and my brother and the impact it has on you and Misa and you are kissing me and saying I am predictable."

Jovan gave an indulgent laugh, then reached out and took her hands in his. "Thank you," he began. "Thank you for being you and caring about me and Misa and other Orthodox families across our nation. I am touched that you are worried. But this is nothing new. These tensions have been here from the beginning of Yugoslavia, and will likely remain."

Ilona shook her head slowly. "But why? We all live here, we are friends and neighbours and colleagues."

"And life is difficult and politicians are fat. And people need someone to blame." He paused and rolled his shoulders. "Look at our families. You come from a farm. Your tata moved to the city to find work, and he and your brother have struggled. Look at me. I was born in a village but my tata is in politics. We moved to the city and lived comfortably. Resentment is natural."

"What about Misa and me?" Ilona challenged. "We are the same, but different."

"Da," he agreed. "But you celebrate Christmas on different days." He grinned.

Ilona pulled a face at him. "Don't joke about the Church."

"Sorry. I don't mean to be dismissive. But you see what I mean? Religion, culture, perceived or real advantage. These things divide us. When people are struggling, they look for an answer. Independence for their nation seems a reasonable option, especially if you believe that Serbia has too much power in our union. The King and the Prince Regent are Serbian after all."

"I can follow that. But why blame people who were born here? Misa, you... you might be Serbs, but you live here in Croatia."

Jovan shrugged. "The history of our region is long and complex. We have been at war, we have been occupied, divided, united, repressed, liberated. It has only been twenty years since the Great War and our liberation from the Austro-Hungarian Empire. It takes time for these things to work themselves out."

It seemed so rational, so understandable. A sense of relief swept over Ilona, but it didn't reach her core. The rage in Ivica's distorted face refused to dissipate in her memory, keeping her on edge.

"All right now?" Jovan asked.

"Da, thank you," she lied.

"Good, because I have wonderful news! Radič and Misa have finally set a date. They are getting married!"

The worries of the world evaporated around her, and Ilona gave a shriek of joy. Then consternation furrowed her brow. "I was just with Misa, she didn't tell me..."

"I asked to be the one to tell you."

Ilona cocked her head at him. "Why?"

"Because, Ilona, my love, I would be honoured if you would accompany me to the wedding."

She went still, and her breathing slowed as his words sunk in. To attend a wedding together as a couple, that felt significant. Suddenly and unexpectedly shy, Ilona glanced down, a small smile on her lips.

"Da," she said softly. "I would love to go with you."

SEVEN

ILONA

A soft knock sounded on her dormitory door. Ilona paused briefly before the mirror, pressing her curled hair into place and checking her lipstick.

Today was a special day. Today, Misa and Radič were getting married.

Snatching up her purse, Ilona walked swiftly to the door. Radmila's friend Petra stood on the threshold. Ilona blinked in surprise.

"Oh, sorry I was expecting——"

"Jovan is downstairs waiting for you. I said I would fetch you."

Ilona cocked her head in question and watched as Petra's face tensed. Finally, she continued. "I know Misa and I have our differences. But today is a special day. It isn't fair," she paused. "To happen today... Tell her, I wish her well."

Ilona frowned. What was Petra talking about? She didn't know, but right now she didn't have time to worry about it. "I will tell her." She brushed past Petra, aiming for the stairs that would take her to Jovan.

"It makes me stop and consider. I have been unfair," Petra said behind her. Ilona turned back to her fellow student.

"It will be a wonderful day," she assured Petra and hurried away.

Jovan stood on the pavement in front of the apartment block, his face turned to the sky.

Ilona felt her heartbeat jump as a smile split her face, as it did every time she saw him.

"Good morning," she called, instantly linking her arm with his.

Sad eyes turned to her and Ilona frowned. "What is it?"

"You haven't heard?"

"Heard what?" Her mind began to race, tension spreading through her body. First Petra, now Jovan. Had something happened between Misa and Radič? Had they called off the wedding? Impossible! They'd been in love since childhood. Ilona schooled her features to calm and prompted Jovan again. "Jovan, what has happened?"

He heaved a deep sigh. "I heard it on the radio this morning. Hitler in Germany, he has invaded Poland."

The world stopped. "England and France have already declared war. Europe is at war, again."

War. Ilona felt the slow creep of panic as it swirled in her stomach, low and acidic.

"Poland is far away," she began, seeking comfort.

Jovan nodded. "The King and the Yugoslavian Government have declared neutrality. We are not engaging."

"That is good, isn't it? This isn't our conflict. There is no reason to assume it will come to us."

"No, no of course not." He smiled, but it did not reach his eyes. The Great War had started small too, and it had engulfed the world. Their lands were no stranger to conflict, they were born under occupation. Even if they had not been old enough to remember it – they knew to fear. The shadow of war was long and dark. It lived in the nervous glances of their elders.

Suddenly Jovan smiled, his whole face lightening, even his eyes. "You look so beautiful," he said.

Startled at the sudden pivot, her face flushed red at the compliment. "Oh, thank you." She held out her skirts and gave a mock curtsey. "It was my mama's, she altered it for me." The dress was pale green with a fitted waist. Ilona had clipped her hair back on the side with a golden clasp. It brought out her eyes, she thought. "You don't look too shabby yourself."

It was true. His suit was perfectly tailored to his slender frame and clearly expensive. A gift from his tata in Belgrade no doubt.

Jovan's expression softened, his gaze shifting to a wistful calm. "Here." He held out his hand, a patterned silk scarf flowed from his grasp. "For church, to cover your hair."

"It is beautiful," she said, taking the soft scarf and securing it beneath her chin.

"Come," he said, gesturing down the street. "We have a wedding to attend. We don't want to miss the train."

Misa and Radič were married at the Orthodox church in Petrinja, the pews of the church overflowing with the people of their community.

After a simple ceremony led by their childhood priest, Radič swept Misa into his arms and kissed her thoroughly, the ornate white scarf that covered her hair almost falling off as he dipped her back in passion. The gathered friends and family roared with approval, and Ilona felt her cheeks grow wet as she watched the glow of joy on her friend's face. In that church, as the voices of Petrinja cheered for her friend, the worries of the world were forgotten, the last vestiges of fear cast away. Nothing mattered but this special moment. This was hope and joy. This was the future.

Arm in arm with Jovan, Ilona followed the flow of the crowd as they meandered along the quiet streets to Misa's childhood home, the occasional person nodding at Jovan in acknowledgement; some of them remembered him. Small houses lined the roadside at odd intervals, their terracotta roofs shining red in the autumn sun. A young child appeared in a doorway, a bunch of flowers clutched in his hand. Spotting Misa and Radič at the front of their group the boy dashed forward, his mama watching from the doorway, a wide smile on her face. Ilona watched as the boy tugged on Misa's white dress and her friend looked down. Bending to the boy, Misa took the posy of flowers and ruffled the child's hair, before waving to his mama over his head.

"Everyone in this village knows Misa or Radič. They are all overjoyed that they have finally wed," Jovan explained. "As am I."

Ilona watched the boy return to his mama and slip beyond the wooden door to his home. A hollowness had opened up within her. All this love and happiness, it was everything she wanted for her dearest friend. Something in her chest shifted, a sense of longing unfolding against her ribs. It was an unfamiliar feeling.

"My grandparents live near a village like this," she said, talking through her confused thoughts. "Ivica and I spent our summers there. My baba makes the most delicious plum jam."

"Do you miss it?"

Faced with the direct question she realised that she did, but deflected. "Zagreb has been my home for longer. What about you? You were born here, do you wish to return?"

"I don't think so. Petrinja wasn't ever really my home. Like you, my family moved when I was young. I grew up between Belgrade and Zagreb."

"And which of those is your favourite?"

A cheeky twist of the corner of his lip and Jovan leaned closer. "Wherever you are," he whispered.

The celebrations lasted into the dark hours. Misa's mama and baba had put on a feast of pastries and cured meats. As the sun set Jovan pulled out his violin and started playing a jig. Everyone joined in, dancing and singing and laughing until the stars covered the sky above them.

When Radič finally led Misa away, turning in for their wedding night, the whole street erupted in raucous jeering. Misa flushed red, hiding her head in Radič's chest. But Radič only laughed and saluted his celebrating guests.

A familiar arm encircled her waist and Jovan pulled her close. "I cannot wait for it to be us," he said as he swayed her to the music.

"You presume," Ilona said, teasing in her tone. "You have not even asked me."

He pressed a kiss to her lips, and Ilona felt her blood heat. "What do you think I am doing right now?" he said.

She stopped swaying and stared straight into his eyes. "Don't play."

"I am not. I mean it, Ilona. I want you to be my wife. Will you marry me?"

"But you are Orthodox and I am Catholic." Her mind was racing. She wanted this, she truly did. But could she give up her faith?

Jovan stilled, taking hold of her shoulders as he focused on her face. "Today has made me realise two things. One," he held up a finger. "That we can take nothing for granted." The announcement from Europe hissed unspoken between them. It was a shadow that hovered at the edge of the day. "And two, that no matter what, I love you. And I will do anything, anything to be with you. I will convert. In fact, I have already begun the process."

"You have?"

The corner of his lip lifted. "Religion doesn't matter to me as it does to you. But you matter to me. From the day we danced beneath the petals, I knew I wanted to marry you, so I took the first steps. Now, I am taking the most important one.

"What do you say? Dearest Ilona, be my wife?"

Ilona stared at Jovan in the moonlight, her whole world expanding before her, and the answer was clear. It was easy.

"Da. In every lifetime. Da."

As the two of them danced away the night Ilona felt that nothing could ever be as perfect as this moment. And nothing could stand in the way. Not even war.

EIGHT

ILONA

Her mama's kitchen was warm and welcoming. All the scents of her childhood filled the space. Ilona couldn't help but feel at home, despite the nerves that curdled in her stomach.

Breathe, she reminded herself. *It will be all right.*

Once again her traitorous, unhelpful mind made a wish that he could be here. But that was silly. She needed to do this alone.

"Ah, my daughter," her mama said. Coming to press a kiss to each of Ilona's cheeks. "You are early."

"I thought I would help you prepare dinner," Ilona lied. It was a nice thing to do for her mama, but not why she arranged to finish her shift an hour earlier than it was rostered for so she could get here sooner.

"My sweet girl. Come, you can watch the stew."

Ilona and her mama settled into the routine of childhood. Ilona stirred the goulash, while her mama mixed and shaped the proja cornbread into small rounds. The smile that crept over Ilona's face was not a lie. It was the truth.

"Mama?" Ilona ventured as Ivana pulled the proja from the oven. She glanced at the clock above the stove. The ticking countdown to her tata's arrival home from work. She needed to tell her mama before that. She needed to know if Ivana would stand at her side.

"Da?" her mama said distractedly, her focus on the searingly hot tray of muffins.

"I am engaged."

The tray clanked loudly, as Ivana lost her grip above the bench top. Instinctively Ilona reached to help, but her mama slapped her away. "Hot!" she exclaimed.

Ilona shrank back. Embarrassed to be reminded by her mama of the heat of an oven tray. But also at the implication of the sharp tone.

Forcing her hands to her sides, Ilona went still, allowing her mama time.

The older woman took it, fussing with the tray and the baked corn breads far beyond what was needed for the small mishap.

"Mama—"

"I heard you!" Ivana snapped. "This is bad timing, Ilona. Very bad timing."

Ilona fell silent, chastised. She knew her mama was right. The war in Europe and the growth of the Ustaše movement had increased the tensions that simmered across her nation. Further, her tata had had to accept an entry-level labourer job or risk starvation, a blow to his pride. Her family had every reason to be angry right now. And the world was telling them to blame Jovan's people.

Her mama sighed heavily. "All right, you will have to help me. I will make another batch, these are cracked. Your tata likes his proja perfectly round. Let's not give him a reason to complain tonight."

And in those words was everything Ilona needed to hear. Relief rushed through her. "Oh, Mama!' She gripped Ivana in a crushing embrace, earning herself a loud 'tsk' of disapproval. But Ilona didn't care. Her mama wanted to make her tata happy and to remove anything for him to grump about, so that Ilona could share her news. It was the best her mama could do to smooth the way.

Bojan arrived home as the darkness of night became complete, his shift at the munitions factory over for the day. Ilona went to greet him. His body was drawn, his large shoulders slumped in fatigue as he walked through the door, the smell of grease and oil preceding him down the hallway. But the moment he beheld his daughter, his whole face lifted in joy. "Daughter! You are early. What a lovely surprise."

Ilona could not help returning his smile as her tata strode toward her. Stopping a few steps back he looked her over, then patted her shoulder affectionately. "I will clean up. You help your mama in the kitchen."

"Da, Tata," Ilona answered, suppressing the retort that she had been doing just that without prompting.

Once her tata was washed and the food set out on the table the family gathered to eat.

"Ah, Ivana, delicious!" Her tata praised her mama's food. Ivana lowered her head modestly, catching Ilona's eye with a shrewd nod.

"Ivica is doing well," her tata continued. "David has been watching over him. He is working late tonight, I am sorry you will miss him."

Ilona busied herself cutting a section of her proja. There had not been a repeat of Ivica's outburst over Ilona's friendship with Misa, but Ilona knew how her brother thought.

For men like Ivica, the military might of Germany was inspiring; if they could lay claim to lands, Croatia could free itself from Serbia. It was not a good time to announce her relationship with Jovan. Despite his willingness to convert to her religion, Ilona doubted Ivica would accept a Serb into his family.

She prayed her tata was more rational.

"It is good to hear Ivica is doing well. He is a hard worker," Ilona said. And she meant it. Like her tata, Ivica was not afraid of toil. But it was tough to make ends meet in Croatia.

"Better times are coming for our people," her tata said, and Ilona stiffened. A glint of resentment shone in his eye. It stilled her heart.

"For all of Yugoslavia," she said, intentionally misunderstanding her tata's assertion.

Bojan grunted and shovelled more food into his mouth, chewing loudly.

Ilona felt a gentle nudge and met her mama's eyes. "Go on," she mouthed.

Ilona took a deep breath in through her nose, willing her rattling nerves to still. Her mama cleared her throat, and Ilona plunged forward.

"I have news," she said, acutely aware of how strained her voice sounded. "I am to be married."

Her tata's knife and fork froze mid-chop, hovering over his plate as he stared at his proja. Pushing forward into the silence, Ilona continued. "Jovan has agreed to convert. He is from a good family with good prospects. He's been offered a tutor's position at the School of Music for next semester. He cares for me and will take care of me. It is a good match—"

A gentle hand touched her arm, stopping the flow of her words. Ilona flicked a gaze to her mama and held her tongue. Her tata still had not moved. Then he dropped his cutlery and pushed back his chair. "Oversalted," he announced, standing and striding to his couch in the adjacent room. He sat and lit a cigarette, the scent of the acrid smoke filling the air.

"Ta—" Ilona began to try and reason with him, but her mama silenced her words.

"Give him time. He has not forbidden this match. This is good. You must be patient, daughter. Times are unsettled and tensions flare. Your tata is just worried for you."

Disappointment sat heavily on her heart, but Ilona knew her mama was right. "I will help you to clear the dishes."

Ivana shook her head. "No, it is time for you to head home before it gets much later. We will speak again soon." The two women rose, and Ivana kissed her daughter's forehead. "Leave him to me," she said. "Good night, my daughter."

"Good night, Mama."

. . .

The day of Jovan's Profession of Faith, the last step in his conversion to Catholicism, arrived. Ilona stood by his side under the vaulted ceiling of Zagreb Cathedral. Radič had travelled up from Petrinja in support, and Misa was overjoyed to have a weekend with her husband. Despite their adherence to the faith of their birth, they supported Jovan's choice for his future with Ilona. A few other worshippers sat in the pews, heads bowed in prayer, some strolling the sides, lighting candles for loved ones. Neither her parents nor her brother had arrived. Resignation settled over her as she scanned the cavernous Cathedral. "I am sorry," she whispered to Jovan. "I truly thought they would come to understand."

"My heart," Jovan said, his hands cupping her cheeks and tilting her face up to his. "It is all right. I am grateful that you tried. It was all you could do. In the end, all that matters is that you are here beside me, now and always."

Ilona smiled, her heart swelling with love for this man who would be her husband. "Have you heard from your parents?"

Jovan's lips curved in a sad smile. "They are, of course, disappointed. But I have their blessing." He shrugged. "My tata was never truly religious. It is more about the cultural side."

"Are you sure you want to give that up?"

His fingers feathered over her cheek. "For you? I would give up anything."

Ilona gripped his wrists, and he slipped his hands from her face to take her hand, pressing a kiss to her palm. The priest appeared from the vestry and Jovan turned to the altar, straightening his shoulders in readiness.

Ilona stepped back to take a seat beside Misa. Jovan had to face this moment alone. Misa took her hand and squeezed. Ilona was grateful for her friend's presence and unspoken support.

That afternoon, the four of them gathered to celebrate in the kitchen of the nursing accommodation. "To the new Catholic!" Radič joked, raising a glass of rakia brandy in a toast.

"Ah, enough," Misa chastised. "To the happy couple."

As the men fell into the easy banter of childhood friends, Misa drew Ilona apart, chewing on her bottom lip. "I have something I must tell you," she said.

Ilona's heart exploded in joy. "You are pregnant! Aren't you?"

Misa released a gushing laugh. "And to think I thought I could surprise you! Da. I am pregnant."

But Ilona was confused. "How can you know already?" Their wedding was only weeks ago.

A shy smile drifted over Misa's lips. "I am further along than that," she confessed.

Oh, Ilona realised, a hot flush blushing her face; they hadn't waited until after their vows. But what did it matter? Misa and Radič were in love and married. And they were going to have a baby.

"I am so happy for you!" Ilona gushed, drawing her friend into a tight embrace. Pulling back, she saw uncertainty flash across Misa's face. "What is wrong?"

Misa licked her lips nervously, and Ilona waited. "Radič wants me to return to Petrinja. We will raise our family there. I will be leaving within the next month."

So soon. A hit of sorrow tapped her heart, but Ilona pushed it down. "I will miss you, terribly. But I cannot be anything but happy for you in this moment," she said.

Misa gave a small, sad smile, her hand coming to rest over her stomach. "I thought I would have longer—"

"What are you two gossiping about?" Radič called from the kitchen.

"Nothing, dear one. We are coming back," Misa called in answer, then, lowering her voice for Ilona only, quietly said, "I promised I would wait to tell you. But I just couldn't."

"Do not worry, I won't let on that I know."

Arms linked, the two friends rejoined the men and their brandy.

Radič took one look at Misa and cocked his eyebrow. "Of course you told her," he said.

Misa flushed red as a beetroot. "I did no such—"

"Jovan," Radič interrupted. "Seeing as my wife cannot keep a secret. We are having a child."

Somehow, the broad grin on Jovan's face split even wider and he gathered his friend into a bone-crushing embrace. "Now, it is time for a real toast!"

PART TWO

NINE

"*The doctor seemed kind. Interested even. He asked me where I was from, if I played sport or liked reading. Then he put the needle in my arm... I don't know how I survived Stara Gradiška. I don't know how anyone lived.*

"*But we did. I did. Then I came back to Mlaka. No one understands that. My first camp, it was just over there.*" He points out the window. Sara's eyes flick across the room to see a peaceful green glade shimmering in the distance. She pushes a lock of her short blonde hair behind her ear. This is not her first interview, far from it. But it still gets to her, how it's all gone. The buildings, the camps, the evidence: gone. Only the survivors remain.

It's why she's here, why she's making this documentary.

The bombs have stopped falling, but her nation cannot heal. Not without a reckoning. They have to face the past. All of it.

"*It was all destroyed. And Mlaka has been rebuilt. I have no memory of my life before. I can barely picture my mama, my tata. But Mlaka was home. When the Partisans came and took us from the camp, Mlaka was the only place I knew.*

"Besides, nothing was as bad as Stara Gradiška.
"My sister never got out."
Daniel stops recording, and their eyes meet across the room.
He came for the work, Sara knows. But it's not why he stayed.
He stayed for them.

TEN

NADICA

Novska 1991

Nadica's mama is talking with her deda when Nadica arrives two days later. She spies her through the window as she leans her bike against the rough stone of the cottage wall.

Nadica frowns. It is past nine o'clock and her mama should be at the shop already. Mr Kovacic will be livid that he hasn't been able to collect his morning paper.

Why is she here?

As she walks into the kitchen Nadica immediately knows something is wrong. There is an unmistakeable tension in the air. A silence that feels as though it has faded from a shout.

They've been arguing.

They never argue.

Nadica watches in shock. She sees the moment her mama crumples, pulling back in on herself, closing off. She sees the flush of guilt that cracks her deda's face, the way his good hand moves to soothe his daughter. And how her mama backs away from his touch, the movement small, almost imperceptible.

Nadica coughs subtly.

Her mama's head whips around, her grey-flecked hair swinging, her dark eyes going wide and then settling.

"Ah, Nadica. You are early," she says.

She's not. But Nadica doesn't argue. Her eyes flick between them. Her deda's normally serene face is flushed, his hair awry. And her mama looks pale, her lips trembling.

"Well," her mama says, pulling herself together and running her hands over her jeans. "It is good, gives me more time to prepare for work." She comes over to Nadica and gathers her jacket from the hook. "Have a good day," she says pressing a kiss to Nadica's cheek and bustling out of the door.

Nadica watches her go and frowns. Turning to her deda she raises her eyebrows, crossing her arms over her chest and cocking her head.

Jovan meets her stare, his face long, then suddenly morphs into an easy grin. "Stop that," he says waving a hand towards her. "It was nothing."

"Nothing? Deda, you are positively red! What were you arguing about?"

"Not an argument," he mumbles, turning away. "Do you want a krofna?"

"Don't try and distract me with food," Nadica says, coming to stand in front of him. "I am not a kid any more."

"No, you're not," he says, suddenly sad. He releases a sigh. "Honestly, it is nothing. Your mama and I just have a different opinion on a few things."

"What things?"

He taps the side of his nose. "That is between me and my daughter. Not my granddaughter," he says.

Heat rises to Nadica's face. "Is this to do with me? Mama wasn't happy when I asked for less shifts at the shop. But I want to be able to come here—"

She loves her work. There is a deep sense of pride that her mama managed to keep the store running after her tata's passing. Nadica knows how much it took. She will be proud to take over from her mama when the time comes. But just now, time with Misa is more important. Family always is.

"It is not about your job," he says gently, then places a hand on her shoulder.

"Then what—"

"No," he says firmly. "Between your mama and me, not you. Now, are you going to help me prepare the wood?"

Nadica's lips purse in frustration, but she knows her deda well enough to leave it, at least for now. Huffing a loud sigh – she might relent, but she will make sure he knows she remains unconvinced – she links her arm with his good one and they start for the door. She doesn't miss the amused smile that crosses his face.

At the shed, her deda fetches his axe, and Nadica selects some wood from the covered winter pile that rests at the shed's side. Placing the first section on the block, ready for splitting, she steps back and waits. Her deda swings with expert precision, and the wood sections into two.

She gathers the pieces and sets the next for splitting.

"How's Misa today? Did she settle last night?"

The axe swings, the wood splits, her deda nods for the next.

"She slept through. Is still sleeping. I don't think you will get much time with her today."

Nadica nods and licks her lips nervously. "I didn't know," she begins. "About baba's family and yours. That they didn't want you to marry."

Wood splits. Her deda straightens, stretching the muscles of his lower back.

"I wouldn't say they didn't want us to marry. I would say it was complicated. Politics, religion and love, they don't mix well."

Nadica sets the next piece of wood. "This farm though," she says. "It was in baba's family?"

"Da, that is right. So you see, it wasn't so simple as it may sound."

"They didn't come to your wedding."

"They did not. But we married all the same. It is all right,

Nadica." He is no longer focusing on the wood, instead his soft eyes rest on her face. Nadica meets that gaze. "Your baba and I, we faced some hard times. There is more to come in the story. But it is all right."

His smile is soft and kind before he asks gently, "What is this really about?"

Nadica wants to deflect but knows her face has given her away. *How does he do it?* She wonders. *How does he make me talk when I don't want to, but shuts himself down at will?* Irritation surges briefly in her chest, swiftly followed by impending relief. The truth is that she wants to talk about Relja.

"We broke up." She feels her body flatten like she's suddenly in two dimensions not three. Everything had seemed so simple before. She would marry her childhood sweetheart, take over her mama's store, live a life in Novska. Then Croatia voted and Slovenia declared independence sparking a ten-day war with Yugoslavia, and everything changed.

Her deda says nothing. He watches her in silence, giving her time to find her words.

"He doesn't agree with Croatia's independence. He thinks it means his family will be hunted. Because they are Serbs. He believes in Yugoslavia."

"And you don't agree." It is a statement, not a question.

Nadica looks up at her deda. "I am sorry. You are Serb. You gave up your religion for Baba. I should be asking how *you* feel."

He shrugs noncommittally. "I do not care what they call me: Yugoslavian, Serb, Croat. It does not matter, so long as my family is safe."

The words are sobering. Nadica pauses, organising her thoughts.

"I know our country is divided. That there is fear. But what happened during the war... we survived it. Right?"

"Your baba and I did not always agree," he says, not answering her question. Then he reaches down and gathers the last of the split wood, turning for the house. Nadica follows.

As they step over the threshold her deda pauses. "More than one thing can be true," he says, then continues into the comforting warmth of his home.

Nadica follows.

For the first time in her life, the scent of her baba's baking does not settle the churning nerves that flutter in her stomach.

The sun is slipping down the sky as she follows her baba out to the vegetable garden. It has been a peaceful day, but Misa has not roused; sleeping off the panic and stress no doubt. Nadica's mind will not quiet. Talking with her deda that morning should have calmed her, but it only increased the tension she feels inside. The tension she sees on the streets of her town and hears about on the news.

She'd expected him to quell her concerns. To agree with her and dismiss Relja's extreme talk. To allay her fears over the skirmishes that have been breaking out across Croatia. To say it will pass and peace will return.

He hadn't.

She feels her baba's eyes on her in the dimming light and reaches down to dig a carrot from the rich soil. They are making root vegetable stew. It is Misa's favourite. Looking up Nadica sees that her baba is still watching her.

"Ask the question," she says.

Nadica heaves a sigh. "I want to," she answers honestly. "But I don't know what the question is."

Her baba plucks a beetroot from the plot and drops it in the basket on her hip. "Ask whatever pops into your mind first. Then ask what comes next. Eventually, we will find the right question."

"I broke up with Relja, I know you like him. Do you think I did the wrong thing?"

Her baba shrugs. "Do you?"

"No."

"Then neither do I. Next question."

"Did you ever doubt marrying deda? With the tensions between your families? Was that hard to do?"

Baba pauses, mouth pursed in thought. "I doubted briefly, but not because of our families. I wanted to be sure I would love him forever. I chose to trust I would." A private smile. "I chose right."

Nadica feels her lips mirror that smile. It is a beautiful thing, the love between her grandparents. And there it is. A tiny snag in her chest.

"This morning deda said you and he disagreed once and that it mattered. What did you disagree about?" The words are out, ringing through the cooling colours of the sky. And Nadica knows. That is the question that hides from her. Because Relja talks of war, but Nadica believes in Croatia's choice. Because her baba and deda faced a war, and Nadica wants to know how they survived. Was that when they were against each other? And if so, how did they make it through?

Her baba meets her eyes and nods.

"Da," she says. "You are right. We disagreed on the war."

Nadica takes a deep breath, her heart beginning to pound.

"And we were both wrong."

ELEVEN
ILONA

Zagreb 1941

The train rocked gently along the tracks. Ilona sat at Jovan's side, her head resting on his shoulder as they made the journey to Petrinja. Misa had given birth to her second child, a girl, two months before. Ilona had only just been able to get leave for a weekend to make the trip. When Ilona finished her training the year before, finally removing the pin from her uniform that declared her a student, Matron had offered her a teaching role. Ilona had accepted. She wanted to stay at the Sisters of Charity Hospital, and teaching was the only way. The work meant long tiring hours, but it was a good distraction from the rising tensions on the streets of Zagreb and the rumours from abroad. The war in Europe that had begun on the day of Misa's wedding now stretched its tendrils towards Yugoslavia's borders.

It wasn't something she should know about. She hadn't read any news articles or heard any of the training nurses or nuns at the hospital discussing it. But Jovan had.

She'd come home early some weeks before to find him and a friend from the University of Science, Goran, talking.

"The tensions are growing," Goran had said. "More and more people call for independence. I worry for our jobs, Jovan."

"There has always been this tension," Jovan had answered.

Goran's voice had dropped low, and Ilona had needed to lean closer to the door to hear. "The war in Europe is building and now Italy threatens our region."

The statement had rocked her to her core. The pause before Jovan answered was telling. Even when his words of reassurance came, Ilona could feel his hesitation.

"Yugoslavia is large and powerful. The defence of our countries is why we exist at all. Together, we can stand against invasion. Besides, what right does Italy have to our lands?"

"What right did the Austro-Hungarian Empire have to our lands?"

"We have been careful not to engage. It is just posturing. You will see." But Ilona had heard the fear in her husband's voice. Later that night as they prepared for bed, she'd longed to ask him about the conversation. To hear it from his own mouth, and not just the snippets of words between friends. But the calm warmth of his body, the comfort of his presence, had stilled her lips. She didn't want that sense of peace to be taken from her, so she closed her ears to it.

And to the rising calls of the new political movement that sought independence for Croatia. The movement her brother was firmly entrenched in.

She hadn't seen her parents in months. They rarely invited her and Jovan to visit. In the time since their marriage the uneasy truce between her husband and her tata only grew more strained. Ivica's politics didn't help that. She hadn't seen her brother at all since before her wedding day.

Now as the trees that lined the railway began to thin, Ilona felt Jovan shift beside her. Lifting her head from his shoulder, she looked up at him and smiled. Today was a special day. She was visiting her dearest friend and would meet a new child of the world, of Yugoslavia. It was not the time to muse on troubled topics.

They found Misa in the front yard of her small home. Her son, Stephan, squatted by a patch of new daffodils, his clumsy fingers picking the flowers from the soil. Misa watched on, her arms full of blankets. She bounced the bundle tenderly. Happiness filled Ilona's heart.

"Misa!" she called, handing her suitcase to Jovan and rushing toward her friend. Tired eyes, red-rimmed from lack of sleep, looked up at her. But from behind the dark circles of fatigue truest joy shone. "Ilona, you are here."

Ilona hugged her friend, careful not to squeeze her and the baby in her arms too tightly.

Pulling away, she looked down into the cradled bundle. A small heart-shaped face, a mirror of Misa's, appeared nestled amongst the swaddling.

"This is Hanna," Misa said, her voice full of pride.

"Oh, Misa," Ilona breathed. "She is perfect."

She felt a small touch on her leg and looked down. Stephan's little face stared up at her, large eyes wide set like his tata's, his fingers gripping her stocking. "Hello, little one," she said, beaming down at him. She knelt quickly and hugged him close. "You have grown so much!" she exclaimed.

"Flower!" Stephan announced, holding up a squashed daffodil.

"It is beautiful," Ilona said.

Jovan came up beside them and ruffled Stephan's fair hair. Ilona looked up at her husband and felt her heart stutter as she noted the longing in his eyes as he gazed at Misa's son. She knew he dreamed of becoming a tata himself. She prayed for the blessing, too. It just hadn't happened yet.

"Come inside. Radič won't be long. We were out of milk," Misa said, drawing Ilona from her worries.

Ilona and Jovan settled themselves in their room, supervised by a very helpful Stephan, while Misa put her daughter down for a nap. Radič arrived home as they made their way into the main living space, Stephan holding Ilona's hand.

"Jovan! Ilona!" Radič's joy boomed around them, and Stephan toddled forward to hug his tata. Scooping his son into his arms, Radič came to greet them, slapping Jovan heartily on the back. Years of living in different places had done nothing to dampen their friendship. Misa appeared and leaned wearily against the door frame, but her face was peaceful and calm.

It was all so beautiful and homely. So different from the worries Ilona had been carrying since overhearing Jovan and Goran.

The men, including a chatting Stephan, peeled off to prepare firewood, and Misa and Ilona settled on the couch.

"So, tell me, what has been happening in Zagreb? How are the new nursing students?"

Ilona didn't miss the intensity of her friend's interest. She knew Misa had been sad to leave the capital. She'd easily have been offered a job as a tutor, like Ilona. And she would have excelled at it. But Misa had had no choice, not with Stephan on the way, and now Hanna to care for.

"They are doing well. Radmila has certainly been putting them through their paces. Marriage hasn't softened her at all."

"Hmmm," Misa mused. "She's never been nice, has she? I always thought it was just me, because I am a Serb. But she's nasty to everyone."

"Everyone," Ilona agreed. "But Dragica has her under control, at least most of the time." The aging matron was a colleague now. The change in that dynamic still felt odd, Ilona would always respect the Head Nurse.

"And you? How are things at home? With Jovan?"

Ilona understood the real question. Pressing a hand to her flat stomach, Ilona sighed. "Not yet."

Silence fell between them, and Misa squeezed Ilona's shoulder in comfort.

"It will happen. You know as well as I do that it can take time for some of us."

"I know." But the knowledge didn't soothe the ache in her heart when she looked at Stephan's soft, fluffy hair, or Hanna's perfect tiny fingers.

"Is that what is troubling you? Why do I see sadness in your eyes?"

Ilona studied Misa's face, studying the lines of fatigue, the bruises of sleep deprivation beneath her eyes. She was exhausted. It showed in her sallow skin, in the dry chaps of her lips. It was just the challenge of a new baby. Ilona understood. Underneath, Misa was full of happiness and contentment.

She could not share her concerns for Yugoslavia, nor the confusion she felt at overhearing Jovan and Goran's discussion of the Italian threat. Misa was her dearest friend; Ilona could not add this worry to her burden. Besides, what was there to say? It was a rumour. It was a feeling on the streets. Nothing had happened. And nothing would. Surely?

Misa reached between them and placed a gentle hand on Ilona's arm. "Has it been tough?"

Ilona felt her face twist in tension and chose to tell a part truth.

"It has been hard, seeing Radmila happy. Her husband is friendly with my brother, they are in the same political circles. But I only know that through Radmila."

"Ivica still has not visited?"

Ilona shook her head sadly. "I have not seen him since before our wedding. I barely see my mama and tata. They are nice enough when I visit, but..."

"You don't feel welcome. What does Jovan say?"

"I don't bring him with me anymore. Tata talks constantly of Croatia's rights. He sounds just like Ivica. I don't wish to put my husband through that."

With the threat of war building along the border the rhetoric of the Ustaše was increasing on the streets, despite the ban on their newspaper. The anger, the frustration. Ilona was scared. Deeply scared.

"Perhaps a baby would be a path through." The words were out before she'd really considered them. But as they echoed through the air, Ilona realised she meant it. A baby. A child like Stephan or Hanna. Her and Jovan's child. Would it melt the tension between her and her family? Would it bring them together? How strange life was. Here Ilona sat with her dearest friend, longing for the children she had, while her friend wished for a life in the city. There really was no simple path in this world.

Frowning, Misa wrapped an arm around Ilona's shoulders. Hanna chose that moment to wake, her piercing cry of indignation cutting through the house. Misa's laugh sounded more like a sigh. "That girl is fierce," she said. "Every time she wakes I swear she is declaring my incompetence as a mama."

"She is not, Misa! You are a wonderful mama." Guilt clawed at her insides as she watched her friend's tired face twitch. There she was meeting her dearest friend and all she could think about were her own worries. Shoving her fear and frustration aside, Ilona stood up. "Stay," she said to Misa. "I will get her."

"Are you sure?" The hope in Misa's tired eyes was palpable. "She can be fussy."

"Don't worry. I will be fine. Besides, it's good practice for the future, right?"

Misa leaned back into the lounge. "You don't have to offer twice. I am more than happy to stay here."

Ilona laughed. Tapping Misa's shoulder, she padded across the house. The bedroom was warm and still, the scent of milk in the air. Ilona approached the crib on light feet, eager not to startle little Hanna. As she looked over the railing of the crib, Hanna's cries sputtered to a stop. Two large blue eyes stared up at Ilona, two little fists unclenching. "Hello, dear one," Ilona said reaching down to collect Hanna into her arms. "There you go. Aunty Ilona is here now." Cradling Hanna to her chest, Ilona rocked her side to side, humming gently. Hanna's mouth pursed making a sucking motion.

"Ah, well, that I can't help you with. Come on then, time to visit Mama."

As she carried Misa's tiny daughter through the house Ilona felt a deep contentment settling over her. *A baby would be a wonderful thing,* she thought. One day. One day.

TWELVE
ILONA

But dreams of the future could not stop the growing threat from Germany.

Ilona sat at the kitchen table, hands entwined with Jovan's. At the stovetop a stew of beets and cabbage bubbled, the warm scent filling the small space.

The newspaper that day had worrying reports from Greece. Italy was engaged in battle there, but were being pushed back. Germany was coming to their aid. It was a building conflict. It was too close to home.

"It will be all right. Tata says the diplomatic threads are all in place. You will see."

Ilona eyed Jovan in silence. It had surprised her, just how much this foreign conflict had settled over their city, their nations, how it heightened their own tensions.

Ilona leant her elbow on the table and rested her head in her hand as she stared out the window at the bright blue skies beyond. It was a beautiful spring Sunday in Zagreb. Outside, the birds tweeted and flittered about, the green leaves of the trees rising for the heavens. A perfect and peaceful day of God. She could not help but wonder what the people of Greece and beyond faced that day. Did the sun still shine over the shadow of gunfire? And if it did, would the citizens notice? Her nation was at peace. Surely this conflict across the continent would not come to their border?

The knock on the door made her jump. The tension of the news and its repercussions had them all on tenterhooks. "I'll get it," she said, rising.

"It's probably Radmila needing flour again," Jovan said. After their wedding the year before, Radmila and David had moved into the same apartment block. The men kept apart. But Radmila and Ilona still worked at the hospital together, a strained truce between them.

Nodding her agreement, Ilona made her way to the front door, swinging it open casually.

But it was not Radmila who stood in the open doorway.

"Ivica?" Ilona blinked in shock as she took in the stocky man who awaited her on the threshold.

"Hello, sister."

Shaking off her surprise, Ilona plastered a smile on her face.

"Aren't you going to ask me in?"

"Yes, of course. Come in." Ilona stepped aside; her heart was pounding in her chest. Her mind was racing. Why was Ivica here? She and Jovan had been married over a year, yet her husband and brother had never met. Why now?

Stepping into the kitchen, she flashed a wide-eyed stare of warning at Jovan. "Husband, my brother Ivica has come to visit."

Jovan rose slowly, extending his hand to Ivica in welcome. "Welcome, Ivica, how lovely to finally meet you," he said. "Please take a seat. We were about to eat. You will join us of course?"

Pointedly ignoring Jovan's offered hand, Ivica pulled out a chair, purposely scraping the legs across the floor in a sharp whine. He sat down.

Jovan caught her eye, a shadowed question in his stare. Ilona gave the briefest shake of her head, willing him to understand, to be subtle, and turned her attention to the stew. Jovan settled back in his chair.

"So, what brings you into the centre of the city?" he began.

Ivica only stared at Jovan, malice dancing across his features. He leaned forward, spreading his arms over the table and placing his rough-skinned hands flat. Filling the space.

Ignoring Jovan's pleasantries, Ivica said, "It has been a long while, sister. You have not visited. Mama worries."

It wasn't true of course, Ilona knew. Since their wedding, she visited when she could, but she did not feel welcome. Pressing down the rising nerves that bubbled from her stomach, Ilona nodded at Ivica. "I am sorry, Ivica, but it has been a very busy time at the hospital."

"Nothing is more important than family."

"Da."

Ivica's assessment moved to the stove. "And what are you cooking?"

"A stew."

"Hmpf, peasant food. I would have thought you'd expect finer fare," his stare found Jovan.

The air went out of the room. Ilona saw the flush of red that was creeping up Jovan's neck at her brother's thinly veiled taunt. Subconsciously, she gripped the ladle tighter and prayed Jovan would not rise to the bait.

"Ilona is a fine cook. She takes good care of me," Jovan said, rolling with the heavy implication from Ivica's lips. "I hope you enjoy."

She spooned out a portion of stew into three bowls, placing one before Ivica. He sniffed then leaned back in his chair, resting a knee on the table edge.

"Thank you, Ilona," Jovan said, cupping his bowl of stew. "It smells wonderful."

"You've been away from your mama's kitchen too long," Ivica said.

Jovan twitched. Ilona flicked a glance at him, willing him to let it slide. To let it go.

"So, what brings you to Zagreb?" Jovan said, steering the conversation. Ilona smiled at him gratefully.

"Does a brother need a reason to check on his sister?"

"I am well, Ivica. Really," Ilona said, trying to calm the moment.

"Besides, I live in Zagreb," Ivica said over her. "Or did she tell you we came from a farm?"

"Apologies, I misspoke. I know you live in the outer suburbs."

"It is not so far. Belgrade is much further to travel." A sneer twisted Ivica's lips.

Jovan nodded, remaining calm. "The capital is certainly a journey. I am lucky to call Zagreb home."

Rage danced in Ivica's eyes. He leaned forward, elbows landing heavily on the table. "Zagreb is *my* capital," he said. "You know we are in the path of the war. Germany is coming."

"Da. They are emboldened. But it is just talk."

Ilona's eyes darted between her brother and Jovan.

Ivica's lip curled menacingly. "We will not give up our country to another foreign force. Not this time.

"This time we will take back what is ours."

Jovan took a sip of stew. Ilona could not comprehend how he remained so calm in the face of Ivica's clear threat.

"It is fortunate that we have each other. Yugoslavia is stronger together," Jovan said. "We have signed an agreement with the Axis forces. So we are protected. A clever move from Belgrade."

Ilona stiffened at his words. Jovan had directly challenged her brother. Ivica's face darkened, and he shoved his bowl of stew away, the liquid sloshing over the rim of the bowl.

A cruel smile smeared his face. "Not Yugoslavia," he hissed. Driving his thumb into his chest, he continued. "We, the Ustaše."

Ilona felt her mouth go dry as panic closed her throat. Ustaše. She knew he had been to meetings with David. But this...

"What do you mean 'we' the Ustaše?" she asked, dread uncoiling within her.

"We rise," he said, coming to his feet. "We will stand up for our people."

"We can do that together," Jovan said softly. "We can stand for all our people, together."

"There is only one people I care about," Ivica said. Fury ripped through Ilona. How dare he come into her home and say such hideous words. She opened her mouth to order him from their apartment but he spoke first. "I am going," he said, eyes aflame with anger. "This is your one and only warning."

"I—"

"You said you were leaving." Jovan had stood up fast, drawing himself to his full height and glaring down on Ivica's shorter frame. She saw Ivica flinch slightly, before he glared at Jovan and strode from the apartment.

They stood in stunned silence until the bang of the front door told them Ivica had left.

Ilona hurried down the hallway and locked it tight. Returning to the kitchen table her heart felt heavy. Tension tugged at her forehead as she sat down. "Jovan, I am so sorry. Ivica is—"

"Correct," Jovan interrupted. "Ivica is correct. Italy is a threat. So is Germany."

Ilona frowned. "But there are agreements in place, you said so..."

"It is just words. Look at the actions. Germany has taken France and Belgium and reaches still further. Aligned with Italy, it will not be long before they turn for us."

"And we will fight," Ilona said. "That is the whole point of Yugoslavia. To work together for our freedom."

A heaviness descended over her husband, lengthening the lines of his face. "Of course," he said.

Something told Ilona he was not convinced.

THIRTEEN

ILONA

Their anxieties were realised on the 6th of April 1941. The King fled, and the Nazis invaded. By the 10th of April, the low, growling rumble of a panzer division filled the streets as the tanks rolled into central Zagreb. Ilona was on shift at the hospital when the news echoed through the wards, whispered nurse to nun, quiet and fearful. The Wehrmacht was here. Zagreb was no longer free.

Ilona stepped out into the cool spring evening, the last streaks of dusk painting the sky in pinks and purples, and relief washed over her. Standing in the glow of a street lamp was her Jovan. Seeing her he straightened, long legs closing the space between them in a matter of strides, hands cupping her face, his eyes searching hers. "You heard?"

Ilona nodded, dread squeezing her ribs. "Everyone knows."

"Let's get home."

The walk home was eerily quiet. The streets of Zagreb were deserted, and her people secreted behind drawn curtains.

"It was chaos only hours ago," Jovan explained. "They were cheering..." He cut off, giving a small shake of his head, and Ilona gripped his arm tighter to her side.

"It will be all right."

His eyes met hers in the failing light, and all she saw in his deep grey pools was rage. Ilona blanched. At their apartment, Jovan locked the door securely, retreating into the kitchen for a chair that he wedged beneath the door handle. Ilona watched on, her concern growing. He took her hand and led her back to the kitchen table. The radio sat on the small table, voices blaring from the speaker.

"I have listened all day."

He helped her out of her coat and pulled out a chair for her, and she sat. The newsreader's voice was a steady hum, oddly familiar against the waves of worry that shook from her husband.

"*Slavko Kvaternik has declared the establishment of the Independent State of Croatia...*" the disembodied voice stated.

A series of cheers sounded from the streets, and Jovan crossed to the window, drawing back the curtain just enough to peer outside.

"Kvaternik... isn't he?"

"The leader of the Ustaše? Da."

Fresh fear gripped Ilona's throat. "The Ustaše, they are in control?"

"Working with the Nazis." He turned to face her.

"We are occupied. But our own people have been placed in charge?"

"The Ustaše are not our people!" Jovan's eyes flashed.

Ilona recoiled from the anger in his stare.

"You know their policies. You know what they want."

She did. Not just an independent Croatia, but an ethnically pure Croatia. God, what would this mean for Jovan? For Misa and her children? For all the Serbs of her country?

"What do we do?" she asked.

Jovan came to her side. Drawing his chair close he pulled her against his chest, his arms strong and firm. "I will keep you safe," he promised.

It was not her life she feared for.

As he walked her to the hospital the next morning, Ilona felt a wreck of nerves. She'd slept poorly, the momentous events of the day before invading even her dreams. The dark circles under Jovan's eyes told her he'd faced the same fitful rest. Around them, the city began to wake. Already, soldiers in grey stalked the streets beside others bearing the navy blue 'U' emblem of the Ustaše, scrutinising the city's citizens as they passed.

The emotion in the hospital was palpable, and an air of excited energy infused the wards. Ilona stood in the hallway in shock. The people were happy. They had been occupied by a foreign force, but they were happy. Only the nuns kept their heads down, their lips still. She fought the rising nausea that burned up her throat. Radmila came into view, and Ilona ducked her head, hoping to avoid the woman's sharp tongue. The click of fast-approaching heels told her she'd not be so lucky.

She raised her head and braced her shoulders, determined to meet Radmila's bullish behaviour with what strength she could muster.

"Why are you here?" she hissed at Ilona, concern furrowing her brow.

Ilona blinked in surprise. "I am supervising my students' rounds today."

"I will cover you, you need to go."

"I don't understand—"

"The university and the schools of education, David says they will start with the academics."

Ilona met Radmila's stare, and saw the panic resting there. "What do you mean?"

"The Ustaše, you know their policies. They want to change our city, our country."

"As do you," Ilona said, her stare hardening on her colleague. For years Radmila had taunted Misa, reminding her daily of her inferior status.

Radmila's face fell and guilt flashed over her features. "My jealousy has been... unbecoming. It made sense before. But now..." a pause, then she gripped Ilona's hands, her fingers ice cold. "Now it is real. The Ustaše, it is not enough for them to rule. They want all of the Serbs gone. *'One third exterminated, one third converted and one third deported'*."

Ilona felt her lips part in horror. "What are you saying?"

Radmila bent lower, bringing her mouth to Ilona's ear. "They rounded up the Orthodox priests last night. They will not live long."

Already? They'd only been in power for a day. Surely Radmila had this wrong.

"David says the academics will be next." Her gaze tightened on Ilona, and realisation stole her breath. "Jovan."

"You must get to him. Get him out of the School of Music. Out of Zagreb."

Panic clutched at Ilona's chest, her heart beat fluttering wildly. Jovan.

"I..." She turned, hands trembling.

"Go," Radmila breathed. "I will explain to Dragica. She will understand. Go."

Ilona didn't wait to let her mind catch up. Energy flooded her, and she pivoted on her heel, racing from the hospital and onto the streets of the city. She had to make it to the School of Music. Fast.

Jovan wasn't at the music school, but soldiers were. Ilona tugged her coat up around her chin, obscuring her face, and hurried away. Back at their home she found their rooms silent and dark. No sign of Jovan and no letter of explanation. Infused with worry, Ilona headed back out, pacing the streets of Zagreb. She went to their regular cafe – no Jovan, to the park where he liked to play violin – no Jovan. Mind locking up with fear she passed the central Dolac market, eyes ranging over the citizens, desperately hoping Jovan would simply appear.

Suddenly, a soldier grabbed hold of a woman's arm and shoved her bodily to the ground, the scarf over her hair falling away. A child screamed as the soldier brought back his boot and swung it into the fallen woman's ribs. Ilona froze in shock as the people around the woman scurried away. The woman looked up, meeting Ilona's stare, the whites of her eyes wild. The soldier shouted something at her, and she scrabbled to her feet, her basket of apples rolling away over the cobbles.

Ilona hurried home.

As the day darkened she made her way to the hospital, thinking Jovan may go there to collect her from her shift. But the space outside the entrance was empty. Giving up as the night claimed the streets, Ilona returned to their apartment. Body exhausted from walking, lack of food and fear, she slumped down at the kitchen table and waited.

Hours after the moon had risen to its zenith, a key sounded in the lock. Ilona's head shot up from her arms where she'd been resting against the table. She hadn't turned in for the night, she couldn't. Not without Jovan. Senses on fire with alarm she listened, muscles trembling.

Footsteps sounded along the hallway, then a figure appeared in the shadows beyond the doorway. Her breathing hitched as a hand reached for the switch, flooding the kitchen in light.

"Jovan!" she exclaimed, coming to her feet and rushing to his side. "Thank God, oh thank God!"

She clutched him to her, heart beating out of her chest as she pressed in close.

"Ilona?" His voice was soft and confused. "I am sorry, I know it is late. I did not think it would worry you."

"Where have you been?" Her voice was high pitched and frantic. "I went to the music school but there were soldiers. So I tried the cafe, the park. I thought... I thought." She cut off as the sobs of fear and relief flooded through her and turned away in an effort to control her outburst.

"You went to the school? Oh, Ilona..."

Jovan pulled her back into his arms, rocking her gently as her body gave in to all the emotions she'd been holding at bay since Radmila's warning.

"My heart," Jovan whispered. "I am sorry. I had to register. I didn't know how long it would take."

His words cut through her tears. Blinking the water from her eyes Ilona looked up at Jovan. "Register?"

He released a heavy sigh. Stepping from her arms, he dipped his hand in his pocket to draw out his wallet and produced a small rectangular card. Showing it to Ilona he said, "Da, we all did. Every Serb in the city, in the country. We all have a number now."

FOURTEEN
ILONA

"I will be safe," Jovan assured her. "Radmila is likely right. David would know, he is firmly in the hierarchy of the Ustaše."

Jovan broke off. Ilona saw the barely controlled rage in the pulsing of his neck. David was her friend's husband. David had always been anti-Serb.

Ilona breathed through the biting anxiety that gripped her chest. The reality of her family and friends. And how they viewed the most important person in her life.

"But," Jovan continued, "I converted years ago – for you. I am not a target for the Ustaše."

What about my brother? What might Ivica do? She didn't voice the thoughts. Didn't allow that piercing fear to be shared. Yet how could she turn it from her thoughts? Ivica was angry. He had followed David to the Ustaše meetings. Even Radmila, who had long taken David's lead, was concerned about how things were progressing.

That night as she stared at the small card that labelled her husband as nothing more than a number, Ilona chose to accept her husband's words. Comforting, reasonable. *"One third converted,"* that was what Radmila had said. Jovan had converted. It was logical that that meant Jovan was safe. But what about the others?

Would they really threaten the lives of innocent Serbs? It was too much to reckon with. Too big to comprehend. Radmila had to be wrong. It had to just be passionate words, not a real plan, surely?

As the darkness of the small hours built around her, she worried for Misa, her husband Radič and their beautiful children. A family couldn't be a target, could they? Two people making their way in life, working for their community, their small children by their sides. No, she was overthinking it. Yes, they were occupied and soldiers walked their streets. But they were all people, at the end of the day. What did the lives of factory workers in the centre of the country matter? The world still turned, even in war. Yet try as she might, sleep did not come, that night, or the next.

The days dragged on, the fear on the streets rising.

As Ilona made her way to work she started to notice everyday people wearing the Star of David on their sleeves. Another order from the new government no doubt: a symbol for the Jewish citizens, a number for the Serbs.

Jovan was fired from the School of Music, his friend Goran from the University of Science.

"It is all right," he argued that night as they lay in bed, limbs entwined. "It will give me more time to watch over you."

Ilona had nodded, allowing the warmth of his skin, the scent of his musk, to soothe her fears. But they both knew it was a bad sign.

Then Goran went missing.

Jovan asked around, but no one had heard anything.

A week later, as Ilona stepped out into the May dusk, the shuffling echoes of the hospital fading away behind her, Jovan was not there to walk her home. Ilona forced her mind to calm. He was just busy, there was no need to fear. He couldn't be there every shift, she reasoned. She still made her way home as rapidly as she could. As she stepped through her front door the low hum of voices drifted down the passage from the kitchen.

"I am telling you, they wanted them hurt!" A man's deep and impassioned voice rose above the general murmur of chatter.

"You can't know that, Josip. It was a youth meeting. Who would try and attack children?" Another voice reasoned.

"The Ustaše." That was her Jovan.

"That doesn't help," the second voice said.

"At least he is listening. My Petar ran home in terror. Those Croat leaders, they were riling them up. There was a whole speech about race theory and the scourge of the Jew and the Serb. Then they asked those children to step forward. Only those children. If Petar's friends hadn't stepped forward with him, and the others, they would have been killed."

"They tried to create a pogrom," Jovan said.

Ilona walked into the room, and Jovan's face snapped up, seeing her standing in the doorway.

"Ilona!" He stood, eyes flicking to the clock that ticked on the side table. "I forgot the time."

Ilona stared into the room. At the table sat two men she did not know, dark-haired and dark-eyed, their bulky jackets filling the small space of her kitchen.

"This is Josip and Slavko," Jovan continued, running his hands down his trousers nervously. "They were just leaving."

The two men pushed back from their chairs and stood. Slavko nodded at Ilona, "Pleased to meet you, Mrs Babic." The other passed without a word. Jovan walked them to the front door, pausing to gently squeeze Ilona's arm as he passed.

"We will see you again soon. If anything happens before then, you know where to find us."

"Da."

The men disappeared beyond the door, and Jovan turned back to Ilona. "Who are those men? What has happened?" she asked.

Jovan tried a deflection. "Just some friends from the university," he said, shrugging past her and heading for the kitchen. "Can I make you a cup of coffee?" He threw over his shoulder.

"Jovan," Ilona speared her words at his back as she followed close on his heel. "Do not hide things from me. Those men were scared, and angry."

He didn't face her, busying himself with the stove. But his hands were shaking, his movements jagged, and he could not light the match. Gently Ilona took his hands in hers, seeking his eyes. Fear tightened his irises. "Tell me," she said softly. "We are under occupation. People are being categorised. We know the Ustaše rhetoric. Are they putting those words into action? If you know something you have to tell me. We have to be honest with each other."

Jovan released a long, sorrowful sigh. "I just don't want to scare you."

Ilona raised her head. "I am a nurse. I see sickness and death every day. I can take it."

He gripped her face and brought their foreheads together briefly.

"Sit," Ilona ordered, "I will make the coffee." She lit a match.

Sitting together at their small kitchen table, knees pressed together, coffee cups steaming, Ilona waited in patient silence.

Finally, Jovan spoke. "Josip is a colleague of Goran's from the university, as is Slavko. They were all retired, like me."

The pain of losing his tutorage flashed across his face, and Ilona reached forward taking his hand in hers. He gifted her a quick smile and continued. "Josip's son is part of the National Youth Guard. He thought about removing him when the Ustaše took power, but we all thought it would be a good thing... a way to show loyalty. But..."

He broke off and sipped his coffee. "Petar said the leadership tried to make the Croatian boys angry. Tried to separate the Jews and Serbs, and..."

"You used a term I don't know. What is a pogrom?"

Jovan's eyes closed. "Rounding up a group and killing them."

Ilona sucked in a sharp breath, her hand flying up to cover her mouth. "Surely not. At a Youth Guard?"

"They are still the wrong race and religion."

"What do we do?"

"We keep quiet and small. We keep our heads down. And I walk you everywhere."

As the height of summer reached for its peak, the tension on the streets was ready to boil over, and the next act in the conquest of the Ustaše was about to begin. Ilona walked hand in hand with Jovan, their fingers laced tight as they made their way to the open-air Dolac market. The tables of produce were already crowded by hungry citizens, seeking to secure what they could. There had been an increase in population in Zagreb as Ustaše military operations in the countryside forced people to the cities. Food was becoming scarce, but not desperate, yet. A light, misty rain began to fall from a weak smattering of clouds above, dusting the bright red radishes in droplets.

Pushing through the crowds, Ilona was able to secure the bread and vegetables she needed, and a leg of pork. She left the cheese; their budget on only her teaching salary was limited. But she bought some plums to make jam to share with her parents. She had decided to visit them the next day. Food secured, they headed home to prepare for her trip to Dubrava.

As the sun rose the next morning, they made their way down to the lower town and Zagreb Central Station, Jovan carrying their paper bag of goods. He would not accompany her to Dubrava, but he would walk her to and from the bus. As the green tree-lined pavilion that stretched before the station came into view, a commotion rang out from the streets ahead. Jovan slowed, instantly scanning around them. Ilona copied but saw nothing out of the ordinary. The sound fell away, and they continued on. Until Zagreb Central Station came into view.

Jovan froze, one arm darting out to press Ilona behind him. Craning her neck around his broad shoulder, Ilona recoiled in shock. Queuing before the station entrance was a long line of men, all bearing the Star of David on their upper arms, and bracing them on each side stood men in the uniform of the Ustaše.

"What are they doing?" Ilona breathed at Jovan.

"Head down," he ordered. "Stay behind me. And *don't* look."

His free hand gripped Ilona's shoulder, holding her firmly at his side as he angled them away from the station.

A scream ripped through the air. Ilona's head snapped up, just in time to see an older man fall to the ground. The soldier standing above him raised his gun, bringing the butt down on his greying curls with a sickening thud.

"Eyes down," Jovan hissed, manoeuvring them into an alleyway and lengthening his stride.

Ilona allowed herself to be hurried along, the pain in the old man's scream echoing in her ears.

Jovan did not let up his pace, not as they raced past the central gardens and on to a bus back up to their upper town apartment. Not as their feet hit their cobbled road and they rushed up the stairs to their second-floor home. Not until they were inside and their door was securely fastened behind them.

"What were they doing?" Ilona asked eyes wide with fear and confusion.

"I don't know," Jovan said, and she could tell he was being honest. "But it won't stop with the Jews."

She would not be visiting her parents today after all.

The transports out of Zagreb didn't stop. Soldiers filtered out through the streets rounding up Jewish and Serb citizens and anyone else they deemed "against" their government.

Over the summer, rumours spread of beatings and the executions of Communists in the prisons. Of terrible conditions.

Then the anti-fascist resistance fighters tried to rescue their men.

The result was blared out across Zagreb through radio waves and gunfire. The resistance had been routed. Their prisoners never made it from their cells. They were rounded up and executed in the streets, blood running through the cobbles. The result was repeated when a group staged an assault on a company of Ustaše near the Zagreb Botanical Gardens.

The radio declared their fate: captured and court-martialled. Though neither Jovan nor Ilona believed there had really been a trial.

As the radio announcer shared the information, Ilona and Jovan stared at one another, and she knew he read the the question in her eyes that had lived there permanently since their occupation: *what do we do?*

"We stay small," he repeated.

Ilona swallowed and sent a prayer to God that Jovan would keep his word.

And he did.

Until the woman arrived at the hospital.

FIFTEEN
ILONA

Ilona was just finishing her midday rounds when she heard raised voices from the reception. Putting down her clipboard, she made her way out to the front entrance of the hospital, hoping to help.

"Please, please. They must be here. They must be." The woman's dress was torn, her shoes scuffed and dirt-crusted.

Behind the reception desk, Dragica stood, palms raised. "No children have been admitted today," she said. "And no Serbs."

Ilona's forehead tightened. "But I got them out," the woman said. "I shoved Lada through the glass. She cut her arm. Igor would have taken her here to be treated."

Stepping forward Ilona listened intently. Got her out? Pushed a child through a window? What was going on?

"I am sorry but there is no Lada or Igor in our wards."

The woman looked around, movements tight and frantic, and Ilona noted the deep gash along the side of her face. Blood had dried along her skin and the collar of her coat.

Dragica stepped around the desk, catching Ilona's eye. "Please, Mrs Davocvic. Let me look at that wound."

But the woman jerked away from Dragica's touch. "They will come for them. I have to find them. They will come for them." She backed away, hands out before her defensively.

"Mrs Davocvic, please," Dragica tried again, but the woman was beyond reason. Her back hit the entrance to the hospital and she turned sharply, crashing her hands against the door and racing into the streets.

"What happened to her?" Ilona said, coming to Dragica's side.

The older nurse shook her head slowly. "I could not make sense of it. Likely a result of that head wound."

"Concussion?"

"Undoubtedly."

"But what of the children?"

Dragica heaved a long sigh. "We can only hope they got away."

"Away from what?"

"Whatever did that to Mrs Davocvic's face."

The streets were quiet as Ilona made her way home from her shift beneath a cloudless sky. It was late, but the air still held the heat of the day. Summer was lingering. By the time she made it up the airless stairwell of her apartment block, Ilona was covered with a sheen of sweat. Opening the door to her home, the stuffy scent of cigarettes and coffee assaulted her nose. As she padded down the hallway, the heat of the rooms increased with that of the words that drifted from her kitchen. Slavko and Josip sat at the table, the grey smoke of their cigarettes hanging above their heads in the stagnant room. Jovan stood at the stove, preparing coffee. The empty cups at his side showed it was not their first round of the bitter drink. He had thrown the window open, seeking respite from the unseasonable warmth, but not even a breath of breeze curled through the open space. Outside the sky hung streaked in shades of blue, the sounds of the city muted by gathering dusk.

And the men spoke of death.

"...It was a slaughter."

"It cannot be true."

"David saw it with his own eyes They rounded them up for conversion. Then shot them all dead. It was an execution."

"Who was executed?"

The men's faces whipped to hers as one. Jovan's mouth

dropped open in shock, his skin paling in the harsh light of the kitchen lamp. His mouth opened and closed, and Ilona could see the war within his mind. He didn't want to tell her.

"Who was rounded up?" She pressed. Josip stood and paced to the window. Perching on the edge of the open frame, he took a deep draw on his cigarette and breathed white smoke out over the city.

Slavko closed his eyes, head shaking. But Jovan kept his focus on her.

She saw the moment he gave in as his shoulders collapsed down. "Ilona, you weren't meant to hear that."

"Jovan. Who? Slavko... he said they were taken for conversion... that they were shot? Oh!" Her eyes flew open in horror as her mind raced forward, joining the dots.

"The Orthodox," she whispered. Jovan winced. "They went to convert? To be baptised and join the Catholic Church? To be safe from the Ustaše. But they killed them." She knew there had been campaigns across the city. The Ustaše pressuring Orthodox Serbs to convert to Catholicism, just as Jovan had done. He had done it for love, and of his own free will. In this case it was about survival. Radmila's words bloomed in her mind again, *"One third converted, one third deported, one third executed."* Oh dear God, they had taken people to church to begin the process to convert and executed them instead. Her hand slapped over her mouth as gravity of the realisation weighted her soul.

"They killed them in a church."

Jovan eyed her sadly, his face sagging in sorrow, and Ilona knew she had guessed correctly.

"Two children escaped. They ran to David."

Ilona's breath left her body. "Children. Oh God! Their mama... she was at the hospital today. Searching. She said she pushed her daughter out of the window. She was bleeding..."

"It is all right," Jovan said, closing the space between them. "Darna is with her children. David saw to it."

"Jovan. Are you telling me that the soldiers murdered people, children, just because they were Orthodox?" Radmila had said they would, but who could believe such a policy? Who could imagine such brutality?

Jovan closed his eyes. "No," he whispered sadly. "They did it because they could."

It was too much. Ilona felt her knees give. What was happening to her beautiful country? Leaning heavily on the table, she sunk into the chair beside Slavko.

"I will make you a coffee," Jovan said, crossing to the stove.

Ilona felt her body begin to shake, her hands blurring where they rested on the table. A steaming cup of coffee was placed before her, and she felt Jovan's closeness as he sat at her side.

"How many?" she whispered.

"Over sixty."

Her eyes snapped to his. "Sixty?"

He reached out, smoothing a curl behind her ear. "We didn't know. There have been other conversions, without incident. We thought it was just the priests."

"The priests?"

"They were sent to the camps. Along with members of the former government."

"We never thought they would attack the converts," Josip said from the window.

A rushing sound had filled her ears. It was blood. The sound of her blood.

"Drink," Jovan's soft command was muted and far away.

"Wait." Josip's words filtered over her. "What do you mean 'we never thought'?" She looked up at the man by her window, but his face was turned away. Slavko coughed uncomfortably. Ilona sought Jovan's eyes.

He blinked, then turned away, raking a hand through his hair. "There have been rumours—"

"We will take our leave," Slavko blurted, pushing up from the table.

"Da," Josip agreed, stubbing out his cigarette on the window sill and flicking the bud into the night.

"I will see you out," Jovan began. But Josip stilled him with a hand on his shoulder.

"We know the way. Take care of your wife. We will see you in two nights' time."

The men's heavy tread softened down the hallway, the door clicking shut, leaving Ilona and Jovan alone in the over-warm kitchen. A line of sweat raced down her spine, and Ilona gulped.

"What rumours?" she whispered.

Jovan released a heavy sigh, his head bowing low. "Executions, in the forests outside Zagreb."

Ilona's mind spun. More killings? She couldn't take it. "Who?"

"Mostly resistance fighters, those who stand up against the Ustaše."

"Goran?"

Jovan shook his head sadly. "No, I don't know. He wasn't a rebel. There is hope."

That was a relief.

But as she put together all the details a terrifying idea formed in her mind. "How do you know all this? You all talked of pogroms. And now it is your friends that Darna came to for her children. And you know of the forests."

"I told you, rumours," he answered evasively.

"Jovan, look at me."

His shoulders bunched, his lips twisting.

"Jovan, tell me you aren't working with the resistance?" Ilona gripped the table, fear cutting deep into her heart.

"We can't stand by and watch."

The air whooshed from her lungs as her mind began to race.

"What are you doing in two nights?"

He met her eyes, confusion scrunching his brow. "Don't pretend. Josip said he would see you in two nights. What are you a part of?"

"My people aren't safe. Innocent people, women and children. I can't sit back and watch."

"What are you doing in two nights?" she repeated, her voice rising in time with her strengthening pulse.

He glanced away. "Destroying the Post Office Telegram Station."

Ilona gasped. "What? Why?"

"Communication," Jovan's eyes were beseeching. "If we take out the telegram system then we cut Zagreb off from Berlin, Vienna, even Belgrade. It gives us time."

"Time for what?"

"Time to fight."

"Jovan! That's too dangerous. The attempt at the prison, they were caught," her throat knotted. "They were shot in the street as a warning. What if you are seen, or worse, get caught? It will be you in those forests with a gun to your head."

"I have a number assigned to me. I am already unsafe." His eyes blazed, and Ilona stilled. "They are murdering women and children..." He continued softly. "I have to do something."

"Jovan." She reached forward, placing a hand on each of his cheeks and bringing his forehead to hers. "Please, don't do this. We have to lay low. Stay small. You said so yourself. It is the only hope we have."

The warmth of his breath brushed her lips. "Innocent people are being slaughtered. Refugees are pouring in from the country-side, thrown from their villages by Ustaše military units. Our resources are stretched."

"And you are my husband," Ilona said, forcing him to look at her.

"I have to do this, Ilona. Our targets are carefully chosen. They will disrupt. Slow the Ustaše down. It will save lives. I need you to understand. I need you in this with me."

Ilona leant back, dropping her hands from his face. The resolve she saw shining in his eyes hurt, punching a hole right through her stomach. His mind was made up, she could see. This wasn't an argument she could win.

"Come back to me," she said, her voice barely a breath.

Jovan's hands slipped around her head to cradle the nape of her neck, pulling her mouth to his in a deep and impassioned kiss.

It was all the answer he ever gave.

Two nights later they sat together in the twilight that shone through the kitchen window.

"Play for me?" Ilona asked.

Jovan smiled softly and went to collect his violin. Soon the aching strains of his beautiful instrument kissed lightly over Ilona's skin, bringing her senses alive and filling her with sorrow and joy in equal measure. As Jovan's fingers danced across the violin frets, Ilona gave herself up to the music, allowing the gentle pluck and sway of her husband's playing to lure her away from the truth before her. A city under occupation, a nation divided, her husband about to risk his life. She let go, and the notes fluttered through her mind, dulling the fear, the panic – releasing the hope, the meaning.

When Jovan held the last chord, a tone that suggested there was more to come, that this story was not finished, not yet, she opened her eyes. He stared at her across the room, his eyes full of love.

She rose and crossed to him, pressing her lips to his. He wrapped his arms around her, the violin and bow coming to rest against her back as he tugged her close.

"I will see you in the morning," she whispered against his mouth.

Jovan nodded, stepping back he handed her his violin, trusting her to pack it away.

"You are always with me," he said, tapping his heart. Then turned and strode from the room.

Ilona watched until the door shut behind his back, then knelt down and slid the violin back into its case. As she set it in the cupboard in their room, she could not have known those were the last notes she would ever hear him play.

SIXTEEN

ILONA

A knock on her door shocked Ilona awake. The strains of a violin playing in her dreams faded from her hearing. Springing up from her pillows, Ilona blinked rapidly, trying to bring her eyes into focus. The light that leaked around the curtain edges was still soft, with barely a hint of sunlight touching the morning sky.

Her hand reached out across the mattress beside her. Cold. Empty.

Jovan wasn't home.

Rolling to the side she clicked on her lamp, her uniform pulled against her skin. She was still fully dressed. But she'd been asleep. Dreaming of music.

Her sleep-stuffed mind began to turn. Jovan was out with Josip and Slavko. They were attacking the Post Office. The memory flooded back. Of his focus and determination. Of her agitation and fear. She hadn't wanted him to do it. But she could not stop him. Unable to calm her nerves she'd stayed up late, drinking coffee, staring out over the moonlit streets of Zagreb. She had only come to bed to rest her eyes...

The banging on her door sounded again, booming and insistent.

Fear seized her breath. Who was at the door? It was barely day, and she was alone. Jovan was not here. Had he been captured? Had they come for her?

Slipping her feet from the mattress she crept along the cool hallway to the front door. She took a deep shaking breath, her hands resting against the solid wood.

"Who is it?"

"Ilona? Oh, thank the heavens. It's Radmila. You must come to the hospital now."

The hospital? Oh, dear God. Her stomach dropped out as panic rattled along her limbs. Had something happened to Jovan? Had the plan for the Post Office failed? Hands shaking she pulled the door open.

Radmila stood in the hallway, expression closed. She regarded Ilona quickly. "You are already dressed. Good. Gather your things, we are all needed at the hospital."

"I am not teaching this morning."

"Me neither, but we have all been summoned. They need all hands – training nurses, nuns, teachers, everyone. There was an explosion at the Central Post Office and there have been several other skirmishes across the city. They are bringing the injured to us."

"The Post Office?" And more attacks? Oh Lord, what had Jovan done?

"There isn't time now, Ilona. Get ready quickly, we must go."

They raced down the silent streets of Zagreb, the dawn gathering gently, a striking counterpoint to the worry in Ilona's heart. Who had been injured? What would she find at the hospital? Where was Jovan?

They arrived to a ward in chaos. Several men in military uniform, both Ustaše and Wehrmacht, lay on gurneys, blood seeping through their uniforms, marring the usually pristine cloth. Their groans of pain filled the room, their wide eyes shattered by agony. Dragica was leaning over the only man in civilian dress, a stethoscope pressed to his chest. She rose as Ilona and Radmila entered, and Ilona's eyes sought the man. Not Jovan. Definitely dead. Her heart cleaved. A civilian. Not a soldier.

Dragica met her stare. "Come," she gestured. "We are needed. Assess each man in turn and stabilise the bleeding. If they need surgery, inform me immediately."

Ilona and her fellow nurses plunged in. At that moment it did not matter that the men beneath her hands were the enemy. They were injured and needed treatment. It was her job as a nurse. She had trained for this. Forcing her concern for Jovan's safety from her mind, she got to work. The young man lay sprawled on the trolley, his lips pale, his face tight with pain. Ilona checked his pulse: weak. "Where does it hurt?" she asked. He stared at her, eyes glazed, and clutched his stomach. Carefully, Ilona unbuttoned his jacket. A bloom of red had soaked into the shirt beneath. Gently she pulled back the shirt and sucked in a sharp breath. His eyes darted to hers. Then he pushed up on the gurney, trying to rise to see his wounds.

"Shhh, be still, be still," Ilona said quickly, pushing him back down. He offered little resistance.

"Dragica," she called. "This one."

Dragica nodded, sending two porters over to collect the writhing soldier and wheel him away for surgery. Ilona watched them disappear down the hall. Would he survive? He was so young.

"Next," Dragica's voice cut through Ilona's paralysis, and she moved to the waiting patient.

An hour or so later, when the last injured soldier was settled on a ward, Ilona collapsed into a chair in the break room. Her hands were covered in dry blood, and the front of her white apron was stained. A quick glance around her confirmed her fellow nurses were equally exhausted and bloodied, staring at nothing as they sat recovering. A group of nuns gathered together against the far wall, heads bent together in silent prayer. Ilona crossed herself.

There had been so much blood. She'd seen injuries before, but nothing like this. The damage an explosion could do... The human body was so fragile. What were they doing to each other? Jovan had been part of this. He'd promised no one would be hurt. But seven soldiers now lay bandaged and broken on the hospital wards. And a civilian was dead. More soldiers were arriving, brought from attacks on patrols on Vrbanićeva Street on the other side of the old town. A fresh cohort of nurses had relieved Ilona and her colleagues, taking over the assessment and treatment of their wounds from bullets and shrapnel. Dragica was still out there overseeing. The old woman was like stone. Immovable and strong.

Ilona rubbed her forehead and felt a crust of dried blood break off from her fingers. Her stomach churned as acid burned in her throat, her stomach threatening to empty its contents. She took a deep, steadying breath and willed herself to calm. How she longed for Misa's steady presence.

The door to the break room creaked, and Ilona looked up. Dragica stood in the doorway, her heavyset arms resting on her hips as she studied Ilona and the other exhausted nurses sitting in the room in various states of dishevelment. "You did well today," she said, fixing each nurse with a stare. "I know this would have been a shock and for some of you a challenge." Her gaze snagged on Ilona before moving away. "Sadly, it likely will not be the last of such injuries we see. But that is tomorrow's burden. For today, well done. Clean up, go home and rest. The roster has been rearranged to allow you to recover. Check your new schedule at reception on the way out."

Ilona stood, weary to her very bones, and filed into the bathroom to wash her hands. Red streaked down the washbasin, pale and watery. She scrubbed at her hands with the carbonic soap, but try as she might she could not get the blood out from beneath her fingernails. Drying her hands, leaving streaks on the towel, she made her way to her locker and collected her coat and bag before heading for the doorway. Her stained apron went in the bin. It was beyond salvage.

The apartment was dark and silent when she returned. No

lights were on, and the curtains were still drawn from the night before. She'd not had time to open them for morning in her rush to the hospital. The dark silence answered a question though: Jovan had not returned.

Worry washed over her, stealing the last of her resolve. Something had gone terribly, terribly wrong. Dumping her bag on the floor she drew off her coat and hung it on the hook by the door, her movements slow and disjointed. She was exhausted.

Footsteps heavy, she made her way to the kitchen. Her eyes were drooping; she needed sleep, but her stomach grumbled, and she knew she needed food too. The chaos on the wards, the stress and fear, had taken a huge toll that needed to be nursed to health. She stepped into the kitchen. A dark figure moved before her.

A cry escaped her lips, and Ilona stumbled backwards. The curtains to the window were thrown open and sunlight blasted through the glass. Ilona squinted against the brightness and her heart leaped.

"Jovan!" She rushed across the kitchen and threw herself into his arms. His body was rigid like stone against her embrace. She pulled back, scanning his face.

"Jovan? Are you hurt?" Her fingers brushed over his torso, down his arms, scanning frantically for any sign of wounds or blood.

"No," he said, voice rasping. His large, gentle hands took hold of hers, stilling her search.

"What happened to you?"

His voice was sharp and urgent as he seized her shoulders moving her into the sunlight. Ilona glanced down and realised the blood had seeped through her apron onto her uniform. "I am fine, I am fine," she said quickly. "They brought them to the hospital..."

Ilona looked up and saw his face crumple, shame lacing his features. His eyes were red-rimmed. "What happened?" she whispered.

His head shook from side to side. "It went wrong," he managed.

"Tell me," she soothed her hand over his brow.

Jovan sniffed, leading her to the kitchen table. He took a seat and drew her into his lap, wrapping her tight against his chest. Questions raged through Ilona's mind, but in that moment all that mattered was his closeness. Jovan was alive. Unhurt. It was all right.

His voice was soft against her skin as he spoke. "We got the bombs in place. There weren't meant to be so many soldiers. The detonation was delayed. It wasn't up to me. They decided to continue."

Ilona closed her eyes and bit her lip. "And the attacks on Vrbanićeva Street?"

Jovan drew back his gaze, searching hers. "What attacks? I didn't know about that."

She turned away, her breath tight. "It seemed coordinated."

Jovan was nodding. "Likely the Partisans. Combined attacks are more effective."

"He died," Ilona said. "The civilian died."

She felt Jovan's body stiffen, then soften as he accepted the news. She folded her arms around him again, drawing him tightly against her. It was horrible. It was wrong. But it was war.

The Ustaše had murdered children. Was more death the answer? What other choice was there?

Jovan ran a hand through her hair and turned her head to face him. "I have to go away."

Ilona frowned. "Go away? What do you mean?"

His eyes tracked over her shoulder, gazing out of the window across the sun-kissed roofs of Zagreb, orange and golden, peaceful and beautiful. And a lie. "Josip was seen. The Ustaše have issued a warrant for his arrest. And for Slavko, they are known friends."

Ilona's breath stuttered. "No," she whispered.

"Da, we don't have long—"

"But wait. You said Josip was seen. What about you? If you weren't spotted—"

"Ilona," Jovan's voice remained soft, but the edges hardened.

"If they are caught I will be discovered. They have more chance if we work together. We are a group. We go together."

Ilona searched his face. "Where?"

He leaned forward, burying his face in her neck. "I can't tell you that. But I will come back."

"No, please, Jovan. Stay," Ilona said, her stomach tightening in fear. "They didn't see you. Stay here with me. Please."

"We can't stop," he breathed against her neck. "We have to fight. We cannot give up. My people—"

"They are my people too," Ilona interrupted.

Jovan drew back and met her eyes. "I know. And you do so much in your work at the hospital. But I am a man; I have to fight for what is right."

"What about your safety? This is dangerous, Jovan! Look at what happened today. That was your plan going wrong. What about when the soldiers come for you?"

"13789."

Her protests died on her lips.

"I am just a number to them, Ilona. Recorded and tracked. It was always a matter of time."

She knew it was true.

"I will come with you."

"No." He lifted her chin gently, running a finger over her jaw. "You will stay and be brilliant, train new nurses and care for the sick. And when this is over, I will come back."

Sorrow overcame her. It was too much. The hours of blood and cries of the injured. The panic over what might have happened to Jovan. And now this. To be separated. To not know what was happening or where Jovan was. "I can't do this," she sobbed. "I can't be apart from you."

Jovan cocked his head at her, eyes twinkling in the sunlight. "You are never apart from me, remember?" He tapped her heart. "We are never apart."

Ilona surged forward, locking her lips with his. His arms enveloped her, fierce and strong, and he stood, carrying her to their room. His step was sure despite the fatigue that must weigh on him, as it had her. But that didn't matter now. There was no time to rest, only time to say goodbye. And it was slipping away.

As he lay her down on the mattress and settled above her, his face hovering over hers, she held his stare. "You promise to return?"

"With all my heart."

PART THREE

SEVENTEEN

"I was in Sisak II. I didn't know that at first of course. To me, it was just a camp filled with children. They made us work, chopping wood, planting crops. We never had a day off. Some children were taken away to the sheds at the back of the camp. They didn't come back. We didn't know why. But we wanted to be chosen. Anything had to be better than where we were, we thought."

Jelena looks down at her knotted hands and takes a ragged breath. Sara waits patiently. They are in the woman's home in Zagreb. Her husband has gone for a walk. He didn't want to listen. But Jelena wants to talk, and Sara wants to listen. It is important, even if it hurts.

"I know now why they didn't come back. The gassings. That stopped when the nurses came. They also brought food and blankets. That was a wonderful day. But I didn't get much time to enjoy it. The next week, I was selected, but not for the sheds. I was old enough for the adult camp. Sisak I. I didn't realise a camp could be even worse than Sisak II…"

"That was hard," Sara says to Daniel as they walk to the van.

"My baba is about Jelena's age. She never talks about the camps, but hearing that story I can imagine..."

She breaks off, the lump in her throat too large to talk around. Daniel places his camera on the ground and pulls her into a hug. Sara leans into his embrace. He is a good friend. She is glad they met at university. Glad he is here with her now.

"We are doing this for her," he says. "Remember that."

Sara pictures her tiny baba and steps back from Daniel.

"I wish she would speak to me about it."

"It's understandable. It can't be a good set of memories."

"True," Sara agrees. She can't help but think there is more than bad memories behind her baba's silence.

EIGHTEEN
NADICA

Novska 1991

A frown forms on Nadica's brow as she pulls into her grandparents' property.

He is there.

The sight of him still quickens her heartbeat, even as it churns her stomach.

Relja.

He is standing with her deda, their heads bent close in urgent conversation. About the unrest no doubt. Despite the agreement to negotiate, the Yugoslav Army has crossed into Croatia, joining with local Serb-led military groups to wall off entire regions of a nation that voted for independence, claiming them for Serbia. There has been a siege in Vukovar since August. So far Nadica and her family have not been directly affected, but the fear grows as tensions escalate. Nadica knows Relja's thoughts on the conflict that surrounds their nation. Knows he is ready to fight. It is one of the reasons she has distanced herself from him. Surely they can find a path to peace?

The wheel of her bike squeaks as she approaches, and Relja looks up. The hard set of his mouth softens momentarily as he sees her. Patting her deda on the back he turns away and begins the walk across the fields to his own plot of land.

He has visited to help her grandparents since he was strong enough to wield an axe. She is grateful for it. Even if she no longer wants his company for herself. Her deda approaches, a knowing twist on his lips. Nadica knows he likes Relja. Knows he wishes for them to reunite. It isn't something Nadica wants to discuss with him. At least not today.

Because today she feels confused. Relja is angry, he has always been angry, seeing his place as an ethnic Serb and Orthodox Christian in Croatia as unstable and insecure.

After listening to her baba's stories of her brother Ivica, Nadica has a new understanding of that hurt. It is something she knows exists. It has always been there in the background of her life. But never in her experience.

She hugs her deda in greeting, pushing away her thoughts of Relja and Ivica. "How is she today?" she asks, as always.

"Brighter than yesterday. She's been asking for you."

That lifts Nadica's spirits. Aunty Misa has been too unwell since her outburst to have company, needing to rest and sleep. Nadica is glad she will get some time with her today.

"I will go in."

"Relja sends his well wishes."

Nadica's step falters slightly. "He could have said so himself," she says over her shoulder.

"He didn't want to intrude."

Nadica nods but doesn't face her deda. She doesn't want to talk about Relja. She just wants to be with Misa.

Inside the cottage is warm, as always. Her baba is knitting by the fire.

"Go through," she says. "Misa is waiting for you."

Nadica gives her baba a quick kiss and heads through to see her Aunty.

Misa is propped up by several pillows. Old and thinning but covered in brightly coloured pillow cases. She looks small and shrunken, sinking into the pink and frills. But her eyes are open, her pupils focused and sharp.

"My dear one," she says, lifting a hand.

"Aunty," Nadica says, taking her hand and settling herself on the edge of the bed.

"Ilona tells me I frightened you the other day. I am sorry."

Nadica frowns. Why would her baba say that? Misa is sick and weak, she doesn't need to worry about unnecessary things.

The old woman pats Nadica's hand. "I see your worry. Do not blame your baba. I knew something had happened. There was an energy in this house when I woke. It felt like the past was leaking through. My memories had all sharpened." She falls silent, her eyes unfocused for a moment, then snapping back to Nadica's face.

"She told you of Zagreb? Of how we met?"

"Da. And of her and deda. And of your husband Radič," Nadica ventures warily, unsure how much of the past Misa is ready, or willing, to drag into the present.

A sad smile drifts over her aunty's face. "He wanted to marry me the moment we turned eighteen, but I made him wait. I wanted to study in Zagreb, to become a nurse and bring that knowledge home. He agreed to wait for me. Two whole years living apart. Two years I could have had him by my side every night.

"I can barely even picture his face any more. Or theirs."

Nadica listens in silence. She doesn't need to ask who she means. Stephan and Hanna.

Misa grimaces. "A reminder to never waste time. I saw your young man in the yard with your deda. He is a good one. You haven't brought him for dinner in a while."

Her keen eyes bore into Nadica's face. It seems there is no getting away from talking about Relja today. No matter how she might wish to leave the topic well alone.

Suppressing a sigh, Nadica seeks the words to answer, without lying. "We are taking some time for ourselves. Time to work out what we want, as individuals."

Misa sniffs in disapproval. "What modern nonsense. If you had lived in my youth, you would not be so flippant with love."

Nadica raises an eyebrow. "We have known each other forever." Perhaps that was all that was between them: familiarity and expectation. "Relja remains a long-time friend."

"Who sees the world a little differently to you."

Nadica shuffles on the bed, uncomfortable under Misa's piercing scrutiny and the accuracy of her understanding. Nadica has never spoken to her about Relja's fervour. Of how it twists inside her when he speaks of their nation and its past injustice, of the war he sees on the horizon. How has Misa seen all that? Especially as she lays here so unwell?

The old woman releases a sigh and points at the chair by her bed. "We faced a lot in my young years. I am only glad I had your baba beside me. And your deda."

Nadica moves to the chair and makes herself comfortable.

"Stephan was just an idea when it started."

"When what started?"

"Hitler's war. Germany invaded Poland the day I married, but I barely gave it a thought. I was happy in the blissful bubble of that life. So I wasn't so worried with events in Europe. It was so far away, another part of the world." She pauses, shaking her head ruefully. "How fast we forget our history."

"You weren't to know. Why would one invasion mean conflict here?"

Misa's attention settles on Nadica. "Conflict spreads quickly. The Great War wrapped its talons around us once. It was naïve to think it would not happen again.

"But I learnt that from experience. At the time I was just like you. Busy with my own life. When France fell, I was a new mama; Stephan took up all my thoughts. I know better now." A sparrow lands on the windowsill and Misa's attention turns to the small, jittery bird. "Don't be too hard on him," she continues. "Relja remembers better than most."

Nadica picks at a fingernail, uncomfortable with what her aunty is implying. "That was a long time ago," she says.

"Yet I only need to close my eyes to return to it. Will you listen to an old woman's rambles?"

"Da, aunty, of course. They are not rambles, they are memories."

"It is not a happy story. But I want..." she pauses, her chin quivers. "I need to tell it. All of it. You need to understand."

Nadica keeps her face neutral. Why do all her loved ones seem to think she needs to understand the past all of a sudden? Mentally shrugging, she nods at Misa. "I will listen, aunty. I will always listen."

"It was this time of year, the trees had just turned. My babies were fat and happy. And I was happy. I was so happy..."

NINETEEN
MISA

Petrinja 1941

Misa bent down and collected up one of Radič's shirts, hanging it on the line to dry in the sunshine. A cool breeze blew through the forests that bordered Petrinja, bringing the scent of autumn and familiarity to her nose. At her feet, Stephan and Hanna played. Hanna had just started to sit up unaided; it was unconvincing but growing stronger with each day.

Excited by something dancing on the breeze, Stephan started racing off towards the trees, legs more confident now he had mastered the movement.

"Stephan, slow," Misa cautioned.

Stephan looked up at her, his large round eyes wary. How he reminded her of Radič. "You are not in trouble." Misa smiled, leaning down to brush her fingers over his cheek. "I am just reminding you to go slowly, my big strong boy!" She tickled him along his ribs, and Stephan squealed in delight.

"Stay with Hanna and me."

Still smiling from being tickled, Stephan plopped down on the grass next to his sister. Hanna lunged toward her brother and toppled into the grass.

Quickly Misa knelt to help Hanna back up to sitting, and her heart swelled with love for her children, for this life they shared as a family.

Radič arrived home well before evening. Kicking off his boots he crossed the lounge to their children, ruffling Stephan's hair and pressing a soft kiss to Hanna's crown. Hanna looked up at him, her pudgy hand offering her tata a bite of her soggy biscuit.

Radič laughed. "Thank you," he said and mimed taking a bite of her proffered snack. He came to Misa's side, winding an arm around her waist and pressing a kiss to her cheek.

"You are home early," she said, turning back to the pot of stew she stirred on the stove.

Radič shrugged. "We got through the delivery faster than expected. Miloje was happy to let me head off."

Misa smiled and didn't challenge the lie.

It had been months since the invasion of the German Army and the establishment of the Ustaše rule. So far in Petrinja the change had had little impact. Yet almost instantly, Radič's routine at the steel factory on the outskirts of town had changed. He left for work later and returned sooner. All the men did. He never said it, but Misa suspected the men had agreed together to be home during the dark hours. They didn't talk about it, the implied threat of Ustaše, but Misa knew they both felt it. It walked the streets of Petrinja.

"Well, it is lovely to have you home. Supper is a way off yet."

Radič pulled her back into his arms. "Can you leave it for a few minutes?"

Misa grinned and followed him to their room.

The sun was high overhead as Misa sat on the porch, folding yesterday's washing and watching Stephan and Hanna picking fallen leaves. The day was mild, but the chill was approaching. It would not be long before the true strength of winter had her wrapping up in shawls and praying for summer sun.

A sudden frown crossed her face, and she turned her head towards the street that led to their small neighbourhood that bordered the forest. She was sure she'd heard something. Ears pricked, she listened.

Marta next door stepped onto her porch, brows furrowing. She'd heard it too.

"Misa!" That was unmistakable. Rising to her feet, Misa set down the cloth nappy she'd been folding. It would be a while yet before Hanna would be able to toilet; her nappies made up a large bulk of Misa's daily washing. Radič's head came into view down the street. He was running.

Instantly in the grip of panic, Misa stepped forward. "Stephan, Hanna, shhh." She held a finger to her lips and cocked her head.

Marta gasped. Misa's eyes flashed to her neighbour. The colour had drained from her face. Her attention snapped back to Radič. Rounding the corner behind his desperate sprint came a truck. Two soldiers, guns slung over their backs, hung from the truck windows.

"Dear God," Marta said. "Get your children and run!"

Misa didn't need to be told twice. Surging from the porch, she gathered Hanna into her arms. No doubt feeling her mama's tension, Hanna burst into furious and confused tears.

"It's all right," Misa said, but her words were distracted. "Stephan!" She grabbed her son's hand; his eyes were wide with fear. She spun toward the backyard. If she ran, they could hide in the forest. She had to quiet Hanna, but that was a concern for later.

"Race me to the trees," she said to Stephan. But the little boy was too smart. He stared at her, fear locking his knees. Radič had made it to their front gate, but so had the truck.

"Tata!" Stephan called, pulling away from her as the two soldiers she'd seen hanging from the truck leapt from the vehicle.

"Stephan, no!" Misa cried. But she was too late. Breaking from her grip, Stephan took off at a run towards Radič. Her husband mounted the front fence, not bothering with the gate, and dived for Stephan as one of the soldiers drew his gun from his back. Son and husband came together in a roll as the crack of gunfire split the air.

"No!" Misa's voice was barely a whisper as Radič found his feet, Stephan tight against his chest.

"Run!" he shouted across to her as his legs began to lurch towards her.

More soldiers were pouring from the truck, the barrels of their guns catching the sunlight Misa had just been savouring.

Misa turned, Hanna screaming in her arms, and plunged toward the forest behind their urban home. A shout sounded behind her, and she chanced a glance back. Two soldiers had Radič on his knees. Stephan was curled into a ball beside him. Her heart stuttered, and her footsteps slowed. Radič's head rose, his eyes meeting hers. She had to help him; she had to get to Stephen. But the moment that their eyes met, she knew she could not. She could only save Hanna.

Swallowing a wail of pain, Misa pivoted back towards the trees. To the left, she heard Marta scream as a gun was thrust into her side. But Misa didn't slow. Legs pumping hard she threw herself towards the forest's edge. Hanna's weight slowed her, but she didn't stop. Breath straining in her chest from panic and exertion, she crossed beneath the line of trees, her shoes sinking into the soft undergrowth. She stumbled, pitching forward. Unable to throw out her hands to break her fall, she twisted in the air to take the brunt of it on her shoulder, shielding Hanna and braced for impact. The ground cracked against her back.

Two hands seized her shoulders, and hauled her to her feet. Blood rushed to her head, fogging her thoughts, her ribs screamed in pain. The hands that had hold of her didn't release their grip. She blinked and came face to face with the blue "U" of the Ustaše and looked up into a face of pure malice.

A slow, cruel smile twisted the man's lips, and Misa knew: there was nothing she could do.

· · ·

The truck bounced beneath her, but Misa barely noticed. They'd been travelling for hours, along rough, uneven roads, the light outside fading from afternoon into dusk. Beside her Marta rocked, a strip of her skirt pressed to her forehead. She'd stumbled and fallen, striking her head when she was taken. The rest of the occupants of the truck were mostly unharmed, only a few bruises but nothing serious. Misa had been sure to check. They were all women, gathered into the truck by the Ustaše, dressed in only their light autumn cardigans. No one had a coat. The men weren't here.

Stephan wasn't here.

She hugged Hanna closer to her chest. At least one child was still with her. Hanna had cried herself to sleep an hour ago and now slept cradled to Misa's heart. Where was Stephan? Where was her husband? Where were they being taken? Were they separating the men? Misa forced her mind to quiet, it did no good to guess.

Sometime after dark the truck engine quieted, the tyres slowing as they turned into a long drive. Through the canvas flaps of the truck, Misa glimpsed a sprawling building lit by floodlights, soldiers pacing at the front entrance. The truck stopped, the hum of the engine cutting off. A murmur of anxiety washed through the women. Something squeezed Misa's elbow, and she looked down to see Marta had gripped her. "We stay together," she said.

Misa nodded.

The back of the truck was thrown open, and they were ushered out at gunpoint. Misa did not lessen her hold on Hanna. She would not be parted from her baby girl. More trucks were pulling up behind them, and more women and children were being filed from their bowels.

Misa scanned quickly, she recognised some more women from her village, though her mama was not there. She didn't see a single man.

A soldier prodded her in the ribs with the butt of his gun, urging her forward. Misa didn't resist. She followed the line of women into the large building, an abandoned manor house perhaps, but it was difficult to tell in the ghostly light of the floodlights.

They were directed to a large central courtyard, flanked on each side by wings of the house. The temperature had fallen with the sun. Misa snuggled Hanna closer, Marta huddled at her side. Women and children milled around the courtyard, all with the same shocked and confused expressions on their faces. Why were they here?

Misa didn't know. Her heart pounded in her chest as she surveyed the people before her, then it stopped.

Relief flooded through her veins. It was hard to make out people's features in the harsh floodlights, but she would know that face anywhere.

"Stephan!" She raced forward, breaking contact with Marta.

Stephan stood alone surrounded by adults, his face lost and bewildered. At her call he looked up, fear twisting his features. Then he saw her, and his face crumpled into tears.

Misa knelt before him in the dirt, reached out an arm and pulled him to her chest beside the sleeping Hanna. Warm tears soaked through her dress as she clutched her son to her heart, breathing in the pinewood scent of him.

"My son, my son," she crooned as his little body shook in her embrace.

Gently she drew back, hand on his shoulder to hold him where she could study his face. Her eyes swept over his cheeks, down his chest. "Are you hurt?"

He sniffed, rubbing the tears from his eyes with dirt-crusted fingers. "Good, good," she whispered, pulling him back into her body and kissing his hair, savouring his soft familiar feel. She surveyed the people around them, her stomach sinking lower and lower as she did.

"Stephan?" she said softly. She had to ask. She knew the answer, but she had to ask. "Is Tata with you?"

His little hands came up around her neck, his fingernails digging into her skin. She didn't stop him as he clung to her, arms shaking with the strain. "It is all right," she whispered. "Mama is here."

She felt his breath against her neck, the sobs that shook his body.

"Stephan," she tried again as gently as she could. "Did you see what happened to Tata?" She knew he could not explain but, hoping against hope, she asked, praying her son would lift his small hand and point to her beloved husband somewhere in this melee of terrified people.

A puff of breath, the slump of his body against hers. "Tata," he cried. "Tata."

And Misa knew. Her husband was not here.

TWENTY
MISA

As the cold of night deepened, the women and children remained huddled together in the courtyard, confused and dazed, with no idea what was expected of them. The Ustaše soldiers didn't help. They stood around the open courtyard, watching the women but doing and saying nothing.

Old Luca, whose husband trimmed the grass at the church in Petrinja, approached a group of soldiers. "Why are we here? Where are we to sleep? What food have you for us?" she demanded.

The soldiers stared at her a moment, then laughed in her face.

Luca recoiled, indignant. "What is funny? We have children here. Babies! You have forced us from our homes. It is your responsibility to provide—"

The taller soldier lunged forward, the back of his hand connecting with Luca's wrinkled cheek. She went down in a heap, her wrist bending at an unnatural angle as it took the brunt of her weight.

Misa hissed in shock. Luca was an old woman. What man would harm a defenceless old woman?

The Ustaše.

The man stood over her, his eyes gleaming, the harsh lighting cutting his face into hardened lines.

"Children? Babies?" he said, voice pitched to carry across the open space. "I see only vermin. We don't feed and shelter vermin. Vermin scurry out of the way, in case we decide to crush them."

Bewildered, Luca peered up at the man, and Misa's throat tightened. Terrified she might speak against the man – or worse, attempt to appeal to his humanity – she passed Hanna to Marta and stepped forward quickly. She kept her eyes fixed on the ground, avoiding the soldier's hateful stare. She would not goad him, she just wanted to get Luca away.

The courtyard around her fell deathly silent. She felt every eye on her as she approached. Dipping down, she scooped her hands under Luca's arms and helped her to rise. The movement jarred her injury, eliciting a soft cry of pain. Misa frowned. Luca was more hurt than she'd initially assumed. Her arm around Luca's waist, Misa took her weight and helped her to stumble away. The nerves across her back jolted with each step, and her ears pricked to hear any hint of movement from the men at her back. Returning to Marta and her children she whispered, "Let's go inside. At least we will be out of the wind."

Marta nodded in silence, the whites of her eyes shining. Misa said nothing more. She didn't call out to the other women, didn't round them up and take charge. She just moved. Slowly and calmly they headed for the closest door. The rhythmic crunch of gravel told her that the other women of her village were taking her lead.

Inside was dark, lit only by the secondhand light of the courtyard. The wooden floorboards creaked loudly, wobbling dangerously under her feet, as if they might split apart. The smell of dust and rot filled her nose, damp with the wet of autumn that wrapped around their country. It had been a long time since this house had been a home, or even maintained. Shuffling slowly along the hallway she passed several doorways, each leading to rooms in disarray, their furniture smashed. Others were simply empty. At the far end of the hall a room opened out, and she spied a worn and faded lounge chair. She decided there was no point searching further. It had been a long, awful day. They could investigate their prison further tomorrow, by the light of the sun. The lounge would have to do. She helped Luca to the chair and set her down. The old woman held her right arm against her chest, her hand hanging limp.

Misa turned to Stephan. "Sit on the lounge next to Luca. Marta, would you give Hanna to Stephan and check the room? See if you can find anything we can use for warmth: old curtains, blankets, coverings of any sort."

"Da," Marta said setting Hanna carefully beside Stephan.

"Hold her hand," Misa instructed her son. Stephan nodded. "Good boy." She turned her attention to Luca. "May I have a look?"

Luca met her eyes in the dim light; they were glazed with pain. Misa stilled her mind, controlling her reaction. It would do no good to add to the woman's panic. Misa was a nurse; her job was to assess and heal. Emotion had no place.

She took hold of Luca's forearm and gently slipped back the material of her blouse. Luca puffed heavily, fighting the pain as the blouse slipped over her wrist, exposing the white glint of bone.

Compound fracture. Not good.

"All right Luca, I can see the break. I am going to need to set it. It will hurt, but it can't be helped." She eyed Luca. The old woman raised her head in determination. Marta appeared at her side. "I found a scrap of what I think was carpet."

"Good, good. It is something. Was there any wood? Beams or ornaments?"

"A few shattered paintings?"

That would work. "Can you bring me the frames?"

As Marta bustled off, Misa tore a length of fabric from the bottom of her skirt. It wasn't clean enough, but it was better than anything in this room.

Behind her, the scrape of footfall told her other women were filing in, choosing this room too. It was good. If they stuck together, it was good. As the women dispersed through the space, seeking warmth and a bed for the night, Marta returned with a length of picture frame. Misa took it from her and aligned it over Luca's wrist. "Marta, can you stand behind Luca and hold her shoulders steady? Luca, this will hurt. Are you ready?"

Luca's lips trembled in fear, but she nodded once. Misa didn't hesitate. Snapping the wood down on the fractured bone and pressing her other hand underneath she forced the wrist to align in one swift motion. Luca screamed, and the room went black.

They'd cut the floodlights outside, casting them all in darkness.

Sunlight shone red through her eyelids. Misa's eyes snapped open, her mind instantly alert. The room around her was quiet, the only sounds were the soft snores and breath of the women of her village. Her body was stiff and aching, the side she lay on was numb. Blinking rapidly to clear her vision, Misa rose on one elbow and craned her neck back to survey the sleeping women. Cast in streaks of light from the splintered shutters was a room of bodies. Women curled in bundles against walls, two children under a table. They'd all had to make their beds in the pitch dark after the soldiers saw fit to extinguish the lights the night before.

Plunged into unexpected darkness, the room had become a melee of panic. Gasps and cries for help. But Misa had blocked them out. She could not help the others; her children were all that mattered. She had managed to settle an unconscious Luca on the lounge, leaving Marta to watch over her before seeking safety for her and her children.

Retrieving Hanna from Stephan, she'd cradled her little girl to her chest and ordered Stephan to hold tight to her skirts. "A big grip, and do not let go," she'd stressed. She'd felt his hands clasp the cotton of her dress then pressed forward. Groping with one hand, she'd shuffled across the space, using her memory of the brief scan of the room she'd made on entry as a map. She wanted a section of wall, she wanted a way to secure her children between her and the house. She didn't trust that the soldiers would leave them alone all night. Eyes peeled as wide as possible in a desperate search for any faint hint of light, she slowly moved across the room. It wasn't long before her searching fingers met the cool wall and she released an involuntary sigh of relief. Small mercies.

Reaching to her side she gripped Stephan's shoulder. "All right, my dear one, now hands up before you and move forward slowly until you feel the wall... that's it. Do you feel it?"

Gently she guided Stephan to the wall.

"Good. Now settle on the ground. I am going to curl around you and Hanna, to keep you warm."

"Tata," he whined.

Sorrow cleaved her heart at the misery and fear in his voice. He was not yet two years old. This was too much. This should not be happening.

"It is all right, darling," she crooned, hating the lie but knowing he was too young to understand. All she could do was offer the comfort of a mama. "It is dark and late. We will work things out in the morning. It will be all right. I am here. I am with you."

She felt his little body sink to the floor. Keeping Hanna pressed to her chest, she stretched out along the rough wooden panels and curled herself around her children as closely as she could. Squeezing them between the wall and her body. No one could get to them without her knowing. It was the best security she could give them. Rubbing her hand along Stephan's arm she began to hum a gentle lullaby. Eventually she felt the rise and fall of his chest slow and deepen as his body gave in to the fatigue, over-whelming the fear. Around them the noises of the panicked women began to quiet as acceptance settled over the room. They had been ripped from their homes, separated from their families. They were in an abandoned building in a forest guarded by Ustaše. They had no food, water or blankets. But they lived. That was all they could focus on. At least until morning.

Now, as Misa observed the women her mind began to race.

Hanna had soiled herself, it was normal and not a surprise. But Misa had no clothes, cloth for nappies or water. What could she use? Surely the soldiers would bring them some supplies. Last night had just been to scare them, right?

The answer came sooner than she expected. The pounding of approaching boots echoed beyond the doorway before three soldiers burst into the room. The women around her cried out in shock as they were startled awake.

"Get up. Outside. Now!" the soldiers shouted, rushing through the room, kicking women at random, grabbing others to haul them from the floor.

Misa had chosen her location well. At the far side of the room, she had time to respond. As one soldier picked up a bawling child from the floor and threw him aside to get to his mama, Misa was on her feet. Arms spread wide, placing herself bodily before her children.

"Mama?" Stephan's terrified voice.

"Shh, Stephan. Stay behind me."

A soldier's cold blue eyes swung to hers. She stood taller, firmer, showing him she was up and ready. She was not an easy target like those still waking from a cold night's sleep.

His eyes slid away, seeking someone else to menace. Loathing filled her belly. Cowards.

"Go. Out into the yard!" the order was repeated. Misa turned her body to Stephan, keeping the soldiers in her sights.

"We are going outside," she explained as she gathered Hanna into her arms.

The soft warmth of her daughter filled her hands, a momentary comfort. "Now give me your hand," she said to Stephan. "And no matter what happens, do not let go."

They were hurried out into the morning sun. A cool breeze blew over the dusty pavement, a promise of icy rain in the currents. The soldiers forced them into a central space, framing them on all sides.

One man stood at the front. He was dressed like the others, but something in his bearing set him apart. He was in control, Misa realised. Terror seized her stomach. Something was happening.

"Children to the front," he ordered. "Women step back."

No one moved. What?

The man's eyes pinched in anger. "Children come forward, women back. I will not ask again."

They all stood still, rooted to the spot. Stephan's small hand rested in hers. She looked down. His innocent face filled her vision.

The soldier nodded, and the world exploded.

The armed men rushed at the crowd of women and children. Pinned between their ranks the women could do nothing. Large rough hands reached out, grabbing people by their clothes and their hair, wrenching babies and small children from arms.

They mean it, Misa realised. They are separating us from our children.

She didn't have time to consider why, only that it was happening. She would not allow it.

Unable to run through the press of struggling bodies around her, Misa crouched down low, covering Stephan and Hanna with her body. Hanna screamed. Stephan sobbed. The mass of panic swirled around her, the stomp of feet, the cries and shouts punctuated by the pulse of her own blood in her ears. *Not my children. Not my children.*

Then someone knocked into her. Misa braced, trying desperately to hold herself steady, but lost her balance. Her grip on Stephan slipped, and the crowd surged between them.

"Stephan!" She screamed, her hand groping forward.

"Mama!"

She was on her knees again in a flash, a bawling Hanna tucked to her side. Scraping her knees over the gravel she lunged for her son, clasping his shirt and dragging him to her.

Hard hands gripped her shoulders, and she knew she had only this moment to do what she must. She thrust the writhing Hanna against Stephan's legs. He dropped into a squat and his arms wrapped around his sister instinctively, his face a ruin of tears and snot.

"You stay together, Stephan. You stay with Hanna. You never part, never!" she said into his ear.

How could she ask such a thing of her son, when she herself could not stay with them?

His bewildered eyes watched her from a rictus of terror.

"Stay with Hanna," she repeated, desperate fear flooding her senses.

The soldier's rough hands pulled her backwards, tearing her hands from Stephan.

"Mama!" Stephan shouted after her, and her heart broke, her whole soul shattering into a million pieces. And her mind rebelled. She would not let this happen. Radič was gone, her mama's whereabouts unknown, but Misa would not leave her children. Not ever. Her body tensed ready to fight, to break from the soldier's grip and get to her children, somehow. Nothing would stop her. Stephan and Hanna were all that mattered. Just a few steps away. Misa could get to them.

Hot breath on her neck, the stench of stale cigarettes. "You comply or they die," the soldier hissed into her ears.

And Misa went still. Heart pounding against her ribs so hard she felt they would crack, her mind locked up.

Stephan's eyes beseeched her, his lips wobbling, his tiny body quaking. Every nerve in her body strained towards him. Every part of her being ached to close the space between them.

But there was nothing she could do.

For them to live, she had to let them go.

"I love you. Always," she said across the unfathomable space that was opening between them, then she straightened. The soldier pinned her arm at her back, wrenching the socket tight, and Misa went slack and allowed herself to be led away.

Stephan's desperate cries echoed behind her, the sound like needles scoring her skin. Her muscles trembled in opposition to the moment, her thoughts trapped in a battle against reality. How could this be happening? How had she failed so deeply?

As they reached the edge of the buildings, Stephan's final screaming protest pierced her heart. Then fell silent behind the walls that separated them.

She would never forget those wails. They would haunt her forever.

TWENTY-ONE

MISA

The ground cracked beneath her feet, the earth encrusted by a layer of ice. The snows would come soon, but Misa doubted that would mean a reprieve for her and her fellow labourers. It had been two months since they'd been forced from their homes, and driven north. Two months since she'd been forced from her children's sides.

Shoved onto a new set of trucks, they'd been sent further north to the farming fields that bordered the edge of the Ustaše rule. Housed in an abandoned manor house outside of Lobor-Grad, with other women and children, at first Misa's mind had railed against the injustice: other women still had their children by their sides, why had she been separated from hers?

But as the months wore on and the daily reality of the camp became clear, Misa's view changed. Her children were too young to survive here.

Each morning the old and the impossibly young were all led out onto the fields before dawn to dig and hoe and scratch in the earth. The first week her hands had been a ruin of blisters. They would form in the morning as her soft skin, used to the toil of a mama, not a labourer, rubbed against the harsh wood of her shovel then filled with fluid. The next day they burst into rivers of sticky liquid and blood. Then came the infections. Misa was not the only one. Most of the women she toiled beside were housewives, mamas and babas, unused to this work. She did what she could for them in the evenings, when they slept on the rows of bunks fitted along the large wings of the Manor. She used what water they could spare to wash their wounds, and tore strips from their clothes to bind them, a small protection against the labour the morning would inevitably bring.

They bled through the material. Misa knew the wrappings should be changed daily, but there were no supplies. It became a choice between hygiene and warmth. Few chose hygiene. Luca was the first to succumb to her fever. Weakened by her broken wrist, and age, the pus that leaked from her skin had taken the last of her strength.

As the clouds of winter darkness and the cold set in, the movement working in the fields was the only thing that helped to warm their frozen limbs. The old building was overfilled with prisoners, yet too large to properly heat. The cold took Marta, leaving Misa alone. At night, huddled together, sharing the few blankets they had been assigned by the soldiers that guarded them, the women told stories of their homes. They were from all over Croatia. Some were Jewish, some Roma, and many Serbs. It was those moments, shivering arm to arm with her fellow prisoners, sharing tales of their villages, their families, their lives, that kept Misa going. That and the promise she'd made to herself, that was rooted in her soul: she would see her children again.

Every week some of their group fell. Taken for medical assessment, few returned. And every week new inmates arrived, from different towns, or from different camps. It mattered little; they would soon learn the rhythms of their days.

Misa came to the line of young beech trees. Bracing her legs wide she gripped a low-hanging branch and angled her saw over the grain. Along the row of trees around her other women took up the beat, sawing into the sapling wood. The branch came free. Too heavy for her to hold with one hand she allowed it to drop to the hardened earth before kneeling over it to begin separating it into smaller more manageable chunks. It was back-breaking work. Her exhausted muscles screamed, her stomach growling in protest at so little nourishment. They were only fed at night, and then it was mostly thin bean soup or broth, some women resorted to eating grass or pumpkin leaves from the ground to try and line their stomachs and strengthen their bodies. There was nothing to be done about it. They had to perform the work that they were assigned each day. Branch sectioned, Misa leaned back a moment, wiping the sweat that had gathered in the creases of her eyes. Around her the women toiled, at their backs the soldiers patrolled, eyes keen, focused.

Someone had run yesterday. Seeing two soldiers distracted and chatting, she'd hitched up her skirts and fled into the forest. She hadn't got far before the blast of a gun stained her back in blood. She'd fallen, injured but not dead, her body twitching on the ice-coated ground. Instinctively Misa had moved to help, but the sharp order of the soldier nearest to her had halted her step. Another man stalked to where the prone woman lay, gasping in pain. Face blank, expression almost bored, he'd hefted his gun, pointed it at her head and pulled the trigger. They'd left her body there. No burial. No final rites. Only an exposed grave. Today, no one would run.

A young fair-haired girl appeared at Misa's side. Slight and small, her sunken cheeks were rosy with cold. She couldn't have been more than fourteen. Misa hadn't noticed her before, but that was not unusual with the constant arrivals. Bending down, she gathered the pieces of branch Misa had chopped into arms so thin they looked about to snap like a twig and lumbered them to the waiting wheelbarrow, before returning for more. Misa watched her slow step, the strain of the work wrinkling her brows. So young, forced to labour in the freezing cold. It truly was fortunate that Stephan and Hanna were not here. Misa could only pray that wherever they were, conditions were better. She had to believe that. It was the only way she could go on.

Misa stood and selected the next branch to chop.

. . .

The soldiers came to Misa's wing that night. It had been a while since they'd visited. Misa rolled over, huddling under her thin blanket, face and body pressed to the wall, and prayed she'd not be selected. She worked to slow her breathing, to draw no interest and be as silent as a mouse. Heavy boots stomped towards her bunk. A whimper sounded further down the long room. Misa felt her flesh begin to crawl, and tension raced up her spine. The footsteps grew louder, and she curled in on herself as they closed in. Then they passed.

A cry of terror filled the night. "No, no! Please no!"

The sharp crack of a fist connecting with a cheek and the woman fell silent. The boots retreated past Misa and out into the night, the woman hustled with them. Misa released a sigh of relief, and guilt churned in her belly. She'd not been taken into the night by the soldiers, yet. Every night it was a possibility. She hurt for those taken, for the prettier women who were favoured. But she could not help but be grateful it was them, not her.

She was out sawing wood again the next day when the pale sunlight caught the blonde streaks in the hair of the young girl from yesterday, drawing Misa's gaze. She made her way along the row of trees, collecting the chopped wood, her movements careful and slow. It made sense that she would be carting wood, she was too small to saw. Normally Misa would simply turn away and continue her work. She didn't engage with the women outside of wing where she slept; she didn't have the emotional energy to reach out to others, not without her children. But something in the girl's movements caught her attention. She was sheepish, curled in on herself more than yesterday. Misa frowned, pausing as she dropped a piece of wood in her pile. The girl came closer, her head lowered, and bent to gather the wood. Misa stepped forward and took her chin in her hand, turning her face up to the light. A vivid bruise marred the child's cheek, her lip split. Misa sucked in a sharp breath.

"When?" she asked.

The girl stared at her with sorrowful eyes, tears swimming along her lids. She didn't speak.

It was too much. Misa could turn away from the horrors of this camp and keep herself tucked small and safe, but she could not ignore the brutalisation of a child.

She released a heavy sigh. "What is your name, child?"

"Kata."

Misa smiled. "Kata, that is a pretty name. Where is your mama, Kata?"

Kata's head lowered, and she gave a small shrug.

Misa closed her eyes in sad understanding. Separated, just like she was from her babies. She could do nothing for Stephan and Hanna but pray and hope. But this child before her? This child she could protect.

"Do you know wing three, Kata?"

The girl nodded slowly.

"You will sleep there with me from now on. Understand?"

Kata nodded again.

"Good, now, back to work before we draw attention," she said, eyeing a patrolling soldier over Kata's shoulder as he slowed his step.

She dropped her hand from the girl's face and turned back to her tree felling. She didn't know what the night might bring, or the next, or the one after. But one thing was certain: no soldier would be taking Kata out of her bed, ever again. Not while Misa was there to stop it.

PART FOUR

TWENTY-TWO

"*We managed to get one of the beds by the window. Of course, in the winter and without any blankets, that wasn't actually a good thing. But we were children. It seemed like we had the best bed in the place.*" Milena smiles sadly.

Sara adjusts the camera to widen out as Natalija returns from the kitchen with a tray of coffee. Daniel didn't travel with her to Belgrade. For this interview she is alone.

"*I remember the frost,*" Natalija says, putting down the tray. "*It fogged up the window. We used to draw pictures on the glass. Stars and hearts.*"

The sisters' eyes meet, and Sara forces herself to remain silent. She doesn't want to prompt or shape their recollections, only to record them. That is her purpose; to document the survivors' stories so they won't be forgotten. Natalija hands Milena a cup of coffee and settles herself on the couch beside her sister. They have matching grey hair pulled back in long plaits down their backs. Their mouths turn down at the corners – from age, genetics or trauma, Sara doesn't know.

"The nurses were very careful to keep us together," Milena continues. "They gave us our numbers on cards—"

"You ate yours!" Natalija interrupts, laughter in her voice.

"I was hungry," Milena protests, eyes darkening slightly. "I wasn't the only one."

Sara has read of this. When the first children were taken from the camps their details were recorded on cardboard. But children are children, and starving children are hungry. Many of the records of those rescued were lost to hungry mouths and fidgeting fingers.

"It didn't matter," Natalija says. "I had mine. And we knew who we were, where we came from. We were the lucky ones. Our mama came back."

"Not that it ended there. The War of Independence in 1991..." Milena stops, shaking her head. "At least Mama didn't live to see that."

Natalija reaches over and takes Milena's hand. "Belgrade is our home now," she says firmly.

"I miss visiting Mama's grave."

"You don't feel you can return to Croatia?" The question slips out. Sara can't stop herself. She wants to understand. Her baba would not leave Zagreb, even when the bombing started, and these sisters won't return. Opposite reactions to the same trauma. Why?

The sisters turn to her as one. "They already tried to kill us twice," Milena says.

"Why would we go back?" Natalija asks.

Why indeed, Sara thinks to herself.

TWENTY-THREE
NADICA

Novska 1991

"I left that time." Misa's voice is a rasping whisper. Her breathing is heavy and laboured. Nadica presses a hand to her forehead. She is burning.

"Aunty, I think it is time for your medication," she says.

"Aren't you listening?" Misa demands, though her rough voice steals the emphasis.

Nadica sits back down, nodding slowly. "Da, Aunty. Of course. I am sorry. I just wanted to check on your well-being."

"Nadica," Misa says, looking at her with utter disdain. "I am dying. My well-being is irrelevant. But time with you... that matters."

A smile touches Nadica's lips, but her heart is sad.

"You are all that is left. Stephan and Hanna..."

Her heavy exhale makes the blanket fall impossibly low over her body, like she is a mere skeleton underneath its weight.

The silence stretches between them, heavy and dark. It presses on Nadica, making her squirm. She doesn't know what to say. Or if she even should speak.

Finally, she tries. "Aunty—"

"Don't," Misa says, her voice a whisper. "I know all the words. All the logic. All the reasons I made the only possible choice. It doesn't make it right. Not in here." A finger taps her chest.

"No," Nadica agrees. Then a question pops into her mind. She tries to ignore it. Tries to trust in all she has grown up with. But it will not be silenced.

"Ask," Misa says.

Nadica rubs her tongue against the roof of her mouth, seeking moisture. "Have you forgiven yourself?"

Nadica doesn't need to ask that question, she already knows the answer. But the need to speak the words forces them from her lips.

Misa sniffs. "I am tired now. Leave me."

Heavy with understanding, Nadica rises and kisses her sweaty brow. "Sleep well, Aunty," she says, then pads from the room.

Her baba is outside, pruning the rose bushes. She likes to trim them low before the winter sets in, then they can flourish with new growth in the spring. Without a word, Nadica bends and gathers up the cuttings her baba has placed in a basket and carries them to the pile where they will be left to decay. Their lives breaking down into a cycle for those that come next. Returning to her baba, she sits on the front step and watches Ilona work. She is ageing, but not old. Her movements remain strong and controlled, her focus sharp.

"Was today about her children?" she asks, not taking her eyes from the bushes.

"Sort of," Nadica answers honestly. "But I think more about Misa herself, at the core of it."

"Hmmmm." Ilona drops more spiny stems into the basket Nadica has just emptied, then moves to the next bush.

"Are you tired?" Nadica asks. "I can do this for you."

"No, no," her baba waves her away. "It is good for me to keep busy."

It is a loaded comment. Does she mean because of her joints and the need to keep the stiffness at bay? Or because of Misa?

Nadica doesn't ask. There are too many unspoken words these

days. Too many conversations without clear meaning. She is struggling to understand. She longs to feel the ground beneath her feet settle, but it just keeps shifting.

"Baba?"

"Da?" Ilona says absent-mindedly.

"Why didn't you and deda have more children?"

Her baba's hands still over the bushes, her body going rigid.

Nadica feels panic rush through her. She's asked the wrong question. She shouldn't have brought it up.

"We couldn't," Ilona says simply. "We tried for years before the war. And after." She cuts a wilted rose from a branch; it falls, its curling petals fanning out from the centre of the bloom. "But it didn't matter. We have your mama. She is enough, as are you."

She has turned to Nadica, her eyes boring into her, intense in a way Nadica rarely sees.

"I know."

Ilona sighs and puts her cutters into the basket of trimmings, then comes to sit beside Nadica, close enough that the sides of their bodies meet and warmth spreads between them.

"Misa has spoken to you of Kata?"

Nadica cocks her head. "You mean the girl in the camp?"

"Da. Misa loved her like family. A little sister to protect and care for. Even though she wasn't."

"It is a terrible story," Nadica says. Because it is. A fourteen-year-old girl, alone in a camp of adults, dragged away by soldiers in the night.

"It is," Ilona agrees. "But it has a beauty."

Nadica frowns at her baba. "Beauty?"

Ilona nods sagely. "In a camp of death, Misa found love. So did Kata. It ended sadly. So many stories of that time did. But for that moment in time, they had each other. A girl who needed a mama, a mama without her children. I believe God brought them together, for a moment of comfort. I believe Misa made it through her time in the camps and the separation from her children *because* of Kata."

Nadica stills, her mind connecting dots. "Like Mama was for you?"

She feels the softening of her baba's posture. It seeps into her, warming her from within. "Your mama saved my life," Baba says. "And then you came along and kept it going."

She flashes a smile at Nadica. "It is a difficult time right now, my darling. Misa's health. The tensions in our country. I don't want you to forget all that you mean to your deda and me."

Nadica smiles and rests her head affectionately against her baba's shoulder. "I could never forget that," she says.

TWENTY-FOUR
ILONA

Zagreb 1942

Dragica stepped to her side. "Walk with me," the woman said.

Ilona looked up from the patient chart she was assessing and blanched. What would the head nurse want with her, specifically? Shoving her unease aside, Ilona handed the chart to one of her students, then trailed along beside Dragica, keeping her head down, avoiding eye contact. The large head nurse led her away from the busy wards, pushing open a swinging door to a far section of the hospital. Patients slept peacefully along the walls, a few older men of the city who were nearing their return to God.

Dragica moved closer to Ilona, her voice barely a whisper as they strolled along the ward. "Have you heard from Misa?"

Ilona jerked in surprise, eyes narrowing on Dragica. The old matron had been their teacher at the hospital before Misa married and returned home to raise her family. But that was years ago. Why would Dragica ask about Misa now?

"Not in a while," Ilona admitted. Not since the early days of the occupation. Misa's letters had stopped soon after Jovan left with Josip and Slavko. She'd not heard from him in months either.

She longed to take a train down to Petrinja and check on her friend and her family. But she did not wish to be away if Jovan returned.

Dragica sucked in a deep breath. "There are rumours... about camps."

Ilona frowned. She knew about Jasenovac. No one could miss the lines of Jewish citizens and other 'enemies of the Ustaše' that were herded onto trains at Zagreb Central Station for transport.

"Da, work camps. The race laws..."

"Your husband is a Serb," Dragica said directly.

"Jovan has nothing to—"

"But he is a Serb. And you love him. Watch yourself."

Ilona blinked as confusion flooded through her. Was Dragica accusing her of something? Did she know about Jovan's activities with the resistance? That he had fled?

She stared at the older woman, but found no malice in her face, only sadness.

"The rumours are of more than work camps... but also camps of women and children."

"You mean where they are housing the Serbs who wish to leave the Independent State of Croatia?" She knew more and more Serbs had decided to leave the borders of the Ustaše's rule. However, all of the states of Yugoslavia were occupied by German allies. It seemed a desperate measure to find safety. There was no freedom left in their part of the world.

"The women and children are not in these camps voluntarily." A heavy sigh escaped Dragica's lips. "The Ustaše. They are rounding up families from the country towns, Serb families. Taking their land. I worry for people like Misa. She was such a talented student."

A chill ran through Ilona's veins as she processed Dragica's words. "Children? In camps, but not for migration? Why?"

Was that why Misa's letters had stopped? No, it couldn't be true.

Dragica's eyes glittered. "They are work camps. Like Jasenovac. The Serb people are being treated as labourers, just like the Roma and the Jews. It is just less visible in the capital.

"I have a contact, she is organising supplies to be sent to the camps. To help... I wondered if you might be willing to donate? I know you and Misa were close."

"Are you saying the Ustaše are holding women and children as prisoners and not feeding and clothing them?"

"As they fail with the Jewish."

She hadn't thought of it before. She'd seen the men lined up at the station, heading away. Had watched the Praška Street synagogue be slowly demolished in a cloud of dust and ruin. A symbol that its worshipers were no longer welcome in the city. Why hadn't she considered what might be awaiting them at the end of the line? And women and children.

Horror sluiced through her. *Misa.* "Are you telling me that Misa and her children are in a camp?"

Dragica placed a steadying hand on her shoulder. "I have no way of knowing. But regardless, there are innocent people, vulnerable people, in those camps. If I have judged you correctly over the years we have worked together, I believe that you would want to help."

Ilona's mind was racing. Children in work camps. It couldn't be true. Could it? No one could be so cruel. Then the woman in a torn dress, Darta Davocvic, who had pushed her children from the shattered window of a church to avoid a massacre, flashed into her memory. Jovan's words: sixty Serbs put to death in a church. The massacres in the forests. Ilona had turned her thoughts away from that knowledge, choosing to believe it was a one-off, the act of a barbarous few. She had been unable to believe such a horror could be repeated. But if the soldiers were capable of such an act once...

She looked up at Dragica. "Who is your contact?"

Relief sagged Dragica's face. "Her name is Diana Budisavljević."

. . .

She was talking with Dragica in the hospital break room the first time Ilona saw her. Small and slender, elegantly dressed in a fitted skirt and jacket, a fur over her shoulders. They were standing by the window, heads bent close in hushed conversation. And Ilona knew the gentile woman had to be Diana Budisavljević. Stealing her courage, Ilona approached.

Two sharp eyes turned to her, and a perfectly shaped eyebrow arched expectantly. She looked older up close. The wrinkles of time sat along the expanse of her forehead and creased at her eyes. Tired, deep dark circles nestled beneath them. But she was still beautiful.

"Diana, this is Ilona, the young nurse I was telling you about," Dragica said.

Diana studied her face, her thin lips pursed. "You know what we are doing?"

"Da."

"And you are willing to help?"

"Da."

Diana paused, a small knot forming between her brows, and then she gave a sharp nod. "We are taking anything people can spare: food, blankets, warm clothes. Here." She handed Ilona a card. "My address. Come any morning before eleven o'clock."

"I will."

The very next day Ilona stepped from the bus into King Petar Svačić Square. Around her, expansive and beautifully detailed homes and gardens rose into the grey and cloud-strewn skies. But the parks in this suburb were the same as those across the city. Dug up to plant crops in a desperate attempt to feed the overburdened city. As the occupation lengthened, food had become scarce. Even Ribnjak park by the cathedral, where Jovan had first kissed her beneath the falling magnolia petals, had been converted into rows of vegetables that struggled under the ice of winter. Still they all went hungry.

She walked along a wide boulevard lined with plane trees, their leaves long gone, their brunches rustling in the stiffening breezes. It was quiet and calm. But Ilona's heart raced. She clutched the suitcase of supplies tightly to her chest taking comfort from the belief she was doing the right thing. She'd gone through their home packing up what she could. They didn't need two sets of sheets or three blankets. She would make do with less, so the people at the camps could have something. She hoped Jovan would agree, even if it would draw the disapproval of the Ustaše.

Her heart told her that he would.

Soon she came to a high stone fence, a polished brass number proclaiming she had reached her destination.

Diana's home was beautiful. The pale stone walls of the large house shone in the muted morning light. The wrought-iron door that secured the front entrance was elegant. Even the dormant vines that clung to the walls could not dim the building's stature. Ilona traversed the gravel drive, placed her suitcase at her feet and pressed the doorbell.

The bell rang in an echoing chime, and Ilona ran a nervous hand over her dress, smoothing her skirts and straightening her coat.

The door cracked open, and Diana's narrow face appeared, her eyes instantly spotting the suitcase at Ilona's feet.

"Come in." She opened the door ushering Ilona inside.

The foyer was cavernous, with high ceilings stretching up and away, creating a wide open space that was lined with bags and piles of clothing and bedding.

"The delivery goes out this morning," Diana explained as she strolled across the tiled floor. "You can put your things by the window. Ilona complied, kneeling down to crack open the suitcase and add her offerings to the pile that sat in a shard of light. Behind her Diana picked up a small booklet. "Can I record your name and donation?"

Ilona nodded absent-mindedly, her pulse fluttering as she took in the room around her. So many donations. So many people cared. It was wonderful.

The doorbell pealed through the foyer again, the chime

bouncing from wall to wall, and Diana motioned for Ilona to stay back. A well-dressed lady stepped through the door, her heels clicking on the tiles. Her eyes darted nervously as she withdrew an envelope from her silken purse. "It was all I could spare," she paused. "My husband can't notice."

"It will be of great help," Diana said, accepting the envelope. It must be money, Ilona realised. Diana placed the envelope on the table and retrieved her notebook. "Can I take your details?"

"Oh, no." The woman stepped back, hands palm out before her. "I... no."

"It is all right," Diana said hastily. "We are grateful all the same."

The woman's lips trembled, then she turned on unsteady feet and left, her back retreating swiftly down the drive.

"She was so scared," Ilona said. "Why?"

Diana shrugged. "She is Catholic and wealthy. She has a lot to lose if her actions are discovered. Much like you." She regarded Ilona pointedly, and Ilona straightened.

"It is the right thing to do."

Diana sighed. "If only it was enough."

Ilona frowned. "What do you mean?"

The sound of tyres on gravel interrupted her query, and she followed Diana out into the yard.

A small vehicle with an open tray already laden with boxes pulled to a stop before the house, and two men jumped down from the cab.

"Abner," Diana said greeting the shorter of the two, his dark curls bobbing as he moved. "I have a full delivery today."

She led him back to the open doorway. His dark eyes studied the piles of donations, and he nodded. "We can take half today. We still have supplies to take to the Jewish camps."

"I understand," Diana agreed.

Abner leaned closer to her, pitching his voice low. Ilona strained to hear. "I am not convinced that the items are making it to the prisoners. The guards, the way they look at the deliveries." He paused, shaking his head. "I do not trust the men of our country who wear uniforms."

"We can only do what we can, and we must hope at least some of our donations make it to those in need. Ilona? Will you help us to load the truck?"

"Of course."

She gripped a large box and hauled it into her arms, before tottering across the drive to the truck. The other man stood atop the truck tray waiting and took the parcel from her with a nod of acknowledgement. Ilona could see the gratitude in his eyes. The men strapped down the extra boxes from Diana's hallway, and Abner climbed into the driver's seat.

"I will try and make another run before the week is out."

"I appreciate that," Diana said.

With a wave of his hand Abner fired the engine and manoeuvred the truck to leave, the contents of the tray swaying dangerously.

As the loaded vehicle disappeared out of Diana's drive, Ilona turned to the woman. "What did he mean about the supplies? That he has concerns?"

Diana breathed a heavy sigh. "I have permission to send donations to the camps I believe are holding Serb civilians. I registered as a volunteer charity with the German Army. Our actions are all approved. Abner and his friends have the same permission to supply the camps for the Jewish. He agreed to help deliver my supplies, but..."

Ilona waited as Diana raised her eyes to the grey sky above, her mouth moving in a tight twitch. "But the soldiers at the camps don't allow Abner and his workers inside. The deliveries must be handed over to the soldiers who are guarding the camps. So we cannot be sure exactly who is being held in the camps, if it is women and children as we suspect, or not. Equally, we cannot know how much gets through."

She turned to Ilona. "I suspect much of our work is ineffectual."

A cold wind blasted down the drive, brushing the debris of winter twigs and dead leaves across Ilona's shoes. She hugged her coat tighter. "They need the blankets, the seasons have turned. The snows aren't far off."

"And the food," Diana agreed. "But I have a plan."

"You do?"

Diana's face hardened in determination for a moment, but she pivoted the topic. "Are you also helping with the soup?"

Ilona wanted to press her on her plan, but read in her focused expression that the conversation was closed. Accepting that she asked, "The soup?"

"Da, Dragica and the Red Cross nurses hand out soup to the men in the trains. They go through Zagreb Station on the way to the labour camps in Germany. It is one place we know we can offer support, food and medical help to those being dragged from our country. She could use more hands."

"They don't feed them on the trains?"

A small shake of her head. "Their health is not a priority."

Ilona could not understand it. To round up people and imprison them, use the men for labour, hold the women and children in camps, and not feed and clothe them? It made no sense. What had any of these people done to deserve such treatment? Why were the Germans – and, worse, her own people in the Ustaše, people that included her brother Ivica – why were they doing this?

Dear Lord, Ilona thought, *please protect my Jovan. Please keep him safe from enemy hands.* Ilona sent her prayer to heaven, making the sign of the cross over her chest. *Please let him be safe.*

"And Dragica needs more help?" She noted how Diana had watched her sending her prayer, the woman's intense stare softening slightly.

"We all do."

"Then I will join her and the other Red Cross nurses. I will do what I can."

"Good." Diana nodded. "The next soup run is tomorrow. I hope you will be there."

With that Diana strode back inside, shutting the door behind her, leaving Ilona standing alone in the barren yard, locked in sorrow over all that was unfolding through her nation. She would do what she could, and prayed that God would look mercifully on them all.

TWENTY-FIVE

ILONA

The air at the station was laced with ice, unseasonably chilled in the dark night of March. A line of Red Cross nurses stood to attention, their uniforms covered by thick cloaks, plumes of white mist puffed from their mouths.

A group of soldiers dressed in the deep grey uniform of Germany milled about on the platform, guns slung casually over their backs. Ilona watched them from the corner of her eye, her soup ladle clutched before her like a shield. Beside her, Radmila stood with a large steel pot of steaming soup, Petra too, with a bowl. The smell of cooked root vegetables wafted through the air. In all, there were five nurses with soup pots, and assigned to each were two women with bowls.

Ilona had been coming to Zagreb Station with the Red Cross nurses throughout winter, offering food to the men within the carriages, a last moment of humanity before they were whisked away to another country. She scoured every carriage she could, looking for Radič or Jovan, praying she would not see her friend or her husband on route to Germany. She'd still had no letters from Jovan or Misa, and her concern for their safety grew daily.

No one on the platform spoke, but Ilona could tell they were all anxious to be done with this task. She shuffled nervously, her eyes darting from side to side. She noted Dragica halfway down the platform, the slender, elegant frame of Diana next to her. Diana looked out of place in this bleek, cold station. Her fur-lined coat and leather gloves enveloped her small stature and set her apart. But she stood straight, face set in grim determination.

The rhythmic rattle of an approaching train echoed down the worn tracks, and Ilona looked up. In the distance the glint of metal, the flash of a train light. The transport was approaching.

Rolling her shoulders Ilona braced herself for action.

As she did every soup run, Dragica warned them they would not have long to perform their task. The train was on a tight schedule across the Independent State of Croatia. Bound for Germany with cargo carriages filled with working-age men to be delivered to labour camps to toil for Germany and Hitler's war effort.

If it weren't for the efforts of the volunteer nurses of the Red Cross the men would go hungry for days. A brutal thing to do to men whose liberty you had stolen. Yet the German soldiers saw no need to make it easy for the nurses to complete their relief effort. The train would halt, the soldiers would swap and the train would be on its way. The nurses had that transfer time to distribute their soup, not a minute more. They would feed as many as they could.

Soon the air filled with the acrid scent of engine steam, the smoke from the train flooding through the station. Loud screeching filled Ilona's ears as the train breaks were applied. She grimaced at the sharp sound, her shoulders bunching towards her ears in an effort to muffle it.

The train slowed, the heat of its engine blasting Ilona in the face.

"Ready, girls," Dragica's voice called.

A whistle blew, and the soldiers disbursed along the train, unlocking the heavy chains that bound the carriage doors and rolling them open. Ilona, Radmila and Petra stepped forward through the steam that still rolled off of the overheated brakes, moving to the open carriage.

When Ilona had volunteered her help to Dragica she'd never have guessed that Radmila would be among the nurses giving up their time to cook soup for prisoners. The woman whose husband was part of the Ustaše leadership continued to surprise Ilona.

"*Does David know you are doing this?*"

"*No. He has moved into the soldiers' barracks. I barely see him any more.*"

"*It is still a risk.*"

"*I do this because it is right.*"

The carriage doors rolled open and Radmila removed the pot lid, and Petra held up the first bowl. Ilona dipped in her ladle, filling their bowls. Warm bowl in hand, she turned to the open train carriage, ready to distribute her offering and stopped in her tracks.

The carriage was stuffed full to bursting. The stink of human waste and body odour was so strong it overwhelmed the smoke of the train and the steam of the soup. But that was not what halted her step.

Before her, eyes wide with fear and desperation, hands reaching out for the bowl she held, were not the rough and dirty arms of men, but of women.

"Please hurry," one woman croaked, her grey hair peeking out from beneath a grubby scarf.

Shaking herself from her daze, Ilona stepped forward and handed the bowl to the woman. Beside her Petra did the same. Then they returned to Radmila and portioned out another round of soup. Moans and whispered thank yous filled the silence, and Ilona worked. Ladling soup and rushing to pass it on to the next pair of grasping desperate hands. Her mind had gone numb. Women. Hundreds and hundreds of women. What did it mean? She didn't have time to think about it now. There were so many hungry mouths to feed.

"Ilona!"

The sound of her name cut through the muffled jostling along the platform. Ilona's head snapped up. "Ilona! Over here, it's me. It's Misa!"

Misa?

The air went out of Ilona's lungs, and she turned towards the voice. Her eyes searched the carriages along the platform, her mind desperate. *I must have imagined it*, she thought.

"Ilona! Here!"

She caught movement in the corner of her eye, her feet moving before she'd fully registered what she'd seen. Pressing her half-filled bowl of soup into Petra's hands she began to run, pushing past the other nurses distributing soup along the train.

"Misa," she called as she dashed past the carriages, ignoring the frowns and curses that followed her flight.

A pale hand reached out, long dirt-crusted fingers clutching. Ilona grabbed that hand in her own and pulled herself up onto the carriage edge. Shaking arms wrapped around her as Ilona gripped her friend to her chest. "Misa," she whispered as she held her friend's shrunken frame, the bones of her spine jutting against Ilona's arms. Her body felt too small, too frail. She shivered as though she was freezing, but her skin felt hot like fire. Misa's fingers dug into her back. Releasing a heavy sigh, Ilona pulled back, clutching her friend's shoulders and staring into her face. Misa's cheeks were hollowed out, her dark eyes sunken into deep pools of black. Her lips were white and flaking. What had happened to her? What was she doing here?

Ilona opened her mouth to ask, but Misa placed a hand over her lips. "There is no time, you must listen," she said urgently. "We were in a camp. A few hours east of Petrinja. They took us all. Me, Stephan and Hanna. They separated me from the children. You have to find them. Stephan and Hanna. You have to get them out."

"But what are you doing here? This is a labour transport."

Misa looked at her sadly, her too-warm palm coming to rest on Ilona's cheek. "There is nothing you can do for me. I will live. But Stephan and Hanna... they are so small. And alone. All the children are alone. You must find them—"

"No talking with the prisoners!" The loud, booming voice of a soldier ordered from down the platform.

Ilona glanced over and saw the young man begin to advance towards them, the corners of his mouth turned down.

"Go!" Misa hissed.

"I can't leave you here on this train. There must be some mistake. Let me find Dragica."

"No. Ilona, please, listen. There is nothing you can do for me. But Stephan and Hanna. Please, you must find them. You must!"

The sharp squeal of a whistle filled the air, and the women around them began to jostle harder, pushing and scrabbling, desperate to secure a bowl of soup before it was too late. Along the train the soldiers began to advance, rolling the heavy doors closed. The young man who'd ordered Ilona away from Misa was closing in on them swiftly.

An elbow caught Ilona in the ribs and she lost her footing, stumbling down from the carriage. Misa caught her flailing hand and helped her regain her balance. They stood a moment, hands together, one woman on the train, one on the platform. Their eyes met. Horror had Ilona by the throat. The young soldier had reached Misa's carriage. "Find them," Misa said, then dropped Ilona's hand and disappeared into the melee of hungry women.

"Misa!" Ilona called, surging forward, reaching for her friend.

A firm hand landed on her shoulder and Ilona spun, expecting to see the enraged face of the soldier. But it was Dragica. "Away," the head nurse said. "Quickly." She gripped the fabric of Ilona's coat and dragged her from the train's edge, shoving her bodily down the platform and away from the angry soldier. And Misa.

Ilona tried to turn.

"Don't," Dragica hissed. "Eyes forward. You don't want his attention."

Realising that Dragica was right, Ilona allowed herself to be ushered from the platform and back to the bus that had taken them to the station. Out on the street, Dragica finally let her go.

Ilona turned to her. "It's true, they have children in the camps. They are taking their mamas away," she said in a panicked rush.

She expected to see shock on Dragica's face. Shock that their suspicions about the camps of women and children had been correct. She expected that the head nurse would demand more information, that she would turn and confront the soldiers on the platform. But Dragica only regarded her from a face filled with sorrow.

Ilona felt her jaw go slack. "You knew?"

Dragica sighed, then nodded. "It is why Diana has come today. She has a plan."

Ilona's mind reeled back to the first time she'd donated supplies to Diana. Diana had said she had a plan then.

"What plan?"

Dragica paused. "Dragica, please. That was Misa on the train. Her children are in a camp. Please, I need to know what Diana is planning."

She saw her words hit home. Glancing briefly back at the station over Ilona's head Dragica said, "Diana hopes to convince the commandant to release the children into the care of the church. To get them out of the camps."

Ilona puffed a shocked breath. "Could that work?"

"I don't know. But Diana has contacts. She is Austrian after all. She speaks German. If anyone can convince the commandant to listen, it is her."

"What about the women? They are sending them to hard labour. Why? They are just people."

"So are the men. And the Jews."

Ilona stopped, shame heating her cheeks. "I... yes, I know. But the children, they need their mamas."

"It is an Ustaše policy. Germany needs workers, the Ustaše want to remove the Serbs. It suits them and our occupiers. They get free labour, and the Ustaše clear away the Serbs."

"And the children?"

"An inconvenience."

"But without their mamas... Alone, they will die. And the women? Hard labour, how can they—"

"Focus on the children," Dragica snapped. "The innocents. That is all we can control."

Ilona felt her brow crease. Innocents? They were all innocents.

Beyond Dragica's back, the other nurses of the Red Cross were filtering out of the station, the click of their heels muffled by the cold of the streets.

"We must hope Diana will succeed."

"Where is she? I want to help." Ilona went to walk back to the platform, but Dragica stopped her with a gentle hand.

"Let her do her work. If she manages to convince the men in power, she will want all the help she can get."

"And what if she fails?"

Dragica regarded her, silently. "Time to get on the bus," she said. "Our work for today is done. But there will be another train soon. And then another."

The unspoken message was clear: we do what we can. That is all we can do. Just as Diana had said when Abner told her the supplies weren't getting through. Months ago. How long had Misa and her children been in a camp? Through the whole frozen winter? Had supplies made it to them? She was alive. That meant something. Didn't it?

"Come," Dragica said, pressing softly on Ilona's back to move her to the bus. Ilona stepped up into the vehicle. Walking along the aisle she felt numb, disconnected.

What was happening to her country?

Where were they taking Misa? Would she be all right?

This was so wrong! Why was this happening?

As she slumped down in her seat the leather squeaked, but Ilona didn't notice. All she was aware of was Misa's face, thin and desperate. And her plea: find my children. Save them.

Save Stephan and Hanna.

That was just what Ilona was going to do.

TWENTY-SIX

ILONA

The roads around King Petar Svačić square were slick with rain. Ilona pulled her coat tight around her body, sinking her mouth behind her thick scarf to escape the misting drizzle. She longed to turn around, to escape the gathering winds and the grey sky above that threatened a storm. But she could not.

She had to try.

She'd returned home the night before in shocked disbelief from seeing the train full to the brim with women, old and young. And Misa. Her Misa.

And what her friend had said.

Children in the camps.

Separated from their mamas.

No food…

The rumours were true. Of the round-ups of villagers across the countryside: men, women, children. Diana was right; her work to send supplies to the camps was even more essential than they'd known. For it was not only the men being sent away but the women too. Anyone deemed strong enough to work was being separated from their children and deported to German labour camps.

What did that mean for the children left behind?

A bitter wind whipped at her skirts, its chill biting through her stockings to prickle her flesh. What conditions were the children left in the camps facing? Alone, without their mamas?

Who was caring for the babies?

Misa's daughter Hanna was not even a year old. Little Stephan only two. Too young to tend to his sister alone. Were they even together?

All night Ilona had tossed and turned, her fears for the children of her nation and for her friend expanding with the hours of darkness. When the first rays of the pale day had struck her pillow, she'd known. There was only one way she could help Misa. She had to find her children and get them safe.

And only one woman could help her to do it.

She came to the grand home, the wrought-iron gates shut firmly against the city filled with occupiers. One hand against the gate, she pushed.

At the front door, she paused. The perfectly polished brass doorbell glowed too brightly, too elegantly. What she was here to do, here to ask – did it belong in the world of such privilege?

Would she be greeted with respect, would she be treated seriously? A young woman from the fringes of society. Worse perhaps, a Croat? She was good enough to donate, to hand out soup. But more than that?

There was only one way to find out. Taking a deep breath, Ilona rested her finger against the doorbell and pressed.

The ring of the bell seemed to boom through the door. She imagined she could hear it vibrating through high-ceilinged hallways and opulent rooms. Finding its occupants relaxed with the morning newspaper and irritated at the rude interruption.

The wind whistled, the bare tree branches newly budding with green shoots rattled, and Ilona fancied she heard a loud curse from inside the house.

Then the door cracked open.

Ilona straightened her back, drawing herself up as tall as she could.

Diana peered at her from the doorway. She looked straight at Ilona's feet, expecting a suitcase of donations. But Ilona had come empty-handed today.

A brief frown creased the patterned wrinkles that crossed Diana's forehead, quickly smoothed away, then understanding sparked in her eyes.

The door swung open further and Diana stepped to the side, gesturing Ilona in. Ilona crossed the threshold. Diana moved to close the door, ducking her head out and looking swiftly left and right before securing the latch and bolting the lock.

"There," she said. "All safe. Now, if you would follow me."

Without explanation or discussion, the slender woman began walking down the tiled hallway, her neat heels clicking as she went. Ilona could only follow. A looming space opened up before her as she advanced through the foyer. A sweeping curved stair led up to a second level, the ceiling above over two storeys high. She took a steadying breath. It rattled from her lips as she released it from her lungs. At the far side of the hall, Diana led her into a side room. Small and cosy, the room was lined with shelves of books, and a large oak desk took up much of the central space. A high-panelled window filled the opposite wall, its ash-grey curtains drawn open, illuminating the small space with natural sunlight.

"Take a seat." Diana pointed to a lounge chair and closed the door behind them.

Ilona did as she was instructed, slipping the scarf from her neck as she sat.

"Here, let me take that." Diana took the scarf and Ilona's hastily removed coat.

Ilona watched as she hung them on a wooden coat rack then crossed to the large desk and perched on its top, crossing her legs neatly. Hands folded in her lap she centred her focus on Ilona, an open expression on her face, and waited.

It took a moment for Ilona to realise that Diana was waiting for her to speak.

"Oh, um, thank you for seeing me," she managed, mind fighting to catch up with the fact she was here, speaking privately with the woman whose attention she had sought, that she could now make her pitch.

She cleared her throat nervously, her eyes flicking up to Diana's face. The woman remained calm and patient. Steeling her resolve, Ilona began. "I was there at the train station last night. I saw the women. I saw my friend." She paused recognising that she was rushing her words. Palms flat on her skirts, she forced herself to slow. "I thought the camps of children were rumours, fears. I donated anyway, whoever was being held prisoner deserved my help. But last night..."

Diana's eyes shimmered with tears. She gave a short sniff and turned her head aside, dashing them away with a flick of her fingers. Composure restored, Diana returned her attention to Ilona, features arranged in a portrait of understanding and empathy. "Last night you saw it was true."

"Da."

Diana took a deep breath, her small body filling up like a balloon and then deflating down to almost nothing. "Sadly, it is not rumours. The donations I came to Dragica about, the supplies like those you handed in, and thank you for that," she added distractedly. "They were needed. Are needed. But as we suspected, little made it through."

Fury surged up from Ilona's core. "What are they doing? Locking up children. Children! Then stealing their parents. It's... it's..."

"Unforgivable," Diana finished for her.

"Why are they doing this?"

Diana's face hardened, and she stared at Ilona. "Is that really a question?"

Ilona closed her eyes, her breath slowing. "No. I know why. I merely..."

"Hoped it could be different?"

"Da."

Diana stood, pacing to the window.

"It is hard to believe the worst of people. I didn't believe it at first myself. But I have seen..." she stopped, turning back to face Ilona. "So, why have you come to me?"

"I want to help."

"You have donated. You have cooked soup. You help."

"It is not enough. Now I know the full truth. I must do more."

"Why?"

"Because I have resources, access to supplies."

"Da, you would be useful, but that doesn't answer my question. Why do you want to help?"

"Because it is wrong. The children—"

"Are in need, yes, but why does it concern you?"

"Because they are children."

"So are the Jewish children, taken long before. Did you seek to support their plight?"

"No, I—"

"So is it religious? You are secretly Orthodox?"

"No, I am Catholic. It's just that—"

"Your friend is in danger."

"I... da." Ilona deflated.

Diana nodded sagely. "Good. We have established the parameters."

Silence fell between them. Ilona felt her skin tingling. Her heartbeat slowed as she realised she had failed. She had come here intent on convincing Diana to help her, and she had not made her case. Not at all. Diana thought she only cared about Misa. As Ilona sat there, she knew that wasn't true. Concern over her friend may have driven her to donate and guided her to Dragica's Red Cross soup kitchen, but seeing Misa on the train had brought it full circle. Horrified her. Given her focus. She was not just here for her friend. She was here for all the children. She didn't know what those left behind in the camps were facing. But she'd felt Misa's desperation, her fear. All night she'd imagined small children alone and cold.

Yes, she wanted to find Stephan and Hanna. And she wanted to free Misa. But she wanted to help all of the children too.

Determination fired through her soul. She raised her head, focusing her gaze on Diana.

"It is true," she began. "I want to help my friend. Seeing her on that train... I did not expect it. It cut me in my flesh." She pounded her thigh. "Her children, as dear to me as if they were my own, they remain in a camp, somewhere in the countryside. Alone, afraid. That horrifies me. So yes, that connection brought me to your door. But it is not just for my friend that I am here. I do not know the extent of what is happening in those camps. Perhaps no one does yet. But I know it is wrong. My friend may have opened my eyes to what is happening. But it is not just her that I care for. It is all the children. I understand you may not believe that. You may see a Croat without a conscience. Fine. But I will help those children. With or without you."

She hadn't realised it, but as she'd spoken her voice had gone softer and softer, more a hiss than speech, her whole body leaning forward as she punctuated her words with the stab of her finger in the air.

When the words dried up, Ilona crumpled in on herself. Hunching down, eyes lowered, hands clasping together in her lap. A moment of awkward silence pressed on her as shock churned in her stomach. She hadn't meant to be so forthright, so rude. She had blurted out her thoughts with no regard for Diana, for the position of power the woman held. She had failed. Diana would never see her as a worthy ally in this fight. Ilona had let her emotions overcome her. Fine. Diana may not want her help, but it would not stop her.

Raising her head high, she stood, brushing her skirts down neatly and straightening her blouse.

"Thank you for your time," she said, nodding briefly to Diana, who remained perched on her desk, face impassive.

She crossed the room, her hands reaching for her coat and scarf. Her fingers had just brushed the wool of her sleeve when

Diana spoke. "You are of course welcome to work alone. But I rather think together we would be far more effective."

Ilona stopped in her tracks. Turning slowly, she stared at the older woman. "I don't understand."

Diana stood, hands tented before her as if in prayer. "It is quite simple. I have secured the support of the German High Command to remove the children from those camps. I do not know how many souls that will mean. But judging by the number of mothers on those trains..."

Her chest rose and fell, a small tick of her eyebrow, then she continued. "I need your help and the help of every decent soul I can find. But it's not just my need, however desperate that may be. I also see you. Contrary to what you think, your personal connection is invaluable to me. You care, I can see it. But you also have a drive, a reason to keep going, even if things become... difficult. You will see this through, with me, to the end. And I would be truly grateful if you would choose to do so."

Ilona gaped at her. She had done it. Diana had done it. Her plan to convince the Germans to act had worked. And she was willing to let Ilona be part of it. Realising she was being impolite, she snapped her mouth shut. "I... I thought I had offended."

A wry smile drifted across Diana's lips. "Honesty works with me. It always will."

Gratitude flooded through Ilona, and her hands began to shake with relief. "She begged me," she whispered softly, almost like a confession. "Misa begged me to find them. She believes their lives are at risk from the treatment in the camps. I wish to discover which camp they are in and bring them home."

Diana nodded. "So let's find them and get them out. And while we search, let's save as many children as we can."

TWENTY-SEVEN
MISA

Somewhere in Germany 1942

The carriage rocked wildly, the rattling through the wooden slates of their prison so violent Misa fancied it might vibrate into splinters.

Then they would be free.

They could run.

But where?

She sat against the corner of the carriage, her legs curled up tightly to her body, for warmth and because there was little space, her head rested against the rough wood of the walls. Around her the women of her village and other neighbouring towns stood or sat, wedged tightly together. There were too many of them for anyone to stretch out in the cramped space. The air smelt of body odour and urine. Someone had vomited the day before, but at least that acrid stench had mellowed. Or maybe her mind had just absorbed it into this new reality.

They had been travelling for days. Peering through the slates of the carriage, she'd seen the sun rise and fall, though she'd lost count of how many times. There were no breaks for toileting or food, none of the usual structures that frame a day. Only the brief pause in Zagreb. The rich and delicious scent of warm soup. The pity in the eyes of the helping nurses.

Misa had been determined to get a bowl. Not for herself but for her little Kata. The girl had withered visibly since they'd first met in the depth of winter. Faster than just the lack of nutrition accounted for. Misa knew it was not just hunger that was making her fade. But she had no way to prevent it.

So, as the train had slowed, she'd pressed forward to the door, forcing herself to the front, to a space nearest the smell of food. Then she'd seen Ilona, and everything changed.

A burst of hope. Not for her, but for Stephan and Hanna. Hope hurt less than despair.

Now, she sat at the rear of the carriage, Kata slumped beside her, her feverish head resting on Misa's shoulder. She'd failed to secured the soup. But the message to Ilona, to search for Stephan and Hanna, that had been worth it. She knew it had.

It didn't fix Kata's growing fever or shrinking cheeks. Nor did it protect them from the coughs and sneezes that ricocheted around the carriage, carried in on the icy winds through the slats in the carriage walls to settle in chests and noses. Hungry, cold and afraid, and heartsick, the women around her had little reserves left to support them against the sickness that deepened around them.

Rolling her head to the side, Misa peered between the gaps in the slats. Outside was covered in a layer of frost that twinkled in the morning light, covering all traces of green or brown ground. Trees lined the far-flung fields, tender spring shoots beginning to pop along the branches. New life and hope, a painful contrast to the reality Misa faced. They'd crossed through varied terrain, farmlands, forests and mountains. No one had told them where they were being taken. They didn't have to. Their guards were German soldiers, the occupiers of her country. The war in Europe raged under Hitler's command. And wars needed workers.

At her side her Kata stirred, a weak groan escaping her lips. Misa wasn't sure, but it sounded like she called for her tata.

Draping an arm around her, she pulled Kata close and tight, willing the little warmth she still had in her body into her icy skin.

"Not long now, dear one," she whispered softly. "Not long now."

Not long until what? She did not know.

A day, a week, a lifetime later the train began to slow, the wheels shrieking as the brakes skidded against the metal of the track. Misa roused herself from a fitful doze, blinking rapidly to focus her eyes and peer beyond the world of the carriage.

The pale sunlight reflected orange off the frost-tipped grasses, blinding her. Slowly her vision adjusted, and a small train station of stone and wood came into view. Along the platform stood a row of soldiers, their breath puffing before them in thick clouds. A light flurry of snow fell from the sky.

Gently Misa shook Kata awake. "Dear one, we are here."

Kata stirred fitfully, her eyelids fluttering open only briefly.

Around them the rest of the carriage began to awaken. Women so long huddled to each other, still but for the rock of the train, stretching and shuffling as they became alert. Anxiety infused the space. They had come to their destination.

The train pulled to a shuddering halt. Bracing her hands against the carriage wall, Misa forced herself up, her legs cramping and stiff after too long bent and cold. Reaching down she hooked her forearms under Kata's armpits and hauled her to her feet. Kata groaned, her head lolling to the side.

"Kata, please. Stand strong, you have to stand strong."

Her time at the camp outside of Lobor-Grad had taught her that. The weak would be separated from the strong. She didn't want to think about what happened to those deemed unfit. Kata was clearly sick, they all where, but Misa did not trust the medical care their captors would provide. Better to keep Kata close and tend to her herself, somehow.

The carriage door rolled open, and a soldier, gun hovering behind his head menacingly, poked his head within.

"Out of the carriage. Out. Out. Schnell!" he shouted, the words angry and impatient. The mass of women moved. Weakened legs stumbled down from the carriage onto the rough stone of the platform. Grimy faces flushed red from the slap of the icy-cold wind that blasted along the tracks, eyes squinting at the light of the sun so long dimmed by the carriage roof.

Misa stepped down first, then reached up to help Kata. Frustrated that she had paused, the young soldier grabbed her elbow, shoving her away from the train. Her feet could not adjust her balance fast enough, and Misa fell, sprawling over the platform.

"Get up!" the soldier screeched. He drew back his foot and kicked her in the ribs, hard. The air whooshed from Misa's lungs as blinding pain shot through her chest. Unable to breathe, let alone speak, she forced herself up from the rough stone of the platform. Turning, she watched as Kata climbed warily from the carriage. Her legs gave and she crashed to her knees. Misa dashed forward. Another pair of hands made it to Kata before she did. A kindly older woman, with grey curls that hung limp around her gaunt face, pulled Kata from the floor.

"Thank you," Misa managed to breathe to her.

"Keep her upright," the woman said, then turned away following the line of prisoners with a determined step.

Misa knew she was right.

She slipped her arm around Kata's waist, taking her weight and leading her forward.

The women streamed from the carriages, pulling their sleeves down to cover their hands, shoulders hunched in seeking protection from the morning chill. The soldiers, keen eyes watching, herded them into a line, ordering them forward. They walked from the small station to a dirt road, patches of green growth spurting from the edges. Misa looked up over the bobbing heads of the women from the train. They stretched out before her down the road turning off in the distance. There were no trucks or buses parked in wait, just a line of soldiers and trudging women. How far they had to walk, she could not guess.

"Come, dear one," she said, pulling Kata closer. "One step at a time."

On they trudged.

As the sun hung on the edge of the distant horizon, a length of barbed wire fencing came into view. Within the fence stood rows of buildings, set out in rectangular blocks. Women milled about between the buildings and the fence line, some stood around large metal barrels, fire flickering from within the cylinders. As Misa's line of women approached, those within the fence looked up. Not one of them approached. Ahead two soldiers unlocked a large wooden gate, gesturing them within. The women filed inside. They were directed to an open space of ice and mud where a large man in the uniform of a commandant stood flanked by soldiers, waiting.

The women gathered before him, feet shuffling from nerves and cold, eyes scanning warily.

The commandant held up his hands and raised his voice. "Welcome, all, to our camp. Thank you for the labour you will perform for the honour of the Reich."

He went on to outline a set of camp rules – curfew at night, the number of wash days a week, and so on. Mind fuzzy from lack of food and the cold, his words slid over Misa. Her attention drifted out over the camp, taking in the ragged women who had gathered to hover on the edge of the new group of inmates, observing, expressions blank.

"Officer Hans will direct you to your barracks. It is your responsibility to keep your bedding clean. We tolerant no nonsense here. Officer Hans."

They were split into groups and assigned to various buildings. Misa helped Kata up the stairs to their barracks. The dim space was lit by a scant selection of candles. The walls were lined with bunks, some already occupied, some empty. At the end of each bunk sat a folded blanket. Misa manoeuvred Kata to a set of two bunks and settled her onto the mattress. Thin, lumpy. Taking up the blanket, she wrapped it around her. It was so thin she could see her hand through the knitting. Frowning she glanced around. The camp women watched from their beds, eyes sunken and dull.

"Are there more blankets?" she asked.

One woman stood, crossing the floor with a swagger. "That depends. What do you have to trade?"

Misa balked. "Trade?"

They'd been forced from their home in Petrinja with only the clothes on their backs, held in Lobor-Grad with scant supplies. No one had anything to trade.

"Stop it, Danica," another woman said, before fixing Misa with a stare. "No one has anything more than what we brought."

She rose and crossed the barracks to Misa. Her eyes swept over Kata. "Fever?"

Misa nodded.

"They won't let her rest," the woman said.

"I know."

The woman looked at Misa, assessing, before saying, "I'm Biljana."

"Misa. And this is Kata."

Biljana nodded at them both, furrowing her brow as she took in Kata's wobbly smile, then turned away. "Get some sleep, we rise early."

"I know," Misa whispered to herself. They'd crossed nations, survived starvation and oppressive labour. And they were right back where they started.

There would be no reprieve.

She could only keep going.

That was all there was to do.

TWENTY-EIGHT

MISA

The frost had broken under the sunshine pouring from a gentle blue sky above. The trees were bursting with blossom in an impossibly beautiful display of life and vibrancy. The ground was covered in rich green grasses and the soil beneath Misa's hands was black with fertility. She scooped some more dirt aside and dropped the seedlings into the hole before covering it over. Kata was bent beside her, trowelling the dirt. There was a lot more field left to finish before sunset.

"Are you all right?"

Kata flicked a glance her way and nodded. It was unconvincing. Her forehead was plastered with sweat, her face ghostly pale. But at least the worst of her fever had passed weeks before, as the two women had settled into the routine of life in this new camp.

Misa had been so afraid. She'd thought she'd failed her.

A soldier stomped behind her and Misa returned her attention to the ground. They had managed to remain unnoticed so far, and Misa intended to keep it that way.

As the sun reached for its midday apex, a whistle sounded from the edge of the field. A soldier stood waving an arm. They were being moved to another field, Misa assumed. She stood, pressing her hands into the small of her back and stretching the muscles that cramped there. Tenting her hand over her eyes she looked out over the field of women. It was just like back in Lobor-Grad and a yet world away. Shoulders slumped, steps unsteady, the women began to trek across to the roadside and the soldiers who would march them to the next field.

"I wonder if we will get some bread before we start again?" Misa said over her shoulder to Kata. "You can have mine if we do—"

A moan cut her off as a soft flopping sound came from behind her. Misa turned around and gasped. Kata had fallen into the dirt.

"Kata!" She dropped her to knees, hands grasping Kata's head and gently turning her face up. The girl's eyes rolled in her head.

"Get her up, now!" Biljana hissed, stalking towards them.

Misa didn't bother to respond. They all knew what happened when they showed weakness.

Biljana crouched down on the other side of Kata and took hold of her, hauling her into a sitting position and slipping an arm around the girl's waist.

"No wait!"

It was too late. Biljana's hand landed against Kata's belly, and her lips parted in shock. She glared at Misa and Misa knew, she knew. She'd felt the small bulge that grew beneath Kata's skirts.

Oh God.

"Please," Misa reached forward, gripping Biljana's hand. "Please don't say anything."

"This can't be," Biljana said.

"It wasn't her fault. She was—"

"I know. They come at night here too," Biljana interrupted. "You can't keep this secret."

"I know, I know," Misa said, her mind reeling. "I just need time."

She had to think of something to help the girl. She was a nurse. She had to find a way.

Biljana fixed her with her eyes. "There is no time. You should have dealt with this already."

Misa knew. She'd tried before they left Croatia. But she didn't have the equipment she needed. Nor the heart. The baby was an innocent, no matter who its tata was. How could she end a pregnancy? How could she take a life? It went against everything she believed in, as a nurse and a mama. But Kata was a child herself, and too weak for this task. It was an impossible choice. So Misa had done nothing and prayed to God for His intervention. She wasn't sure why she prayed any more. With all the horrors they were enduring, it was clear God was not with them.

Despite the work, the malnourishment, the deprivation, the child growing within Kata remained. Misa understood. God had chosen to make Kata fight. She hated Him for it.

Misa glanced up quickly. A soldier was watching them from a few paces away.

"Help me get her up," she whispered, eyes begging Biljana.

The woman adjusted her squat and together they drew Kata up to stand. Her head lolled on her shoulders, but her eyes opened. Blinking rapidly she faced Misa. "What happened?" she asked, dazed.

"You fell. It is all right. We will help you. Can you walk?"

Kata's gaze swung between Misa and Biljana and she lifted her leg and took a step. "Da."

"Good, now, let's move before that soldier comes asking questions."

Bracing Kata between them, Misa and Biljana started towards the road, the soldier tracked their every move. Gradually Kata's coordination settled, and her steps strengthened.

"I am all right now," she said as they neared the roadside. "Thank you, both."

Biljana dropped her arm and stalked away, not looking back.

Kata turned a questioning look on Misa. "She knows," Misa said softly. "But she won't say anything. I am sure of it."

"What am I going to do?" Kata whispered.

"We will think of something," Misa promised. *I just need time to think.* "For now, let's get through the day."

They fell in line behind the others and made their way to the next field to work.

There was no time. That very night the soldiers came to Misa and Kata's barracks. As she had countless nights in Lobor-Grad, Misa bracketed Kata between herself and the wall, hiding the young girl away, protecting her just as she had her own children when they were first driven from their homes, what seemed a lifetime ago.

This time the boots stopped behind her. Holding her breath, she closed her eyes. She would go with them, willingly. She would offer herself to spare the child that lay shaking with terror in her arms.

"Up," a gruff voice said. Misa squeezed Kata once. "Stay still," she whispered and rolled over. The soldier's face was blacked out by the darkness, the lights from outside framing him in white.

She sat up, swinging her legs over the bed's edge and stood.

The man pushed past her and grabbed Kata's arm. The girl screamed.

"No," Misa said, clutching his arm. "I will come with you."

His face swung to her, lines appearing between his brows. He didn't speak her language. Few of them did. Heart racing she searched her mind for the German words. "Nein." Then she tapped her chest. "Me."

His hand released Kata, and relief flooded through Misa even as fear locked up her muscles. It was the right thing to do, it was the only thing to do.

He straightened, then shoved her, roughly. Not expecting the violence, Misa tumbled backwards, smacking onto the floor. The soldier pivoted back to the bed and seized Kata with both hands, lifting her as if she were a sack of flour.

"No, no, no!" Kata screamed, arms and legs flailing. But she was too small and the soldier too strong; her weak fight did nothing to stop his determination.

It fired something in Misa and she surged upward, hands flying out before her, but something pulled her back. Her head whipped around. Biljana was beside her, holding her firm.

"Let go!" Misa cried. "I can't let them take her. Not again."

Another soldier appeared in the doorway as the first manhandled a screaming Kata towards the exit.

"You can't do anything," Biljana hissed. "They know."

"What?" Misa whipped her head around at Biljana as rage filled her chest. "You told them?"

"No," Biljana said, her eyes never leaving the soldier who had now reached the door. "They worked it out."

"Misa!" Kata's anguished cry tore Misa in two, and she lurched forward, fighting against Biljana's restraint and against the terrible ache in her heart that told her there was nothing she could do.

"Be still," she called to Kata as the soldier's bulk blocked the light beyond the door. "It will go faster."

The soldier and Kata disappeared, and the door slammed shut, plunging Misa into a darkness beyond the black of night as her blood hammered against her fear for Kata. For what the soldiers might do to her. Biljana's hand dropped from her shoulder, and the soft sound of her retreat echoed away. Misa stayed on the floor. Curling in on herself, she hugged her knees to her chest, rocking herself gently. She wanted to pray. To beg God to protect Kata. But the words could not come. You can't pray if you no longer believe anyone is listening.

Kata wasn't back when the dawn whistle blew to call them to their work. She didn't join them in the line before the march to work detail, nor in the fields as they toiled. Misa worked, there was no choice, but her mind was in turmoil, her eyes constantly scanning around her, looking for any sign of the girl. Night fell, and they were locked into their barracks. Still no Kata.

In the deep silence of the night, Misa felt an angular body slip into the bed beside her and enfold her in an embrace. Biljana's soft whisper met her ears. "She's not coming back."

The rock in her throat expanded, swelling so tight she could barely breathe around it. Because she knew Biljana was right. They hadn't just taken Kata for their nightly entertainment. They had taken her to remove a problem. A pregnant worker was a slow worker. An infant was a liability. Kata and her unborn child were expendable.

Tears, locked away in her soul since she'd been dragged from her children's arms, spilled down her face as Kata's final desperate cry for help blended with her son Stephan's high-pitched scream.

Biljana held her firmly to her chest, soothing her ragged hair, whispering, "Shh," against her temple. And Misa's heart cracked open, a final brutal rendering, tearing through to the very edge, a gaping wound within her that nothing, not even time and distance, would ever heal.

PART FIVE

TWENTY-NINE

The old man swings his axe, expertly splitting the wood in two. His toughened hands gather up the pieces, and he strides for the door. "Just let me get the fire going, then you can ask me anything."

Daniel and Sara follow him through the door into his small forest cabin. The air is laced with ice, and Sara is glad to get inside. Inside is small and cramped, every available space occupied by a piece of wooden furniture, or an ornament.

Ivanco drops the wood onto the kindling he has already gathered in the fireplace and strikes a match. The smell of woodsmoke finds Sara's nose, comforting and familiar.

Ivanco breathes in deeply, the flames reflecting off his dark eyes. Leaning a hand against the wooden frame of the fireplace, he swings his gaze to Sara and Daniel.

"You will record?"

"If that's okay?"

"Da, da."

He crosses to a worn chair by the fire and sits. Daniel begins to set up the camera as Sara takes a seat opposite Ivanco.

A thumbs up from Daniel.

"So, what do you want to know?"

Sara smiles. "Whatever you want to tell me."

Ivanco huffs, clearly unimpressed. "I don't want to tell you anything. You knocked on my door." His voice is gruff. His arms cross over his chest, closing himself off.

Sara nods. "That is true," she agrees. "But you invited us in."

Ivanco pierces her with a stare. "It's cold out," he says. "Of course, I invited you in."

But it's there, she sees it. The tiny glimmer of longing behind the mask of indifference. The need to speak. They all have it; she just has to say the right thing. It is why her mama is wrong. She is angry at Sara for doing this, angry in general, but she won't explain why. Maybe one day Sara will find the words to help her open up too.

Swallowing softly, Sara picks her words carefully. "Thank you, it is cold. Especially in the countryside."

Ivanco continues to stare, but his arms have slackened. "City folk don't understand the ways of the land," he says. "I learnt. When I was fostered out here."

"You were orphaned by the Ustaše?"

"Da. Well, I guess so. No one ever claimed me. The nurses took me out of Jasenovac. My brothers were not so lucky." His face darkens and his mouth forms a thin, tight line.

Sara breathes through the shock. Ivanco is the first survivor she has met from Jasenovac. They experimented on the children there. They killed so many. It was a true death camp.

So many answers lay behind those hooded eyes. But Sara won't ask. What Ivanco shares is up to him. That is the promise she has made herself. On that, she will not bend.

"The nurses took me to one of their camps. It wasn't good there either, but it was better than Jasenovac. They left my best friend. I heard the doctor say he wouldn't survive the transport." His mouth works as he fights an internal battle. "So they left Dejan. Other kids they took died." He shrugs. "Seemed unfair they didn't give Dejan a chance. He should have died with me."

Water lines his eyes. He turns away, dashing the tears from his cheeks.

"When no one came for me they sent me away to a farm. A foster family. They had three children already, they didn't need me. Not for that anyway. There was no room in the house for me. They put me in the barn with the cows. I was just free labour. At least they fed me..."

As the van rattles its way back to Zagreb, Sara stares out at the fading sun. She feels heavy. She wants to stop. Why did she start this in the first place?

She can't stop.

She needs this.

THIRTY
NADICA

Novska 1991

Nadica places the tinned tomatoes on the shelf. A knock sounds from the shop door. She looks up to see the newspaper delivery man wave through the glass. She waves back. Leaving the crate of tinned vegetables, she heads to the door and unlocks it. Outside is still dark, only the faintest glimmers of blue are beginning to lighten above the trees. Bending her knees, she squats down and gathers up the pile of newspapers held together by rough twine.

Back at the counter, she slips her Stanley knife under the twine and cuts the bindings. The string springs free. The front page headline catches her eye: Vukovar Siege – Defence is Failing. Below that article, an image of the streets of Zagreb, windows taped over in a futile attempt to secure them against the regular bombings the citizens are enduring at the hands of the Yugoslav army.

She takes a deep breath and turns the newspaper over, hiding the article.

She doesn't know how to feel or what to hope for. Battle lines have been drawn across her country based on ethnicity and religion. It should have been simple: Croatia voted for independence, that should have been that. But things are never simple, she is coming to understand. Nadica doesn't know what will happen, or even what to hope for. She's just terrified.

So far her region is untouched, but how long can that last?

The thought snags in her mind, and she feels momentarily out of place. Her baba and Misa's stories over these past weeks, of Zagreb and studying to be a nurse. She knew her baba and aunty Misa had lived through the war. Why had she never asked them about that time in their lives before?

Or had she? And they'd turned the conversation?

Leaning against the countertop, a frown tightens her forehead. Another knock on the door distracts her musing. It is Mr Kovacic, here to purchase his morning paper as he does every day. He is early, it is not opening time yet. But Nadica doesn't mind. She returns to the door to unlock the store for opening.

"Good morning, Mr Kovacic," she says in greeting, bending down to scratch the ears of his dog, Shuma, panting at his side. He is a good old dog, well-named too. Shuma means forest. Nadica hopes he can run through the trees forever in the afterlife.

"News from Zagreb?" he asks, as he does every morning.

"Da, more violence. They are bombing the city. People are taping up their windows and praying to God."

Mr Kovacic grumbles to himself as he strides into the store. "Too close," he says. He is right. "Croatia wants independence, it is time that Belgrade stepped aside. It won't be long before the international world stands with us," he proclaims confidently.

Nadica barely manages to stop her words. What good does the opinion of a foreign country do? Her people are against each other now. She's known Mr Kovacic her whole life. He has always been old, and grumpy. But he is a good customer. She's not getting into this debate with him.

"Just the paper this morning? Or does Shuma need some treats?"

"Shuma is getting portly. No treats. But I will take a bag of carrots if you have them."

"Da... I tried," she whispers to Shuma, patting his head once more. The greying muzzle shoves against her hand in affection. She ruffles his ears.

"Are you staying?"

The question feels out of time. Yet it is exactly the right question.

"Da."

Mr Kovacic regards her a moment, and nods once. "Your mama needs to start locking her doors."

She heads home under a bleak sky. The autumn darkness is gathering.

Her mama is home; she's cooked štrukli. Nadica feels the smile on her lips before she reaches her mama.

"Why?" she asks gently. The delicious cottage cheese-filled balls of štrukli are a treat for special occasions.

"Because we both love them," her mama replies, and Nadica can't help but enjoy the swell of happiness that radiates through her.

They choose to sit in front of the TV, watching Croatia's version of *Pop Idol*. The singer on the screen is talented enough, but Nadica's not listening. It's background sound. It's a filler for their stressed minds.

"Mama, is there something we need to discuss?" she ventures warily.

Mama chomps on her štrukli, then laughs riotously, pointing at the judge on the TV screen as he delivers his assessment of the performer, her mount full of food. "He is a hoot," she says.

Nadica smiles and nods. "Da, da. So funny," she agrees. She knows when she has been told to stop asking questions.

Later when Nadica rises to make her way to bed, her mama grabs her arm, halting her by the couch. "You are visiting your baba and Misa tomorrow?" she asks.

"Da. Or did you want me to take the shop so you can go again?"

"No, no," her mama says, releasing her arm and patting it absentmindedly. "You go. It is important."

THIRTY-ONE
ILONA

Stara Gradiška Concentration Camp 1942

The bus bumped over a pothole, bouncing Ilona uncomfortably against the worn seat. Sweat traced a line down her spine as the high summer sun beat down on the airless cabin. She glanced around herself nervously, hugging her satchel to her chest. Beside her, another young nurse caught her eye and offered a small smile of support. They were all tense. It was their first trip to one of the Ustaše camps, and none of them really knew what to expect.

Diana sat three rows ahead of her, her neat curls bobbing with the movement of the bus, Dragica's solid presence pressed next to her. The two of them had worked wonders over the summer. Diana secured the approval of Officer Gustav von Koczian to allow their little force of Red Cross nurses to enter the camps and remove the children to the care of orphanages and churches, starting with Stara Gradiška. Dragica enlisted the help of bus drivers and locals with trucks to transport the children to safety. Ilona had been humbled by the number of men who had agreed to help without pay. There was humanity left in the Independent State of Croatia after all.

The bus connected with another hole in the road, and Ilona's body swayed, her eyes swinging to gaze out the window at the forest of beech and spruce that stretched around the road, limbs covered in a riot of green. And their destination came into view. The trees thinned out, revealing a looming structure of brick and mortar. High walls ended in haphazard roofing, partially collapsed along the left side. The windows that remained in place were cracked and covered in grime, soaking the sunlight into their dirty surfaces and leaving them dull.

The bus turned into the drive, slowing to a halt before the massive structure. Walls surrounded a compound. Large towers were constructed into the corners, the glint of gun barrels shining from their tops.

"Must be an old factory," Petra whispered. Ilona nodded, her eyes tracking up a series of grand chimneys, their walls coated in the black stains of soot.

"All right, girls," Diana said, coming to her feet. "Remember our directive. We are here for the children and the children only. We are not allowed to cross into the adult section of the camp. Keep to yourself and avoid the soldiers. Record each child's details with as much precision as you can, give them an identity card on a string with their name and number and send them to the transport. Efficient, not rushed, is the best way to be fast. Is everyone clear on the task before them?"

"Da, gospođo," the gathered nurses chorused in unison.

"All right. Let's go. Follow me."

Diana turned, Dragica on her heels. Ilona stood and filed out with the others. As her feet hit the gravel of the drive a warm wind picked up off the surrounding grasslands. Her skin flushed against the warmth, and Ilona unbuttoned her cardigan, seeking relief. Dragica and Diana strode ahead towards the imposing grey building. The sound of rattling filled her ears, and Ilona glanced up, realising it was the shaking of the broken window seals in the strengthening winds.

"It is a ruin," Petra whispered beside her.

"This is just one side, the rest must be in better repair," Ilona reasoned.

"Hmmm," Petra hummed, but she did not look convinced.

As Diana and Dragica neared the large double doors that led within the facility, two soldiers in the grey of the Ustaše uniform strode forward. They placed themselves before Diana. From this distance, Ilona could not make out their words, but it was clear from Dragica's posture that she was unimpressed. The rest of the nurses paused in wait. Dragica's hand flashed out in obvious irritation, gesturing at the buses gathered behind her. The soldiers looked up, shoulders tight. Then the shorter one gave a nod and stepped to the side. His companion followed suit, and Diana and Dragica advanced.

"Guess that's our cue to continue," Ilona said.

Petra didn't even look at her, just stepped forward, fearful eyes set on the guns on the soldiers' backs. Suppressing her own fear, Ilona followed, passing under the large arched doorway. Darkness enveloped her, then the bright sun returned as the building opened out into an expansive central courtyard. Ilona could not stop the gasp that sounded her shock.

The courtyard before her was dust-strewn and unkempt. Pockets of dried-out brown grass and weeds lay dead around the space. A few logs of splintered wood were piled at one end beside some raised garden beds, where perhaps flowers once grew, now barren. The wind whipped down from the open sky above, blowing the dirt and loose gravel stones from the paths. And there, in the centre of the dirty, overheated space, were the children. Hundreds of children.

They milled about in small groups. Some were standing close together, others hunched in the dirt of the raw ground. Around them a few soldiers patrolled, the smoke of their cigarettes hung thick and pungent in the air. The children's faces were gaunt, grime marring their too-thin cheeks. Their heads were shaved to the skin, with only a light stubble of regrowth left to catch the sunbeams. Their clothes were stained and torn, hanging off them like rags; they likely fitted once, months ago when they were first brought here from their homes. But now, as their bodies had withered from malnourishment, their shirts and trousers hung loose from their limbs. The children looked towards the nurses, sunken eyes collectively turning to them. Flies hovered around them, the children shuffling gently to avoid their buzzing. The silence stretched. No shouts of play, or laughter. Just eerie quiet.

Ilona's hands began to tremble, tears building along her eyelids.

"Control yourself." Ilona glanced to her side, meeting Diana's eyes. The elegant woman stood rigid, her face a mask of calm. "It is not their job to shoulder our emotions," she continued.

Ilona gulped, nodded and forced her features to go blank, pressing down the ever-growing swell of horror and despair that built within her soul. So many. How could anyone do this?

A man in a tailored suit approached, a pair of round spectacles sliding down his long nose.

"Guten Tag, Diana Budisavljević?" he enquired, turning an expectant face to Diana.

"Da," she replied, stepping forward. "In our language please."

"Of course," he said, switching from German. "I am Doctor Hoffman. I will be assessing the children's health, to ensure they are fit for transport."

Ilona watched as Diana paused, her eyes sweeping over the courtyard of children.

"And if you determine that they are not fit for transport?" she inquired.

"They will remain."

Shock sluiced through Ilona. Remain? No. They all had to come. Every single one. They could not stay here. They would die.

"They will all travel," Diana stated.

"I will be the one to decide the suitability—"

"They will all travel," she repeated.

Ilona watched in awe as Diana lifted her head, an expression of pure defiance lighting in her eyes. "Every child will travel. Remaining in these conditions is unacceptable."

The doctor's mouth opened to argue, but Diana pressed. Leaning towards him she lowered her voice to a whisper, "Look at them. Look at the conditions here. They have to travel."

The doctor's eyelids twitched, and he raised his hand to push his glasses back up his nose, the gesture nervous and ashamed.

"Da," he agreed, stepping back.

Diana nodded once firmly, then turned to the nurses behind them. "Set up. We have much to do. Tables in a row. Children split between us evenly. Work efficiently and accurately. Go."

The nurses broke into movement. Those with tables and chairs set them out in rows across the courtyard. Others spread out between the children, organising them into lines by each table with gentle, reassuring gestures, their voices soft. The children complied, gathering into groups. Some pressed closer to each other, clasping hands with their friends. Others simply stared, eyes unfocused.

Ilona took up her spot at a table and drew out her record book. Dipping her pen in ink, she looked up and smiled at the first child in her line, a boy, maybe nine years of age, dark circles beneath his hollow eyes.

"Hello, dear one, can you tell me your name?"

The boy shuffled forward, eyes darting nervously. "Dušan."

"A lovely name." Her heart stuttered; Dušan meant "soul" in Serbian. Collecting herself, Ilona focused on the boy. "And, Dušan, how old are you?"

"Eleven. No, maybe twelve."

Ilona nodded through her shock. He was so small. "We can write both. And, Dušan, do you know where you came from?"

"Gređani."

"Well done, Dušan," Ilona said, recording his details in the record book before her. She took up a small piece of card on a string and wrote down a number and Dušan's details before slipping the card around the boy's neck. "Keep this safe," she explained. "It is so we can find you when your mama comes home."

Dušan's eyes snapped up to hers. "She will come?"

Ilona's heart seized. She'd said the wrong thing. She didn't know. Couldn't know. "We must keep track of you," she deferred. "Now, follow the others to the bus. You are safe now, Dušan. I promise."

The boy looked towards the line of children making their way back through the looming entranceway and into the world beyond the camp. He hesitated, and Ilona felt her composure crack. The last time he'd been ordered to a truck to be transported had brought him here, and separated him from his mama. How could he trust this now?

"Go on," Ilona prompted gently. "There will be a soft bed and soup soon."

Dušan's dark eyes met hers once more, wide and edged with hope. He was so small, so young. He still needed to believe that adults would keep him safe. She could see the longing to trust shining from him, and she smiled kindly. He turned and walked towards the buses. What horrors had these children endured? Yet they were still ready to hope. Sorrow squeezed Ilona's heart as she watched him making his way to the exit, but she pressed it down and turned to the next child in line.

For the next hour or so she worked, recording the details of each child. Some, like Dušan, knew their information. Some, however, did not. Too young, or too traumatised, many children could only be assigned a number and a prayer that a description of their appearance – fair, dark, tall, short – might be enough for an identification in the future.

As the sun tipped over the horizon a small boy stepped forward.

"Hello there, what's your name?"

Ilona recorded his details: Andrija, from Sisak, seven years old. Ilona went still. Sisak was the next town over from Misa's village. Keeping her movements calm, she nodded, hoping that her face did not betray her emotions.

"Well done, Andrija. Now, here is your card, follow the others."

"What about my sister?' Andrija asked.

"Oh, thank you for telling me, Andrija. Is she in line? Can you see her?"

The boy shook his head. "No, she's in the sick room."

Ilona frowned. "The 'sick room'? I don't understand."

"Back there," Andrija turned, pointing beyond the courtyard. Ilona looked back where he pointed and saw a dark doorway on the far side of the complex.

"Andrija, are you telling me that not all the children are in this courtyard?"

"No," Andrija said. "The sick ones aren't here. Like my sister. They are back there. I want to stay with my sister."

Ilona swallowed. "The sick ones". All these children were sick. *Dear God, how unwell were those who had been separated?* Taking a deep breath, she faced Andrija. "You will not be separated from her," she said, praying to God it was true. "Will you wait here for me while I go and see the sick room?"

Andrija nodded, his small hands resting on the edge of Ilona's table. "Thank you, Andrija."

Ilona stood, pacing across the gravel to where Diana stood, supervising. Ilona whispered, "Have they told you about the 'sick room'?"

Diana raised quizzical eyes to Ilona. "No. Doctor Hoffman assured me all the children were here in the courtyard."

Ilona pressed her lips together. "I think there are more. A boy says his sister is in a separate place." Ilona pointed to the back of the building.

Diana's mouth flattened in aggravation. "Let's find out."

She strode across the courtyard, Ilona stepping quickly to keep up.

"Wait, stop!" one of the patrolling soldiers called, his boots slapping against the gravel as he rushed towards them. But Diana did not so much as pause. Smacking her hands against the rough wooden door she shoved through into a darkened room. Ilona hurried behind her, stepping into the space, her shoes scraping against rough cement. And stopped in her tracks.

The breath left her lungs as the scent of human waste and sickness filled her nose. She barely noticed, however, as the dimmed room came into focus. Along the rough, bare floor lay children. Stripped naked, not even a blanket to cover them or to line the rough cement beneath them. Tiny bodies, the bones of their limbs poking painfully through stretched skin. Skeletons. Flies buzzed at their mouths and eyes, the children too weak to lift a hand to swat them away.

"By God," Ilona gasped, her hand covering her mouth in purest horror at the sight before her.

Footsteps sounded behind her, and the young soldier who had raced after them stepped inside, Doctor Hoffman on his heels.

"Mrs Budisavljević," the doctor began. "You are not to be here."

Diana rounded on him in palpable fury. "You told me all the children were in the courtyard!"

The doctor nodded. "All the children who can travel. These ones are... too far along."

"What has happened to them?" Ilona breathed in horror.

"Dysentery. Disease."

"Starvation and exposure!" Diana hissed, eyes aflame. Her rigid composure had shattered. Wrath rode her words as she stared at the doctor. "What kind of man are you?" she spat.

The doctor met her stare with surprise, then his face shattered into cracks of shame.

"I arrived too late to help them."

"They are naked and starving. You could have done so much more."

"I..." he trailed off, a hand running through his hair.

"We are taking them."

"They won't survive—"

"We are taking them. Every. Single. Child," Diana said, voice shaking with rage.

The doctor only nodded.

Ilona turned back to the rows of emaciated children, her whole body locking up in horror at the scene before her.

"I will fetch help," Diana said at her side.

Ilona barely heard her, for a girl, so tiny that she looked more like a sparrow than a person, had opened her eyes and met Ilona's. Whipping the cardigan from her shoulders Ilona stepped to the child and knelt beside her. The girl looked up, eyes dull, lips chapped from dehydration. Gently, so, so gently, Ilona gathered the girl into her lap, her limbs so thin and frail she feared she would snap. Carefully she swaddled the girl in her cardigan, covering her nakedness. Running a hand over her shaved scalp, Ilona whispered. "It is all right, small one. We are here now. It is all right."

The door creaked, and two more nurses entered the room.

A sob of disbelief filled the room, then the scent of fresh vomit as one nurse lost her stomach to the sight and scent of the room of horror. Ilona rose to her feet, cradling the small girl to her chest. "It is all right," she crooned, over and over as she crossed the room and headed for the buses now almost full of children, ready to return to Zagreb and leave this place of death behind.

THIRTY-TWO
ILONA

Zagreb

Ilona shut her apartment door behind her. The quiet of her home enveloped her. Silent and still. Alone. Kicking off her heels, she padded into her bedroom and flung herself down onto her mattress. Burying her head in her pillow, her mouth opened in an anguished scream as her resolve broke open and the horror of all she'd just witnessed at the camp shattered within her.

She could not contain it. She could not hold it within. But she couldn't get it out either.

Sobs wracked her body, her blood pulsing painfully in her temples as every muscle within her tensed, waves of hopeless fury spasming through her.

What she had seen, all those innocent children, alone, starved, dying? She would never free her memory from that evil.

So many children, their parents taken away to labour camps in Germany, left to fend for themselves. The older ones responsible for the younger ones. Babies still in nappies, filthy and soiled, no fresh cloth provided and no water to clean. Many of the older children too young still to even know what to do if they'd had access to hygiene. Barely any food or water. No medicine. No blankets.

On Diana's orders, Petra had been sent through the rooms where the children slept, to seek out any other hidden children. Mercifully there'd only been the sick room, but that was beyond hell. She said the bedrooms were no more than palettes of wood fixed to the walls. No mattresses, no blankets. The wind crying through the broken window panes.

"The children said they snuggled together on the hardwood," she'd explained. "Their body heat was all they had to keep them warm through the winter. I don't know how they survived to see summer."

Those in the sick room hadn't even had that luxury. They were too weakened by illness and malnourishment to even shuffle closer together on the cold concrete floor they'd been dumped on.

How had any of them lasted long enough to be saved?

A fresh sob choked her throat, her body seizing at the memory. Doctor Hoffman had been right; most of the children from the sick room hadn't survived the bus ride back to Zagreb. But at least they had passed to God wrapped in caring arms, whispered words of tenderness sounding in their ears, rather than alone and abandoned on a hard, rough floor.

Her little girl had made it, though. As tears flowed from her colleagues' eyes as their tiny charges had released their last breaths, Ilona had prayed and prayed and prayed. And, somehow, the girl kept breathing. Her large round eyes fluttered fitfully as they bumped along the rough roads to the city. At Saint Jerome's Hall orphanage, Ilona had passed her to a waiting nun, Sister Marija, her heart full of regret. She hadn't wanted to leave her side.

The nun had smiled sadly, understanding flooding her face. "I will watch over her," she'd promised.

Ilona roared her anguish, clutching her pillow against her open mouth to muffle her screams, seeking comfort, anything to soothe her. But there was nothing. Nothing could heal this new wound within her soul. Not even Jovan.

How she longed for him. It could not fix this, nothing could.

But he would hold her, wrap her in his strong arms and bear the pain beside her. He would mean she was not alone.

But he wasn't here. And she didn't know where he was or if he was all right. If he still breathed.

No. She shoved the thought away. No. He had not left her on this earth alone. He wouldn't. He wouldn't. She couldn't face that possibility. It would break her open, split her in two; all that she was would be shredded and irreparable. She could not allow that. Jovan lived. He had to. That belief was all that held any part of her together.

Hours later as the first rays of dawn peeked through her curtains, Ilona rose. Eyes red-rimmed from tears, throat raw from sobbing, she made toast, spreading it thickly with plum jam she'd made herself. Her baba's recipe. It was a small comfort, something familiar from the safety of the kitchen of her childhood. Something to hold on to against the turmoil of this war.

She was due at Diana's by nine o'clock to review the records of the children that the nurses had faithfully noted and help compile them into Diana's card-file. Radmila was covering her teaching rounds so she'd have time. Diana was determined to list every single child, to ensure no one went missing and should their parents return, they could be reunited.

A beautiful hope.

After what she'd witnessed in that camp, it was a hope that felt futile and weak in the face of it all. How many children hadn't even known their own name? How many would pass away in the care of the nuns? How many were still languishing in other camps around Croatia?

A pitiful thought. The scent of plum jam melting over her toast met her nose, and a sudden decision seized her mind. Grabbing up her toast, she made a sandwich and wrapped it in paper. She threw on her coat and raced into the street as she shoved the sandwich in her satchel.

A short bus trip later and Ilona stood on the steps of the church orphanage they had delivered the children to the night before.

Straightening her shoulders and schooling her features to calm, she pushed through the door. An older nun, head lowered in diffidence to God, approached. "Can I help you?"

"Hello, I am sorry to come by unannounced. I was here last night, with the children. I wanted to check on their well-being," Ilona explained. The nun regarded her through eyes milky from age and full of sorrow.

"You and your fellow nurses have done God's work," she said. "Please, wait here, I will fetch Sister Marija. She is managing the children's care."

"Thank you."

"May God look down on you with peace and love." The nun turned and disappeared into the depths of the building. Impatient, nerves frayed from terror and fatigue Ilona paced, hands rhythmically tapping her satchel. She had to see the little girl she'd gathered from the floor of the sick room. She had to know if she had made it through the night. Her lips moved in silent prayer, *Please God, please, watch over her, keep her safe, make her well.* Time stretched around her, and Ilona's tension increased. What was taking so long? Why hadn't the nun returned with Sister Marija ?

She was about to abandon her manners and sneak into the rooms beyond when a door cracked open and the old nun appeared, Sister Marija at her side.

"Ilona," she said. "It is good to see you."

"Thank you, sister. I..."

"You wish to know of the children?" Regret shadowed the sister's face. "It has been a long night." Her words were heavy with sorrow, and Ilona's heart cleaved.

"I believe this is yours." The sister held out a folded parcel. It was Ilona's cardigan.

"Oh," Ilona breathed, tears springing to her eyes as she recognised her garment. The one she'd wrapped around the child. Her stomach plummeted like a stone through water. She didn't make it. *No, no, no.* She'd been so strong, lasted so long, and made it to the orphanage. How could God be so cruel? The girl's wide eyes, so full of longing and need, filled Ilona's mind and her tears fell, hot and wet, staining her cheeks in grief once more. It was so unfair. It was too much.

The sister cocked her head at Ilona, then her mouth dropped in shock. "Oh no, I am so sorry. I didn't think... The girl you brought last night, she made it."

Ilona sniffed loudly. "What?"

The sister shook her head. "Forgive me, I have not slept, I didn't consider what returning your cardigan would suggest. I only meant to give it back to you. The girl lives. She is extremely weak. But she is still with us. God has not called her home yet. Few have her strength."

Relief and despair flooded through Ilona, making her knees wobbly and unstable. So many children had not made it through. She thought of little Andrija and prayed his sister still breathed. But the girl lived. It brought unfathomable joy to her ravaged soul.

Sister Marija eyed her, clearing her throat with a gentle cough. "Would you like to see her?"

Unable to speak past the well of confused emotions that swirled within her, Ilona simply nodded. The sister led her through the orphanage and passed a room of children sitting in groups playing games. Those from the camps were easy to spot, their thin cheeks and shaved hair set them apart. But Ilona was pleased to see them clean and warmly dressed, even if they were silent and withdrawn. They continued through a dining hall and into a series of dormitories. The beds were lined in neat rows, each covered with thick, warm blankets. All the windows were intact and clean. Leaving the dormitory, the sister said, "We have kept the sickest children from the camps in a separate room. It is better for them and the other children."

Ilona understood. The healthy orphans had no need to see the cruelty of the camps. It would only scare them. They were too young for that. Even Ilona, an adult and a trained nurse, could barely withstand the truth of it.

"Through here."

Ilona was led to a back room, long and dimly lit, the curtains drawn despite the morning. Her face must have betrayed her thoughts, for Sister Marija explained, "We think sleep and rest are most important for now."

That made sense. Ilona studied the beds noting how insubstantial the tiny children looked beneath the woollen blankets, impossibly small, engulfed by the covers.

Then she saw her.

Tucked tightly in her bed, the little girl lay resting. Yet her eyes were open, watching. Ilona crossed the room and perched on the girl's bedside. Glancing up at Sister Marija, she asked, "Has she spoken? Do we know her name?"

The sister shook her head sadly. "She is very weak. But we are watching over her."

Ilona returned her gaze to the child, a soft smile touching her lips. "Hello, little one. I came to check on you." Reaching out she feathered her fingers across the girl's face. Her skin was dry and thin, blue veins showed through her pale complexion. The girl's eyes closed, and she leaned her cheek into the touch. "Shall I sit here with you a while?"

The girl's eyes opened again, but she didn't answer.

"Would you like something to eat?" Ilona reached into her satchel and drew out the plum jam sandwich.

"She is too weak for solids yet," the sister warned.

"What about just the jam?"

"That should be all right."

Ilona opened up the sandwich and folded the bread, squeezing the jam out between the crusts, and held it to the girl's mouth. A pink tongue flashed out, licking up the sweet treat. Ilona grinned. "Yummy, isn't it? I made it myself."

The girl only stared at her. Putting the sandwich away, Ilona settled herself more comfortably, folding her cardigan over her lap. The girl's eyes locked on the garment, her small hands inching forward. Ilona frowned and looked down at her cardigan. "Would you like to keep it?" She plucked it from her lap and held it before the girl. Their eyes met. Two black pools of desolation stared into Ilona's heart. She steadied herself against the rush of anguish that clenched her chest.

"Here," she said, and gently lifted the child's hand, placing the cardigan beneath her palm. "It will keep you warm, always."

Small fingers curled into the woollen cardigan as the child's eyelids drooped from fatigue.

"Sleep now, small one," Ilona crooned, tucking the blanket tighter around the child. "I will visit again soon." She waited, gently humming a lullaby as the child's eyelids grew heavier, her blinking longer, and finally, she drifted to sleep. Ilona rose quietly, smoothing her skirts, and tiptoed away. Sister Marija smiled at her. "You are welcome anytime," she said.

THIRTY-THREE
ILONA

Ilona finished reading the final page of Diana's official card-file records that listed the details of all the children removed from the camps, rolling her shoulders to release the strain from crouching over the desk.

"All finished?" Dragica asked.

"Da."

"And no Stephen or Hanna?"

"Plenty of them. But not the right ages, or from Petrinja. They are not recorded here yet."

"We have only emptied two camps. There are more. We will find them."

They were sitting in Diana's elaborate private office on the second storey of her home. The walls were lined with shelves of books and a large oak desk sat in the middle, the same one Diana had perched on that fateful day when she agreed to allow Ilona to work with her. Diana had had two smaller desks brought in so that everyone had a place to sit as they worked through their records of children and performed the work to save more. There were phone calls to make to orphanages and institutions, seeking housing for the children, food and supplies. And recently, there were the letters. Somehow, word had reached the labour camps in Germany, and desperate mothers from across the lands of Croatia wrote to Diana personally, begging for information about their children. Ilona knew Diana worked tirelessly to find the children that matched the missives and stayed up night after night to reply to each request by her own hand. Ilona had offered to help, but Diana insisted: each woman had to hear back from Diana herself. "It is the least I can do," she'd said.

Too often, there was no record to find. Or worse, an entry in Diana's book of the deceased. Diana kept that separate. A simple leather-bound book tucked in a drawer. But the room was dominated by the large wooden concertina of drawers in which Diana secured the records of those children who lived and had been brought to the city, becoming children of Zagreb. As often as they could they took a photo of each child and affixed it with their assigned number and details. Anything that might help in the effort to reunite them with their parents.

Ilona looked away from Dragica's optimism, seeking the light of the streets outside. It had been months since they started, but still, so many children remained in the inhuman conditions of the camps. Diana and Dragica worked tirelessly, seeking out places to house the children. But the churches and orphanages of Zagreb that were willing to help were nearing capacity. Others, too many, could not be convinced to help. They'd freed over 6000 children, yet there were still more. It was overwhelming. Ilona felt the challenge pressing against her daily. A camp specifically for the children, run by Red Cross nurses, had been set up in an attempt to solve the issue of space for the children. Dragica had offered Ilona a place working there, but she chose to stay in Zagreb because of the girl, Stephan and Hanna, and her ongoing hospital work. The only moments of happiness in her life came from her time with little Lina at the orphanage.

That's what the sisters had decided to name her. They'd given out monikers for every child too young or traumatised to remember what their parents had called them. But they had their numbers and their details recorded. If their parents returned, perhaps their names would too.

Lina had gone from strength to strength since Ilona had carried her from the camp in her arms, her cheeks filling out and her eyes brightening. She was out of bed now and sitting with the other orphans, eating solids and sleeping regular hours. But not playing, not yet. She loved Ilona's jam sandwiches, waiting patiently, her eyes on Ilona's satchel every time she visited. She'd not yet spoken. Not one word.

"We need to change the cards," Dragica said, drawing Ilona back to the present. "The cardboard doesn't work. It's too fragile. And the children eat them."

"What do you propose?"

"Printed metal—"

The door to Diana's office opened, and Dragica fell silent as Diana stepped in.

Ilona opened her mouth to greet Diana, but something in the woman's face stilled her tongue. Ilona watched in silence as Diana made her way to her desk and sat down, the lines of her body slumped in defeat.

Dragica noticed too, shooting Ilona a quick glance that told her to remain quiet.

She crossed the room to Diana and stood at her friend's side, saying nothing. Her presence was an unspoken offer to talk should Diana wish to unburden herself. It was harrowing work, and no matter how strong any of them were individually, it got to everyone. Even Diana. The least they could do was support each other.

Silence stretched as Diana sat, hands resting on the table, eyes staring unseeing into oblivion. Then she took a deep breath. "He has been assigned a number."

Dragica sucked in a sharp breath. "When?"

"Yesterday."

Ilona was confused, who had been assigned a number? Jovan and the other Serbs had been recorded over a year ago when the

Ustaše had first taken power. What had changed? She didn't understand.

"What did he say?" Dragica asked.

Diana released a heavy sigh. "He says it is a warning. He is right. His status at the hospital has kept him separate, but things are ramping up. Our position in society is no longer the shield it was. We are no longer above suspicion."

Understanding flashed through Ilona. Position at the hospital. Oh! They were talking about Diana's husband, Julije. An ethnic Serb, but powerful and talented. He was a surgeon at the School of Medicine and highly respected. When the Serb population of Zagreb had been rounded up, numbered and deported or sent to camps, men like Julije were overlooked. Until now. Ilona took a deep breath, working to steady her heartbeat as the full implication of this escalation began to come together in her mind.

Diana looked up, meeting her stare. "No one is safe," she said. "I warned you from the beginning. Collaborators are in danger. Your nationality will not keep you safe. They have rounded up plenty of ethnic Croats and executed them."

Ilona swallowed hard. She knew it was true. But surely this work would not be so condemned?

It seemed Dragica had a similar thought.

"We have written permission from the Commandant," she argued. "The Germans openly talk about you. 'Aktion Diana B', that's what they call your work. They are grateful to you for fixing their problem."

Diana snorted. "And the Ustaše make their own rules. You've seen it. The Germans have long decried their brutality and sort to separate themselves from it. They won't take any responsibility if the Ustaše decides to change their minds. I fear this is a sign of escalation. I fear for the children."

"The children in the camps, we will get them out."

"I mean those we have already freed."

A hush fell over the women.

"What do you mean?"

Diana shook her head, her face tight with concern. "We have permission to remove the children, and there are so many more to liberate. But who says the Ustaše will allow them to stay free? If they change their minds, I doubt Germany would step in."

"But to re-imprison children. Surely not," Dragica whispered. "That would be…"

Diana's face darkened. "I put no faith in their humanity, not after all we have seen. As long as they remain in Zagreb, the children are not safe. They are too easy to find. We have to find an alternative. We have to hide them."

"What are you thinking?" Dragica asked.

Diana blew out a heavy breath, shaking her head.

Ilona was blinking rapidly as her fear curdled in her stomach. Little Lina, so quiet, just starting to fill out, just starting to stand straight, to move without crouching in on herself, shrinking small. A return to a camp? She wouldn't survive it, body nor soul. None of the children would.

"The countryside," she blurted, mind rushing ahead of her words.

Diana and Dragica eyed her. "Go on," Diana urged.

Ilona licked her lips, eyes flicking side to side as she thought. "I am not the only Croat to reject this heinous policy. And the Church is not the only place of refuge against it. The people of our nation, families, farmers and villagers, they lived side by side with these children and other Serbs for decades, whole lifetimes. The hatred the Ustaše has for Serbs is real, but it is not the view held by everyone in our nation."

"So what are you proposing?"

"We send them home."

Dragica crossed her arms over her chest, a deep frown marring her brow. "They cannot go home. Their parents are in labour camps or dead. Their homes were burned down or were requisitioned by the Ustaše. They have no homes."

"No, but their neighbours do. Everyday people from the villages and cities. They may know the children from their regions or at least have a heart that cares. So we should look for volunteers in the country areas. Families who are willing to house a child until their mamas return."

"It is a nice idea, Ilona, but will people take the risk?" Dragica asked.

"It could work," Diana said, coming to her feet. "Some children are from Serb-only towns that have been completely destroyed. But many do have neighbourhoods remaining."

"And some people will just want to help. It is the Catholic thing to do."

Dragica snorted at that but remained silent.

"We could reach out and ask," Ilona pressed. "I am sure my mama's family would take on a child or two." Her mind reeled back to her summers spent playing in her deda's fields, making jam with her baba. "For others, we could remind them that the children can help in the fields."

"A labour force?"

Ilona shrugged. "It is the way for farmers. All children help on the land. Extra hands are welcome."

"It would be a risk for them. Make them collaborators," Dragica said.

"Not if I get express permission from the German High Command," Diana said. 'That will be at least some protection. And for the Ustaše, it is a deterrent. Rounding up children from an orphanage in Zagreb is one thing. They are easy to find and all in one place. But hunting them across the farms of Croatia... It is a level of protection."

"Yes," Ilona said, her heart in her throat.

"And it solves the problem of our rapidly filling churches and orphanages."

"There won't be homes for them all. But—"

"It will make a difference," Diana said.

"Da." Ilona gripped her hands before her, her chest rising and falling with her sense of hope.

"I will make some calls," Diana said. "In the meantime, can I leave you both with the plans for the Mlaka camp next week?"

"Of course," Dragica agreed.

"Good," Diana said, standing and crossing to the door. Her hand on the handle she paused, looking back. "Well done, Ilona," she said. Then strode from the room.

Ilona could only hope it would work, and that it would be enough.

THIRTY-FOUR

ILONA

The train to Novska rocked gently as it made its way out of Zagreb Central Station. Lina sat curled against her side, her small hands pressed together against her chest, as if in prayer. Beneath her hands her new metal ID tag shone.

Ilona smoothed a lock of the child's hair back from her face; it had grown well in the months since she'd been liberated from the camp, almost reaching her eyes. It needed a trim. Ilona turned to the window, watching as the tight streets of Zagreb gave way to the plains of the countryside, a wide, flat expanse of green interrupted by pockets of forest that reached north to the mountain peaks beyond, and settled in. It was a familiar journey, one she and Ivica had taken together throughout their childhood.

Ivica.

Tension spread along her limbs as she thought of her brother. Once her companion. Now a soldier for the Ustaše. Was he involved in the camps? Had his hand separated children from their mamas and tatas, ruining families and lives across their nation? Or did he fight the resistance, men like her husband who worked in the shadows to free their people?

What would Ivica do if he and Jovan crossed paths?

Where was her beloved husband?

She'd heard nothing from Jovan: no letter of reassurance, no surprise visits. Every time the newspaper reported a skirmish or an act of sabotage, she scoured the article for his name. So far, she'd never found it. She chose to believe that meant he was safe, and free.

She huffed a breath through her nose and set those thoughts aside. It was too much to bear, and Ilona could not be weakened. Not now. She had to do as Diana always said: manage what she could. Forcing her breathing to slow she tucked Lina closer to her side and closed her eyes. She didn't need to watch the trees beyond. She knew this route by heart.

Three hours later the train pulled in at Novska station.

"Come now, Lina," Ilona said, gently prompting the girl awake. She'd slept through most of the journey, lulled by the steady rhythm of the train. Rubbing her eyes sleepily, Lina came to her feet. Ilona bent down and helped her into her small coat, fastening the buttons to her neck.

"All warm and snug," she said, smiling briefly. Lina only stared at her in silence.

Picking up Lina's suitcase, Ilona took her hand and led her from the train. The streets of Novska were quiet, the residents keeping indoors to avoid the biting chill of autumn. The season sat in glory on the trees, the leaves an explosion of reds and yellows and golds, shimmering in the midday sun. Ilona turned down the familiar road that led out of the village, heading for the farm.

About half an hour into the walk, Lina slowed. Her short legs, still weak from her time at the camps, were struggling. Ilona paused. There was still a way to go. Setting down the suitcase, she lifted Lina up into her arms, securing her on her hip before gathering the suitcase up again and continuing on. Her feet rubbed painfully against her heels as the extra weight affected her gait. But there was nothing for it. Lina needed to rest.

As the sun slipped beyond the tips of the beech trees, the small cottage came into view. Ilona slowed, setting Lina back down on her feet. She knelt before the girl and smoothed her coat. Cupping Lina's cheek, she said, "We are here. Are you ready to meet my baba?"

Lina watched her in silence, her deep brown eyes wide. Ilona smiled softly. She knew Lina would not speak, but she'd hoped for at least a smile. The girl understood her, she was sure. But she never showed any emotion, not really. The trauma of the camp was simply too much and too recent. How Ilona wished the child would open up and speak. She longed to know what the girl remembered of her life before the camps. Did she remember her name? Her village? Did she have siblings? Could she picture her mama?

Ilona suppressed a sigh and sent a prayer to God that time in a home, with a loving family, would help to bring Lina from the darkness of her memories. That healing was possible. For Lina and all the children brought to Zagreb and all those still waiting to be rescued. Standing slowly, she placed a hand on Lina's shoulder and guided her to the cottage. It was small, but on two levels, only as wide as a door and a window at the front, built from the forest wood that surrounded it, cut and shaped by her deda's strong hands. A curl of smoke rose into the cooling air, a promise of the warmth and comfort Ilona knew waited within. She knocked once.

The door swung open, and her baba stood in the doorway. Her face had sagged, the lines around her mouth deepened. But in her pale eyes, the sharpness of her mind still shone.

"My granddaughter," Ludmila said, drawing Ilona into a firm embrace. "Marko, they are here!"

Ludmila released Ilona as her deda came into view behind his wife. Slender and stooped, he shuffled forward. Ludmila stepped back so Marko could see his granddaughter, a beatific smile splitting his hardened features.

"You are even more beautiful," he said, raising his hands to pat her on the shoulder. "Always more beautiful."

She knew it for the lie it was. The strain of occupation weighed on her face, dulling her skin and hair, and lining her forehead with worry. But it was a nice lie. Ilona smiled at her doting deda, calm settling within her chest. This was the right decision for Lina. She knew it in her bones. Here she would be safe and loved, just as Ilona had been.

"And this must be Lina?" Ludmila said, looking down at the small girl standing rigid by the doorway.

"Da. Lina, these are my grandparents, Ludmila and Marko. They are going to take care of you."

Ludmila beamed down at the girl, her the lines of her face softening in sorrow.

"She still hasn't spoken..." Ilona explained.

Ludmila nodded. "That is no matter. I am sure she eats!" A cheeky glint had come into Ludmila's eyes. "Come in out of the cold. I have fresh bread and soup. You will stay to eat?"

Ilona nodded. She still had a long journey home, but just the thought of her baba's cooking reminded her belly of how long ago breakfast had been.

They were ushered into the comfortable central space that made up the kitchen and dining space of her grandparents' home. A large fire blazed in the hearth, filling the wooden walls with comforting warmth. The smell of soup and baked bread found Ilona's nose as her baba gestured for them to sit at the table. Her deda went to the stove, helping his wife to portion out the bowls of soup and slices of crusty loaf. "Pumpkin," he said, placing a bowl before Ilona and one for Lina.

Lina looked to Ilona, a question in her stare. "You may eat, darling," Ilona said. Lina gripped her spoon in a fist and clumsily scooped the soup into her mouth, her eyes never leaving the bowl.

Ludmila looked on, a small frown of pity forming between her brows. Ilona understood that look. Lina was still so very thin. "She eats well," she said. "And is growing fast." No need to use language that may upset the child. Ludmila leaned across the table, cutting a second slice of bread, thicker than the first, and slathered it in butter before placing it on Lina's plate. "That is good," she said.

"We like big appetites here." Despite the food restrictions in the cities, her baba had found a way to keep her pantry well stocked.

Lina looked up at Ludmila, meeting the old woman's eyes for a moment before reaching forward and snatching up her bread. Taking a great bite, she chewed noisily.

Later, Ilona took Lina to show her her bedroom, the same one she'd slept in as a child. She left Lina there with Ludmila to settle in and returned to her deda to help tidy the dishes.

"She is a small one," her deda began. "I can still see the hollows of her cheeks."

"She has filled out so much since we found her."

"She has?" he looked at her incredulously. "She was smaller?"

Ilona grimaced as the memory of the first time she laid eyes on Lina flashed through her mind. A small, skin-covered skeleton. How had she survived? Ilona shook her head, clearing away the vision.

A gentle hand warmed her shoulder, and she looked up into her deda's face. Sorrow was etched through his greying skin. "She will be safe here. What the Ustaše has done..." he fell silent, head lowered. "She will be safe."

"Thank you," Ilona whispered.

The sound of footsteps turned her face and she dashed away the errant tears that had sprung up at her deda's kindness. Her baba and Lina stood by the fire, chatting quietly.

"Well," she said, crossing the space between them. "It has been so wonderful to see you. But it is a long way home and I need to start."

"Of course," her baba said. "Lina is all settled. I have a story we can read by the fire."

"Thank you," Ilona mouthed to her baba. She turned to Lina and knelt before her once again. "You will be safe and warm here. Ludmila and Marko will care for you, just as they did me as a child. And I will visit when I can."

Lina met her eyes and Ilona tried to read the thoughts that must be racing through the child's mind. But Lina's expression remained blank. Ilona gathered her tiny body into a hug, breathing deeply the smell of soap and cotton that was Lina.

Releasing her she stood, farewelling her grandparents each in turn.

"Safe travels," Marko said, following her to the door. Behind him, Ludmila was guiding Lina to the chair by the fire, storybook in hand.

"She will be all right," her deda said.

"How?" Ilona whispered. "How do you understand when my own tata does not?"

The kindness of her deda and baba, this sanctuary for Lina, for herself – it was all she ever wanted. It was what she needed from her own parents.

Her deda released a heavy sigh, setting an arm over her shoulders and tugging her close. "Your tata isn't a bad man," he began. "But life here was tough. He wanted more for you and your brother. Yet, even in Zagreb he saw Belgrade as the block to that." Ilona felt him shrug, his body sinking. "Here, we live and work beside everyone: Croats, Serbs, Roma, Jews. We make our way on the land or we don't.

"But, seeing our neighbours forced onto trucks and driven away against their will? Nothing makes that right, whatever tensions may exist between us."

"That is what is happening on the streets of Zagreb. Tata sees that every day."

"And he is also being watched. As are you. Not everyone is as brave as you are, my granddaughter."

Ilona breathed, trying to take in her deda's words. She was doing so much. It never felt enough.

She forced herself to smile and nodded. "I will visit."

"When you can. But the child is our responsibility now. You must help those still not free."

A heaviness settled over her chest at his words. He was right, she knew. So many more children, just like Lina, still languished in the camps, their parents lost to Germany. How many of those parents would return? How many children were already orphans?

Releasing a breath, Ilona hugged her deda one more time and stepped into the cool afternoon.

Mind forward, she reminded herself. It was time to return to her work.

PART SIX

THIRTY-FIVE

The winter grasses crunch under Sara's feet. She glances over at Daniel. He is bent over the camera, adjusting the focus. He raises a thumb to her. He is ready. She crosses to the camera to check the frame for herself.

Peering through the lens the man, Jakov, comes into focus. He sits in a worn plastic chair, the lake stretching behind him, its ripples striped in the pale sunlight that casts between the bare branches of the beech trees. His puffy jacket envelopes his small body, his wizened face a crumpled mass of wrinkles. Two blue eyes shine out from beneath thick, curling white brows. Old before his time.

Blinking once to settle her nerves, Sara straightens and smiles at him.

"Mr Padocvic? Are you ready to start?"

Jakov stares down at his dirt crusted hands, turning a small metal plate over and over on his palm. He looks up and nods once.

Sara settles herself behind the camera. "In your own time," she says, and Daniel presses record.

The wind rustles through the branches above. The cry of a dove sounds. And Jakov begins.

"They tell me I was three years old. That I was short for my age. They say I might have grown bigger if it wasn't for..." He pauses, turning away towards the shimmering lakeside.

He chose this location. He comes here often. Sara follows the line of his eyes and sees a small rowing boat. It is dark blue. The painted sides are peeling.

Jakov coughs and returns his attention to the camera. But his eyes aren't focused. The irises expand as though he is looking far away.

"They gave me this." He holds up the small metal plate. It looks like a dog tag. Sara knows there is a number etched into the side. Jakov's number.

As if he has heard her thoughts, Jakov says, "13432 – that is all I was to them. All I am. I thought it held the answer. I thought it would lead me home."

Tears slip from his eyes, and he lowers his head, his fingers pressing into the sockets as his shoulders shake.

Sara swallows, watching on. Her heart cleaves. She longs to stop recording. To cross the barren earth and embrace this man. To find a way to soothe his pain. But this is important. This is history.

Slowly Jakov calms. He fixes the camera with a stare, leaning forward intensely. "I do not know my birth name. The name my mama gave me. I do not know where I was born, who my family were or if they lived. I believed this would have the answers." He shakes the metal tag violently and continues. "That one day my identity would be returned. But they took it all. They took everything."

He sighs heavily, lips wobbling dangerously close to a sob. "And they never gave it back."

THIRTY-SIX
NADICA

Novska 1991

"Wait," Nadica says. Her mind is stuck like a bike cog in mud. "Baba, are you saying that mama isn't your natural child?"

Her baba faces her in the fading light of the evening. "Does it matter?"

"Da! It is about who I am!" Her stomach has plummeted through her body, her world shattering into an explosion of emotions she cannot begin to understand. "I am not your granddaughter."

"Don't you ever say that!" Baba turns eyes of fire on her. The intensity is enough to shock Nadica into silence.

"Your mama is my daughter in every way that matters. You are my family in here." She beats her heart with a fist. "I would do anything for you and your mama. *Anything*. Never say that, for you tell a lie of the soul." The old woman glances away. "It is also dangerous."

"Dangerous? What do you mean? How can it be—" But her words dry up as her mind races ahead, putting it all together.

"I am not a Croat. You are not my blood. Oh..."

Her baba sighs heavily. "No, you are the grandchild of an Orthodox family. One that died in the Ustaše camps. Your mama, my Lina, was so, so fortunate to survive. Her parents, any siblings she may have had... we know nothing of them. If they lived or died."

"So you and Deda made her yours? Catholic."

"And part Croat. Part of me. It was a shield in a time of upheaval."

"And during the long peace... you never felt that you could share the truth?"

Baba sniffs. "Peace is a fragile word. We were never truly free. And that hate and fear, the division of ethnicity and religion, it has not left us. Seeing our nation now, I know we made the right decision."

Nadica works to keep her breathing calm. Her baba agrees with Relja about the risk to their safety. Just like her deda. They are terrified. Now that she has heard their stories, she understands. And there is more. She knows there must be. Yet...

"Mama knew."

"Of course. But we helped her to forget. When you were born, we discussed it all together: your mama, Jovan, Misa, me and your tata, Davor. We all agreed."

"Tata agreed?"

She nods sagely. "The past is the past. You are part of this family, as is your mama. We are a blend. What Yugoslavia stands for. Or what it should stand for, at least."

It is all so confusing. Her tata and mama kept this from her? They all kept this secret. The secret of who she is, of her ethnicity. Her past.

Her body succumbs to a mild trembling as her mind fights to bring it all together.

"What about honouring where Mama came from?" she says. "Sharing all you did for the children in the camps? Those stories, we must remember them. They are our history, my history."

It hurts, this realisation. To know her mama was left to die on a cold concrete floor. That she lived only because of luck. Or was it God? Can that thought bring her comfort?

She watches as her baba's throat bobs, her wrinkle-rimmed eyes swimming with tears. "It wasn't enough. It was never enough."

Sorrow, bone-deep and crushing, has descended over her baba. Nadica can feel it in her own soul. All this pain, the pain of her country, it was hers too. She just never knew.

"Baba—"

"Go home to your mama now, before it gets too dark," she interrupts. "You are always welcome here, but she will be fretting."

"She knew you would tell me?"

A flutter of amusement crosses her baba's smile. "Of course. I would never have shared this secret without my daughter's blessing. Go and be with your mama. Tell her it is all right, that you understand."

"You assume that I do understand. This is a big secret, Baba."

Baba fixes Nadica with a piercing stare, then cocks her head in question. No words are needed, her meaning is clear. And Nadica realises her baba is right; she does understand. She understands too much.

"What about you?" she manages to ask through the swell of sorrow that has flooded her chest.

Baba's expression softens. "I have my Jovan and Misa. I will be all right."

The cold wind is biting against her bare cheeks as she cycles home. The dark sky above is littered with sparkling stars. A clear night. A cold night. It was hard leaving the warmth of her baba's hearth. But she needs to get home to her mama.

She knows now.

Her mama needs to know it is okay.

The outskirts of their small village come into view, the warm lights of people's lounge rooms and kitchens shining out across the lawns between their houses. Several sit in darkness. Their occupants have already left for the safety of Serbia or Slovenia.

Pulling up at the front, Nadica leans her bike against the white-painted bricks and heads inside. The door is not locked; it never is. No one locks their doors in Novska, even now.

"Mama?" she calls as she walks in, grateful for the rush of heat that stings her cold cheeks as they rapidly warm. "I'm home." She pulls off her gloves and jacket, hanging them by the door, and makes her way towards the lounge.

Her mama is sitting by the fireplace. Nadica knows she is nervous before she speaks. It is in the line of her shoulders, the stoop of her head. Her pace slows. The butterflies that have fluttered in her stomach since her baba's confession suspend within her.

She loves her mama. She loves her baba.

Nothing has changed. And everything has.

She walks across the room, the carpet muffling her steps, and comes to stand before her mama.

"Mama." Nadica sinks down to sit beside her mama and wraps her arms around her. Lina leans into her embrace, and Nadica feels the trembling that runs along her body. She holds firm against the shaking, walling off her own confusion. Her mama needs her to be strong, so Nadica will be. After a while, the trembling calms, and Nadica withdraws and looks into her mama's face.

"Why didn't you tell me?"

Scared, dark eyes meet hers. "Which part?"

"All of it."

Lina blinks, head shaking. "It was too awful. It was too much. And Ilona and Jovan, they are my parents, in all the ways that matter." She pauses. "I never meant to lie to you. I wanted to protect you."

"It is okay," Nadica says. "I am not upset. Just confused."

"That I didn't tell you I nearly died in a camp? Or that I was so young I don't even know who I am?"

"You know who you are," Nadica says firmly. "You are my mama."

A grateful smile drifts over Lina's lips. "That will always be true." She releases a long sigh that resonates through the room like a lifetime of release and leans forward, pressing her forehead to Nadica's. "I don't remember it. I have dreams, sometimes, when I am stressed. A grape vine, a woman with soft arms. But it's indistinct, watery. Your baba is the first real memory I have. Her kind face, her plum jam."

She draws back. "I wavered so many times, thinking I was wrong to keep this from you. But your tata, he was determined."

"To protect me? Why was tata so scared?"

"Davor came from a camp too. But he remembered."

Nadica can't help the hiss that passes her lips. Her tata was in a camp too? Dear God, this history, this trauma... "What did he remember?"

Her mama presses her eyes closed, her face crumpling. "He was in Jasenovac. There were... experiments. Your baba and the nurses rescued me. Your tata had to wait for the end of the war."

The air between them thickens and sours with what her mama has left unspoken. What her tata endured. What he witnessed. She thinks of her baba's words, of the children she rescued in the camp. Of how close to death her mama was when Ilona found her. Nadica struggles to breathe through it. She had known the war was bad, but what she has learned today... She never understood the full gravity of the pain that hid within her country.

Somehow her tata survived that. And within that knowledge, his choice makes sense. Why Davor turned from his past and forged a new one by her mama's side. Why Nadica has always believed she was Serb and Croat, when she is not. It is so obvious. What other choice was there for him, really? To keep his family safe, he and her mama pretended to be Croats. And her baba helped them.

"So his family..."

"Died in Jasenovac. They were war deaths. That wasn't really a lie."

But it was. It really was. Dying a soldier on a battlefield is not the same as being tortured behind a barbed-wire fence. Nadica pictures her tata's face. The sad lines that always sat along the sides of his smile. A smile that never reached his eyes. He never looked at peace, not even in death.

"Is that why he died young? Why his heart gave out?"

The corners of Lina's lips turn down and she shrugs. "It was why he wanted to be buried on Baba's land. It is the only place either of us feel we belong."

"I didn't know."

"He didn't want you to."

"But I need to now, don't I? Because it matters. I am not a Croat. I am a Serb."

It shouldn't matter. She was born in Croatia. She was raised Catholic. What line really divides a Serb from a Croat? Religion? Birth? Politics? Fear? Nadica doesn't know. But her parents' history, the violence that hides there, obscured by time: can she be sure it won't repeat?

"All this, this is why Deda wants us to leave."

It is why Relja is right.

"Da."

The pieces are falling into place. A history, too dark, too painful. A history that her family have shielded her from. The reason her tata was always more alert than he needed to be. The way her mama always defers to others, closing into herself when challenged, retreating behind a wall Nadica now knows is built of trauma.

The reason Nadica has always felt unsure, that prickle that shimmered along her back in the dark. The sense of uncertainty. Her need for routine, for a simple life here in Novska. Her subconscious knew that her parents were afraid. They never truly left those camps behind. They were shaped by them. So was Nadica.

"You don't trust the government. Now that Croatia has asked for independence from the union. Now we are at war within ourselves. You don't think we are safe. You think the government will come for the Serbs once again."

Lina's lips tremble. "They tried to exterminate us once before. Your deda wants us to go. But—"

"Baba won't leave Misa, and Deda won't leave her." Nadica says for her mama. She knows, she sees, finally.

"Misa would never leave, sick or not. Her children are somewhere on these lands. Alive or buried. She won't leave the soil that cradles them."

Nadica blinks. She remembers Misa's words and the tears that ran down the creases of her cheeks as she shared the haunting nightmare of Stephan's wails and Kata's scream. No, cancer or not, Misa would never leave.

"And what do you want to do?"

Her mama reaches between them and cups Nadica's cheek. "I want to keep you safe."

An understanding opens up within her. "It's why they told me, isn't it? Baba and Misa. They want us to go too. They want me to understand. They want me to choose to leave with you."

They know you can't make this choice, Nadica realises. Her mama is too far within the tangles of their country's history and her own pain to decide.

"This is your home," Lina says. "It is where you were born, where your tata is buried. If we go, we leave behind everything we have ever known. We go where we have no friends, no family. We leave Ilona, Jovan and Misa behind. The very people who saved my life... After everything we have been through and endured. After everything we have overcome and rebuilt. It is just..."

"Unfair." The word feels too small for the understanding that now sits heavily across Nadica's heart. Because it is more than unfair. It is monstrous. A people brutalised simply for existing on the wrong side of politics and religion. Massacred for who they were. A resilient people who stood up and pushed back. Who survived and rebuilt. And despite it all – the trauma, the fear, the loss – they kept going. Shaped new lives. Formed new families. Overcame it all.

Only to be threatened again in the same lifetime.

She had no idea how little she knew, how little she understood.

"I have to put you first," her mama's words turn her head. "I want your deda to come with us, and Ilona and Misa. But they won't. He is angry that I haven't already left. He wants us safe. And I want that too."

"But you feel conflicted."

Her mama nods sadly. "Ilona risked everything to save me. She is why I have had this life. Why I have you. How can I leave her now?"

Nadica understands her mama's dilemma, how the horrors of her past have shaped her fragility and indecision. But Nadica is not her mama. She grips Lina's shoulders and holds her still. "Because it is how you honour everything."

She sees the twitch of her mama's eyebrow, the rejection in the widening of her pupils, and presses the point. "Ilona risked her life for you and the other children. So you could live. The best way to thank her is to do just that: live."

Her mama deflates, pulling in on herself, a hand patting Nadica's knee absent-mindedly as her gaze turns to the fireplace. "Da, da. Give me time. I need to speak with Ilona and Jovan. I need to work this through."

"Of course, Mama," Nadica says. "Of course."

She needs time. And maybe that's a good thing. Maybe it will be all right. Maybe the tensions around them will settle, the gunfire and outbreaks of violence will stop. There doesn't need to be conflict and war. It can be done through diplomacy and agreement.

Maybe it will all be all right. They can stay, wait it out and it will pass.

Maybe.

Something deep within Nadica already knows that hope is a lie. Resolve firms within her. When the time comes, she will make the choice her mama cannot make. She will get them to safety. For her tata and all he endured in Jasenovac, for her mama and her hurting soul, for Misa and her loss and for her grandparents – for saving them all.

THIRTY-SEVEN

ILONA

Zagreb 1943

The repeating blast of a car horn ripped through the streets shocking Ilona awake. She jumped from her slumber, hand clutching her chest. Tyres screeched to a halt, the sound vibrating up, seemingly from below her apartment window. Blood pounded in her ears, her throat closing up and choking her breathing.

A car door slammed shut, then the shouting began.

"Ilona!"

What? Horror sluiced through her. Someone was shouting her name.

"I have a gift for you."

The voice was familiar, hauntingly familiar. It couldn't be?

Rising cautiously from the bed, arms wrapped around her waist protectively, Ilona approached the window, her body a trembling mess of fear. Drawing back the curtain she released an audible gasp.

Standing in the rain on the street side below her window, cast in the glow of a street lamp, was her brother Ivica. The light of the lamp caught on the emblem on the chest of his jacket. His Ustaše insignia.

Dropping the curtain, Ilona crouched down quickly, her knees hitting the carpeted floor. *Maybe he didn't see me?*

"Ilona," Ivica's voice was mocking, cruel. "Don't hide from me."

Pulse quickening, Ilona's mind raced. What was Ivica doing here? She had not seen or heard from him in years. Not since the occupation of Germany and the formation of the Independent State of Croatia under the Ustaše.

"Ilona. Show yourself or I will be forced to come up there."

Bracing her shoulders, Ilona rose from the floor and pushed back the curtain. Sending a prayer to God that some small part of the boy she grew up with still lived within her brother, she swung open her window.

The cold of autumn dawn met her face, making her skin tingle. Ivica stared up at her, his face set in grim determination. But when their eyes met, Ilona went still. The cold resolve, the burning hate she'd come to expect from Ivica was edged with softness.

He raised his hands to the dark sky, palms out, the lines of his body cocky and self-assured.

"Don't say I never do anything for you," he quipped, the tone dripping with sarcasm. But the malice did not reach his eyes.

He was acting, Ilona realised. Putting on a performance for the other soldier in the car. Why?

Ivica's strained eyes held Ilona's, a silent plea swimming within their cool colour, and he gestured down. Bundled on the street at his feet lay a mass of black. Ilona frowned.

Ivica stepped back toward the waiting car. Then, swinging his leg, kicked the mass – hard. The shape groaned, curling in on itself. Ilona gasped. It was a person. Ivica had brought someone to her home.

A shock of terror and reckless hope shot through her.

"Consider this your last warning," Ivica drawled up at her. But she saw the worry, the fleeting sadness that crossed his face. He climbed back into the car, and the engine revved, the scent of burnt rubber filling the night as Ivica and his accomplice tore away into the darkness.

Ilona was on the move. Snatching her coat from the hook by the door she flung herself from the apartment. Her bare feet slapped down the stairs, her knees so weak from impossible and terrified hope that she stumbled, catching herself awkwardly on the handrail, but did not fall. Shoving the door to the apartment block open she burst into the night. A sprinkle of raindrops touched her cheeks, but the air was still. The black shape hadn't moved. Ilona paused, the cold of the cobbled path biting into her bare feet. Ignoring the cold, she inched forward, fear and longing warring within her.

Could it be? Could it really be?

Reaching the mound she knelt down, her hands shaking violently as she reached forward. Gently, so gently, she gripped the dark coat the figure was huddled within. "Jovan?" her voice was hoarse, rough from yearning. The black mass moved. A face appeared within the folds of dark wool. It was gaunt, a thick beard, greying on the edges, covered the mouth, but the eyes – the eyes were clear.

"My Ilona," he breathed, then passed out.

Jovan slept on their bed. Ilona still could not believe he was home. After he'd lost consciousness on the street Ilona had tried to rouse him, but his mind and body were too depleted. She'd waited, impatient in the glow of breaking dawn, desperate to get him off the street and behind the safety of their closed doors. What if Ivica changed his mind and returned? What if a patrol of soldiers happened by?

Eventually, she managed to wake him. She'd forced him to his feet, head rolling unconvincingly to the side, and braced against her side he'd made it up the stairs, step by painful step into their home.

What had happened to him?

Why had Ivica helped him?

He was cold and smelt of human odours and waste, his breathing ragged and his body so, so thin. Even the bulk of the dark coat that cloaked him could not hide the wastage of his strength.

But the worst of his injuries was yet to be revealed.

Once inside, Ilona drew the coat from his body. As she tugged the sleeve over his right hand, Jovan bellowed, his eyes rolling back in his head in agony.

"What?" She'd reached out and gasped.

His right hand, his playing hand, was a mass of flesh and blood. Horror slashed through to the core of her being. He'd been tortured. Worse, the focus on his right hand told a story: he'd been tortured by someone who knew him.

Leading him to the kitchen, she'd taken up a wet cloth and tried to tend to his hand. But Jovan was beyond his strength. "I can't, I need sleep," he'd muttered, and Ilona had relented. Helping him to shuffle the final steps to their bed, the bed she'd slept in alone for more than two years, Jovan had collapsed onto the mattress and into an unyielding sleep. Unable to think and with no idea what else to do, Ilona had drawn the blankets up over him as gently as possible and, slipping between the sheets, curled her body delicately around him. The sound of his breath, uneven and rasping, tormented her ears, but the feel of his body back beside her wound a comfort around the core of her being and soon sleep claimed her too.

She woke well after dawn, the strengthening light of midday warming the pastel colours of the room. Jovan still slept beside her. She sat up, careful not to wake him, and studied his face. More evidence of sustained beatings was clear in the new light. There was a bruise, going yellow from age, that covered his too-prominent cheekbone, a raw red split through a nostril. The flesh of his neck that peeked from his collar was pale and streaked with dirt. What else lay beneath the folds of his stained clothes? She could not guess. The thought filled her with horror. But perhaps nothing could surmount his hand. It lay across his chest, too raw and broken to bear the weight of the blanket. Ilona stared at the broken flesh, the bones so misshapen that she could not even define the fingers.

His body twitched suddenly, his eyes jerking open as tension infused each muscle of his body. A cry escaped his mouth as he surged up, arms rising before him in a defensive posture.

"Calm, calm," Ilona said quickly. "It is all right. You are home. You are safe."

His eyes roamed the room as if searching for a trap, his lips parted in a panicked pant. Slowly his breathing settled, and his gaze fell on her.

"Ilona?" Disbelief hushed his voice.

"Da, my love, da. You are home."

His face collapsed into a wreck of pain as sobs shook his body. He reached for her, and Ilona clutched him to her, firm and fierce. His body quaked beneath her hands, his sobs shattering her heart. When he sat back the grime that lined his face was streaked with tears.

Ilona took his face between her hands. "My love, what happened?"

He watched her face as he answered. "Your brother."

They sat in the kitchen. Jovan had taken a slow bath, alone. Ilona had wanted to help him, to sit with him, to never let him out of her sight again. But he had been decided. She knew he didn't want her to see the extent of his injuries. Even in his feeble state, he was putting her before himself, trying to protect her.

Unable to sit still, she'd gathered fresh clothes for him from their cupboard, her mind distantly aware that everything would now be several sizes too large. Placing them on the floor outside the bathroom, she retreated into the kitchen to sort her medical items, readying herself for the treatment she knew he desperately needed.

He'd emerged clean, but bleeding, his shirt hanging loosely

from his shrunken shoulders, his trousers pooling at his ankles, and Ilona went to work.

She dabbed the cut on his nose, ensuring the open wound was clean.

"Are there more beneath your clothes?"

"Only bruises."

"Can I see?"

He looked away, and Ilona waited. Shame laced his features. Sorrow cracked her open, but she didn't push. He would let her in when he could. But his hand – that she would not allow him to ignore.

"Please," she said, gently taking his arm and moving his hand, laying it delicately on the tabletop.

He sucked in a hiss of pain as the pressure of the table pushed up through the broken bones.

"It needs to be cleaned and set," Ilona said. "It will be extremely painful. I will take you to the hospital, they can give you something for the pain—"

"No!" Jovan's head jerked up. "No hospital. No place. Nowhere but here. No."

She stared at him, and saw the abject fear in his eyes.

God what had they done to him?

She looked back down at the hand. It couldn't wait. If there was any chance that he could regain the use of the hand again, she needed to act. Pressing her lips together, Ilona stood and moved to the cupboard. Glasses chinked together, and liquid sloshed.

"Then drink this," she said, placing a bottle of spirits and a glass before him. He popped the top and took a long sip straight from the neck of the bottle.

Ilona settled herself back on the chair. Taking the bottle she poured the clear spirit over the raw flesh of his hand.

Jovan gasped in pain. She handed the bottle back to him and began to gently move the limb, trying to find the line of the bones. It was a wreck.

"What did this?" She asked.

"Hammer."

Her eyes shot to him. He read the question there.

"No, not your brother. David was there. He told them I play."

David, Radmila's husband. Ilona didn't know what to do with that information. It was all unfolding too fast. She set it aside for later and continued her work cleaning the open wounds and moving the broken bones as gently as possible. Jovan took another swing of the spirit and gritted his teeth. His breathing was shallow, his eyes pressed tightly shut. Tears leaked down his cheeks, gathering in his bushy, unkempt beard.

"What happened?" she said, not looking up from her work. She held her breath, willing Jovan to speak. To tell her everything. Where had he been since he walked out their door? What had he done? Why hadn't he written, even once? Why had Ivica dropped him at their door?

"You can tell me," she continued. "You are safe here."

"What about David? And Radmila?"

Ilona kept her voice steady. "David is never home any more, he lives in the soldiers' barracks, and Radmila is not a threat. You can trust me. Now, tell me, what happened?"

There was a long pause before Jovan spoke. "We ran a mission in the Gornje Vrapče neighbourhood near Zagreb... I was captured. The Ustaše are not kind to their enemies."

"Who is 'we'?"

Jovan paused, mouth twisting.

"Please, tell me."

He nodded reluctantly and explained, "After I left with Josip and Slavko, we didn't know what to do. But Josip knew some fighters. They were part of a resistance movement called the Partisans led by a man named Tito. They are fighting for Yugoslavia, for all of us. So we joined them."

Ilona kept her focus on his hand. She knew of the Partisans. They were regularly in the papers for various attacks on soldiers and infrastructure. "And they have been running missions against the Ustaše?"

"Da. And our numbers have been growing rapidly alongside our strategic success. The plan is to advance on Zagreb in a coordinated series of attacks. Gornje Vrapče was just the beginning."

Not for you, she thought but did not voice the idea. The darkness that shimmered in Jovan's eyes, the emptiness. Something had been taken from him in captivity. She would take nothing more. He didn't need her doubt or fear. He needed her love.

"How long did they hold you?"

Jovan released a heavy sigh. "What month is it?"

"November."

"Weeks then."

Weeks. Her brow knitted as she drew a strip of bandage around his hand in an attempt to secure the bones. "There," she said. "It really needs a doctor—"

"No." The refusal was hushed, more a plea than an order.

Ilona laid her hand against his cheek. "You are home, my love," she said. "No one is going to force you to do anything."

He nodded stiffly, head lowered. Ilona took a steadying breath. This man before her? This was not her Jovan. He was a shell, broken down, torn apart. Anger fired through her in a surge of fury she could barely contain. What had become of her country? First the Jewish, then the Serbs. The children. Now her husband? Was there no end to the cruelty of the Ustaše regime?

She stood, pacing to the pantry, the movement helping to calm her rattling rage. She could not show this pain to Jovan. He needed her strength. He had been stripped to nothing. He needed time to regain himself, to find his dignity. And she would help him do it.

She took up a loaf of bread and a pat of butter, returning to the table.

"Are you hungry?"

A grateful nod, the easing of tension across his shoulders. Ilona felt the relief flow through him as he understood. She would not push. She would not demand. She would stand beside him. She would hold him strong as he healed. They would face this future together.

THIRTY-EIGHT

ILONA

But that healing could not be done in Zagreb. As the year 1943 drew to a close, the Partisans pushed closer and closer to Zagreb. Pressure was mounting on the Ustaše regime and on Nazi rule across the rest of Europe. And pressure breeds cruelty and desperation. Rumours swirled, of mass executions across the prisons of the Independent State of Croatia, of men and women marched into the forests that surrounded Zagreb and gunned down beneath the grey clouded skies.

Then the Partisans attacked an ammunition depot on the outskirts of Zagreb.

Ignorant of the horrors that attack unleashed in retaliation, Ilona and Jovan made their way to visit her parents on the morning of the 20th of December. It was a crisp day. The grey clouds of an overnight storm had parted, allowing the sun to shine down, illuminating the frosted stone of the pavements. Ilona turned her face up to the gentle sunlight that beamed down from above. Jovan's good hand in hers, his injured in a sling against his chest, she smiled, a sense of hope filtering through her. Blue skies always made things feel possible, and Jovan was here with her. Broken, mending, but with her.

They turned into the main square in Dubrava, and the world overturned. Beside her Jovan stopped dead, his fingers going slack, dropping her hand as his whole body recoiled. Ilona looked up at him. His face was a mask of horror. She followed the line of his eyes and felt her soul crack.

A smattering of people stood in the square, frozen in horror by the hellscape before them.

"Dear God," she breathed.

For there before them, presented in a neat row through the middle of the square, hanging from butcher hooks driven into wooden posts, hung sixteen men.

Ice twinkled in a thin layer over the dangling bodies, their eyes staring out unseeing across the square.

The men were thin, the signs of malnourishment clearly visible on their blank faces. Prisoners.

"We have to go," she whispered, gripping Jovan's hand and tugging him back. But he didn't budge. His feet remained locked to the paved square as he stared at the hanging men.

"Jovan, please. We have to go. This... we can't be here."

Ignoring her, or simply beyond hearing, Jovan stepped towards the bodies.

"Jovan," Ilona begged, but it was no use. He was moving. Across the square, steps halting but determined. He walked past the bodies, one, two, three, then paused. His good hand reached up, gripping the man's shoe. Ilona cast her eyes wildly around the square, fear tightening her chest as realisation slammed into her. He knew that man. Somehow, Jovan knew the man hanging from a pole, a hook through his neck.

Dread locked up her limbs. What if there were soldiers watching? What if someone saw Jovan's obvious gesture of grief? They would come for him.

Pushing past the terror that held her rooted to the spot, Ilona forced herself forward. The square was silent. Everyone had drawn back in abject fear. The sound of her heels crunching over the dusting of ice on the pavement seemed impossibly loud. She kept her focus on Jovan and turned away from the spectre of death that hung above her. A breeze blew, and a set of feet tapped against the wooden pole beside her head. Feet that belonged to someone's son, brother, husband.

Her traitorous eyes flicked up, and her stomach bottomed out. Dead eyes stared down at her from a head that was crooked at an unnatural angle. Dried blood crusted over his neck. Her stomach rebelled, the acid burn of bile racing up her throat as she realised what that blood meant. He'd been alive when they hooked him up on the pole. She bent over and lost her stomach over the ice. The sound of her retching filled the square, but nobody looked at her. The horror hanging from the poles was all-consuming.

Straightening, Ilona drew a hand across her mouth, wiping away the traces of her physical reaction and hurried the last steps to Jovan. He hadn't moved. He stood like a statue, fixated on the man. Ilona didn't look up. She wouldn't make that mistake again.

A commotion sounded on the edge of her consciousness, and Ilona's head whipped around. Three soldiers appeared on the edge of the square, their eyes snapping straight to Jovan.

She clutched Jovan's arm. "Jovan, we have to go."

He didn't move, just stared. "Goran," he whispered.

Ilona's lips parted in a sorrowful gasp as her heart plunged through her. Goran. Jovan's friend from the university. Oh God. He'd been missing since the Ustaše were given the rule of the country. More sounds were building behind her. No time to grieve, not now.

"Jovan," she tried again. "We have to go. There are soldiers. Ustaše."

That got his attention. His eyes dipped to hers and then tracked over her head. A fire ignited in them, a blaze she'd not seen since he left for war. His hand released Goran's shoe and his arm wrapped around her, obscuring her from view. He had lost weight, but he still managed to shield her with his body. His long legs stretched, his strides racing them across the square. Ilona scrambled to keep up. But Jovan's strong arm kept her firmly pressed to his side. They ducked into a side street, but his pace did not relent. On and on they hurried, all the way to the bus stop and onto the bus. As the bus bounced away from Dubrava, Jovan scanned the streets they passed, his grip on her unrelenting. It would be the last time she would try to visit her parents.

"It is the right decision," Ilona said, folding a dress and placing it neatly into her suitcase. "You know the fight is coming to the streets. The Nazis and the Ustaše are failing. The Partisans are advancing. We have to go."

It had been hard resigning from her work at the hospital, but Dragica understood. So did Diana. Still, the decision hurt her deeply, even if it was the right one.

Jovan stood before the cupboard, selecting jumpers for their journey. His back was to her, but she could read his emotions in the tension of his stance, the slump of his head.

"My love," she said softly. "There is nothing you can do."

It was true. Painful but true. His shattered hand was far from healed, rendering his arm all but useless. Even if he could return to the Partisans to fight, Ilona wasn't sure she could let him. Not again. Not after what had happened last time.

But that didn't mean she didn't understand. Jovan was a good man. He believed in his duty to his people, to those who suffered – had left to fight for the cause, for the freedom for all of the southern Slavs.

Guilt flowing through her that she was happy he could not fight, not for the injury, but for his relative safety now, Ilona crossed to his side. Sliding her arms around his waist, careful not to knock his injured hand, she hugged him close. His good hand came to rest over hers. They stayed that way for a moment, a minute, an hour, just holding each other. Then Jovan turned in her arms and brushed a strand of her hair behind her ear. "It isn't that I can't rejoin the Partisans that upsets me."

Ilona cocked her head at him, a small frown tightening her forehead. "Then what?"

Jovan released a deep sigh. "I am upset... ashamed because I am glad not to."

Ilona suppressed her surprise and remained silent, allowing him time to find his words.

"When I left with Josip and Slavko, it was the hardest thing I have ever done in my life. Walking away from you, leaving you alone while the Ustaše roamed the streets uncontrolled." He paused, his eyes closing against an unspoken emotion. "I believed I had no choice. That it was the right thing to do."

"It was," Ilona assured him. "What they have done... We had to stand up."

"We?"

Giving a small shake of her head, now was not the time for that conversation, Ilona repeated, "It was the right choice," returning him to the topic at hand. They were discussing his choices now. She would tell him about Diana, about her work to save the children of Zagreb, later, when the time was right.

"I know. But in that prison cell, when David walked in... then your brother... I don't know how to come back from that. Nothing mattered then. Not the Serbs, not my family. Not even you." Shame laced every word. "I just wanted to live. And now. I never want to be parted from you. Not ever."

Ilona took his face in her hands, bringing their foreheads together. "And I would never allow it again."

"I was wrong to leave. You were alone. What if they had come for you?"

"They didn't," she reminded him, trying to anchor him to the present, to this moment. "And you are here now. These years, this reality, we had no say in it. It came and took control of our lives with guns and violence. And we had to fight back. We had to stand up and do what we could."

"There's that 'we' again," his eyes fixed on hers. "What aren't you telling me?"

Ilona braced herself; she didn't know how he might react. But she'd done what was right, little Lina was proof of that. Even if she'd failed Misa...

She met his stare. "Did you hear about the camps for women and children?"

Jovan nodded slowly. "Da, the Ustaše rounded up whole villages of civilians. There was little we could do."

"I helped get them out."

Shock slacked his jaw. "You... you got the children out?"

"I met a woman, Diana. She's from Austria." She broke off, shaking her head. "That's not important. She speaks German. She convinced the commandant that the camps were inhumane. That the children should be freed. I helped. We went to the camps and brought the children to churches and orphanages here in Zagreb. We made a mistake with a camp run by the Red Cross," she paused. "It was awful there. But we moved the children into homes as soon as we could—"

Jovan pulled away from her in disbelief. "You went to the Ustaše camps? Ilona. You are married to a Serb!"

"They didn't know that. Or care. We were there for the children."

"And what if they realised? You were right there, they could have taken you—"

"But they didn't. They took Misa though."

Jovan stared at her. "What?"

Fresh sorrow swamped Ilona at the memory of Misa's terrified face, the grip of her hands as she begged Ilona to find her children. And she'd promised. A promise she had failed. She'd looked, oh how she had searched. In every camp, on every record in Diana's archive. No Stephan and Hanna. No children of Petrinja.

"The Ustaše, they raided her village. Separated her and Radič and the children. Misa was sent to a labour camp in Germany. I don't know if she lives. Her children were left in the camp. Alone."

Jovan frowns. "What do you mean 'alone'?"

He doesn't know, she realised. How could he? How could anyone understand the full horror of those camps? Ilona had been there, had seen it with her own eyes, and still she doubted her memory. Still struggled to comprehend it was true.

"The Ustaše, they took the women, anyone old enough to wield a shovel. They were sent to work camps. And the children were left behind. They didn't feed them or clothe them properly. The older children were left to care for the younger ones and the babies. But they had no sanitation… They had an infirmary, where they left the sick ones to die alone on the hard floor, and I had to help. I had to—"

His arm closed around her, crushing her to his side, enveloping her in his love and strength. His lips were by her ear, his breath warm. "I didn't know," he whispered. "I didn't know."

Tears flowed down Ilona's face as the truth of those camps tore at her heart once more. "It was… I can't…"

"I understand," Jovan said, drawing her back and looking right at her. And she saw that he did. He truly understood. What she'd seen in those camps and what he'd experienced in the prison were horrors that could never truly be explained. They had both faced something unspeakable. Through those experiences, they shared an understanding no one else could.

He grasped her hand and pressed it to his heart. "I am sorry," he whispered, tears threatening to spill down his cheeks. "I am so proud of you."

"Thank you."

A small huff of a laugh escaped his lips. "To think, I ran off to fight and achieved nothing. You saved the lives of children."

"You fought for freedom!" Ilona insisted. "I read every news article about the attacks, the sabotage. Praying every time that I would not see your name. And I never did. Now I know you were involved. You were part of the Partisans. The group forcing the Ustaše into a rage."

"I was caught."

"And you survived."

"Because of your brother."

Her breath released in a rush. "Because of my brother."

Jovan is shaking his head. "I don't know why… When I saw him, I thought my life was over. David had already crushed my hand. I was holding on to hope, desperately. Then Ivica—"

He cut off, clearly working to steady his breathing. "He strode in shouting orders at the others, I don't know what. My mind was not working properly." A pause. His throat bobbed up and down as he faced the memory. Ilona squeezed his arm, willing all the love and strength within her to shine through her touch. Jovan continued.

"He beat me. I lost consciousness," he said softly. "The next thing I knew I was on the street, Ivica standing above me shouting your name. I thought…"

He didn't need to say it. She knew the fear that must have seized him at the sound of her name. The possibility that she had been brought to the hell of a prison he was trapped in. Ilona raised her fingers to his lips and stopped his words. "He brought you home."

"I still don't understand."

"He brought you home," Ilona repeated. "Nothing else matters."

She could see he didn't agree, but he didn't argue.

"And now we are leaving," he said, changing the subject.

"After Dubrava, and knowing that the Partisans are coming, it is time. Zagreb is not safe."

Dubrava. The newspaper had reported the details the next morning. Sixteen men from universities around the city, held since the beginning of the Ustaše rule, roused from their sleep at midnight, driven to the square and hanged on metal hooks while they still breathed. Brutal. Unforgivable. All to seed fear. Two men had managed to escape. Ilona could only pray they remained safe.

"We should have run at the beginning."

"We did what we did."

"Are you sure your grandparents will allow us to stay?"

"Da."

"But I am a Serb."

A small smile curved Ilona's lips. "There is something more I have to tell you."

THIRTY-NINE
ILONA

Lina crashed out of the house, her hands up waving frantically.

Ilona paused on the drive, surprise raising her eyebrows as the little girl ran full speed towards her. It had been more than a year since she had seen Lina. Ilona had expected the child to be shy and nervous. Lina barrelled into her in a shock of limbs and squeezed her tight. Ilona's arms came around the child, hugging her close.

Her baba came up behind her. "She has been watching for you all day. From the window." She pointed to the front of the house. Ilona's deda stood on the porch, watching.

Ilona straightened from her embrace of the girl, one hand soothing Lina's hair. "It's got so long," she said, smiling at the child. "And you have grown so strong."

Her baba gave an affectionate sniff. "She eats enough for two." Then her attention lifted to Jovan, hovering just behind the welcoming scene. "It is good to meet you, Jovan," she said. "It is overdue."

Ilona glanced back at her husband, noting the tension that bracketed his eyes. But he nodded to Ludmila.

"Come inside. I have made krofna pastries with plum jam."

Settled at the table, Lina reached for a second krofna, her legs swinging happily from the chair.

"You have done so well with her," Ilona said to her grandparents, joy and relief calming her overburdened mind. The girl looked happy and content.

"We have experience with children," her deda said, his face softening as he glanced down at Lina. "Our own of course and then after your tata moved you to Zagreb, you and Ivica always stayed for the summers. It has not been so long since we had small ones running around the house."

Her tata. A deep sigh escaped her lips as she met her baba's questioning stare.

"We tried to see them," she answered honestly. "But after Dubrava, Tata is scared. We are... You are..."

"Standing up for the innocent," her baba said proudly, though sadness whispered on the edges of her words. A Croatian family and a Catholic one, her baba and deda had set aside religion and politics and taken in Lina. Now they opened their home to Jovan and Ilona. A Serb with a number and a woman who helped the Orthodox. It put them on the wrong side of the Ustaše. It made them a target. Her tata had chosen differently. The men hanged from the meat hooks in the square had had the intended impact on many of the citizens of Zagreb. A show of brutality and power, the Ustaše had displayed their disregard for human life, their willingness to murder anyone who stood against them. Some people of her city had looked to their German occupiers, hoping they would intervene. The Germans simply looked away. So her parents closed their doors and made themselves small.

Ilona and Jovan fled.

She hoped her grandparents' ethnicity and Jovan's Catholicism would shield them. It had to be enough.

"Ivica?"

Ilona glanced down at her plate, every part of her being suddenly too heavy to carry.

"We know he is Ustaše," her deda said, tone sharp with disapproval as he regarded little Lina. Anger simmered, barely contained, behind that gaze. Ilona understood. The men her brother fought beside had locked Lina up, left her for dead. She had seen those camps. She knew better than anyone just how vile those places were, just how grotesque the Ustaše were.

Jovan's warm hand encircled hers on her lap, and he leaned forward. "Ivica saved my life," he said.

Ilona watched her deda's face turn to Jovan, his mouth softening. Flashing a glance at Ilona, Jovan continued. "I was captured, held in a prison. It was... bad." He shuffled, subconsciously rearranging the angle of his broken hand where it lay strapped to his chest.

"Ivica got me out, I don't know how. Only that I woke up to the cold of fresh air on my skin, the touch of rain, and Ilona's face."

Silence stretched around them. Her deda looked up at Ilona, eyes wet with tears. "Why?"

The question stilled her breath. It was the same question that had haunted her every night since Jovan had come back to her. The picture of her brother standing in the rain, face turned up to her in the light of the street lamp. The boy she'd grown up beside. The man who'd shunned her for her marriage. The soldier who'd been party to mass killings based on hideous ideology.

Ivica.

Her brother had brought her husband home.

She shook her head silently. She had no answer for her deda, nor for herself. But she had her husband back. Broken, lowered by suffering, but alive. If he breathed, he could heal. Ilona was determined to keep it that way.

Her baba stood from the table, the scrape of the chair jarring in the sombre quiet of the room. "It has been a long day for you both. Come, I will get you settled in your rooms. You can freshen up and rest before supper."

"Da, Baba. Thank you," Ilona said.

They'd passed the afternoon helping with the daily chores. Jovan accompanied her deda to chop firewood while Ilona joined her baba and Lina in the kitchen to prepare stew. From the kitchen window, she watched as Jovan fought to manoeuvre the axe one-handed. Her deda stood to the side, giving him space. Ilona wanted to call out to her deda, to tell him to chop the wood. Jovan was still healing after all. But he didn't interfere or make suggestions, just allowed Jovan to work through the new challenge.

"He will find his new way," her baba said quietly.

Ilona felt her tension fade. Ludmila was right. Jovan's injury was severe. He would need to learn to adjust.

"He was a musician," she found herself saying. "He played so beautifully." The sorrow that flooded her chest shocked her, stealing her words. Would she ever hear him play his violin again?

"He is alive. It is enough," her baba said.

Shame heated Ilona's cheeks. After everything she had seen, all the death and loss, she should remember that nothing else mattered.

"Da, Baba. You are right," she said.

That night Ilona tucked Lina into bed. The little girl took her hand, leading her to her room in a mirror image of the first day Ilona brought her here, when it was Ilona showing Lina to her room. Climbing into bed without a fuss, Lina snuggled down beneath her blankets, wrapping her arms around a woollen toy of some sort. Smiling to herself, Ilona perched on the bedside and tucked the blankets snugly around Lina's shoulders, just as she had so long ago at the orphanage.

"It is so good to see you," she said honestly. "I have missed you."

Lina's bright eyes shone from her face as she watched Ilona. Then she gripped her toy and held it up for Ilona to see. Ilona's brow furrowed as recognition dawned. It was not a toy that the child hugged. It was her cardigan.

"She won't sleep without it." Ludmila's voice drifted from the doorway. "I am allowed to clean it, occasionally. But only because I told her that it would last longer if I did. She won't be parted from it. I think it reminds her of you."

Ilona's heart swelled to bursting as she looked down on this small child she rescued from a camp.

"Thank you for taking such good care of it," she said, running a hand over the rough wool. "I am glad you still have it. It is yours now."

Lina stared at her a moment, two, then hugged the cardigan back against her chest, nestling down into her bed.

"Sweet dreams, little one," Ilona said, pressing a kiss to her forehead. "I will see you in the morning."

Lina eyed her a moment, then her lids began to droop, her breathing slowing, and peace enveloped Ilona's very soul. As quietly as she could Ilona stood, careful not to disturb the sleeping child. Lina's hand shot out from the blankets, clutching Ilona's sleeve. "Stay?"

Her voice was small and hushed, rough from disuse. Ilona stared down at Lina as her baba's audible gasp sounded from the door.

"I have never heard her speak," Ludmila whispered, stunned.

But Ilona did not turn to her baba's words, her attention remained fully focused on Lina. She felt her lips curve in a gentle smile. "Da, dear one. I will stay. We won't be apart, not ever again."

The end of the war in Yugoslavia came on the back of the Partisans and the Serbian Chetniks, supported from the sidelines by the Western Allied forces. Brutal, cold and vicious. Seeing the inevitable, Germany withdrew. The Ustaše, driven by ideology and fear of reprisal, fought on. But by the spring of 1945 the outcome was inevitable.

When the victory and reunification of Yugoslavia under the leadership of the Partisan leader Josip Tito, was officially announced Ilona felt nothing. The expected rush of joy and relief didn't come. Instead, her body was simply numb. A letter arrived from her mama in Zagreb, informing her of her brother Ivica's death. He had fought beside the Ustaše to the very end and lost his life at the hands of a Partisan soldier in the final push for the city.

Despair leached from her mama's words, yet Ilona could not bring herself to care.

The years of the war had worn her down. The horrors she had seen, the terrors Jovan and Lina had endured, all that pain and death and loss could not be swept away by some pleasantries on a page. Her parents had never fully accepted Jovan. Their concern for the politics of the city, and their fear of the Ustaše, had closed their door.

It was understandable.

It had let Ilona down.

They wanted her to visit. To bring Jovan to supper. They didn't know about Lina so she was not included in the missive.

Ilona put the letter in a drawer. She never replied.

Another letter came, this one from Diana. It became the first of a lifelong correspondence between the two women who had worked together for the children of Zagreb. The letter was to inform, and to warn, Ilona knew. As the survivors of the camps across Croatia and Germany drifted home, they would begin the search for their lost children.

Someone may come for Lina.

Ilona wrestled with that. Night after night as she sang the child to her sleep, she felt her heart becoming a withering, fragile thing. And a truth she'd known from the moment she gathered Lina's tiny body from the floor of Stara Gradiška blossomed within her: that Lina had become the daughter of her heart. Caring for the little girl was all that had got Ilona through the darkness. The process of their survival and healing had grown a bond that reached between their souls. How could Ilona survive giving her up? Even if it were the right thing to do.

At night when the fear of parting from the girl overwhelmed her, Jovan tucked her against his side, her tears wetting his chest with her sorrow.

"We will be all right. We will be all right," he whispered against her ear. But Ilona knew it was a lie.

In the end, she had nothing to fear. No knock ever came.

No news of Misa's Stephan and Hanna emerged either. No new record, no miraculous discovery of the siblings alive and well under a Croatian roof, or in a newly liberated camp. As the country tried to rebuild, its people finding their way in a new fragile world, there was still no path to uncovering them.

As the hot summer days began to lengthen into autumn, Ilona's world continued to turn. Her grandparent's cottage was her sanctuary, Jovan and Lina her strength.

Then Misa came home.

FORTY

ILONA

The back of her shoe rubbed against her heel. Misa paused. Taking a deep breath to calm her billowing lungs, she ran her forearm over her head to clear a slick of sweat. It was hot, the sun beating down mercilessly on her pale skin. The walk from the train station in Novska to the address she'd been given was longer than she'd expected. Or perhaps that was more to do with her physical condition.

It had been two months since the British soldiers arrived at the labour camp in Germany. Misa and her fellow prisoners had been huddled in their barracks. The day before, the German soldiers had ordered them inside and locked the doors, then disappeared. They hadn't understood what was going on. But no one had been brave, or strong, enough to attempt to break out. The years of toiling in the fields on a diet of bread and porridge had thinned them all to their bones. Those who still lived at least. Their numbers had dwindled with their flesh, but not their workload.

Misa had been buried beneath her blankets, trying to warm her very bones when she'd heard the shout. Male, booming, and not in German. The others had heard it too, rising from their beds to peer cautiously outside. A group of soldiers, guns at the ready, stalked down the muddy path between the barracks, eyes alert and scanning.

"They aren't Germans," Misa had whispered. She'd tapped on the glass of the window. Two faces turned to her, and the women beside her ducked out of view. But Misa had held steady.

Their imprisonment was over.

They'd been transported to a makeshift hospital camp, treated for their wounds and starvation. Not everyone made it. But Misa did.

Arriving back in Zagreb she'd found Ilona and Jovan's home empty. Fortunately, her knocking had roused their neighbour, Radmila.

Misa's one-time tormenter had the decency to gasp at Misa's emaciated state, her eyes lowering in shame. "You are alive," she'd breathed. "I prayed for you."

Misa had turned away. She had no need of Radmila's prayers.

"Wait! They left me their address, for you. In case..."

She'd disappeared back into her apartment, then produced a letter in Ilona's neat handwriting. Misa recognised the town name: Novska, where Ilona's grandparents' farm was. Her friend had spoken of it so fondly. The thought of Ilona somewhere that made her happy should have brought a smile to her lips. But no emotion came.

"Thank you," Misa had said, more than ready to end their interaction and move on. But Radmila placed a gentle hand on Misa's arm.

"I am sorry, truly. I was angry and..." she paused, clearly searching for words. "I was wrong."

Misa regarded her suspiciously. "David?" she asked.

Tears brimmed along Radmila's lashes, and she shook her head.

Something shifted in Misa's chest. It wasn't forgiveness or even understanding. Just a small crack of feeling, an opening. Misa met Radmila's stare. "Take care of yourself," she said and walked away.

Now, standing on the outskirts of Novska, Misa rechecked the address scrawled on the paper in her hand and heaved another lungful of air before trudging on.

The air was hot, the earth dried to dust beneath her step, the perfectly blue sky offered no hint of a cooling breeze. But Misa didn't stop. As the afternoon heat continued to climb, Misa came to a dirt drive. A small cottage stood at the end of the path, surrounded by a cultivated area of green that gave way to a wild forest of trees. Consulting the now-worn piece of paper that held the address, Misa decided she was at the right house.

She paused a moment, working to calm her rattling nerves. It had been three years since she had seen her friend Ilona. Three years of war and death. Three years since she had begged her to find Stephan and Hanna. What would she find in this cottage surrounded by beech and spruce trees?

Forcing her limbs to move, Misa stepped onto the drive.

The front door of the cottage banged open, and a little girl ran out into the garden, dark braids flying behind her. Misa's heart beat outside her body, tears welling in her eyes as her hand came up to cover her mouth. "Hanna?" she whispered, the hope too great to contain. She surged forward so fast her feet nearly tripped themselves up. The girl was skipping, face turned away from Misa. Everything seemed to slow down as Misa drew closer. Her fingers burned with the need to clutch her child to her heart, her limbs aching to feel Hanna's soft body against her chest.

Then the door banged again. Ilona stood on the front porch, hands on hips. "Lina? Not too far."

Lina?

Misa stopped dead.

The little girl turned giving Misa a perfect view of her oval face. Not Hanna.

Misa's heart stuttered, and her knees wobbled. The powerful surge of hope snatched away so fast, was too much for her fragile body. Her limbs locked up, and she crashed to the ground. A grunt of pain sounded from her lips as she fell.

Palms in the dirt of the drive, Misa tried to push herself up.

"Misa?" A gasp, then hurried footsteps and two firm hands gripping her shoulders. Misa looked up into the face of her dearest friend. "Ilona," she said.

Ilona helped her to her feet, one hand remaining on her shoulder to steady her. Misa brushed down her skirts, a wave of embarrassment warming her face even more than the sun had. The little girl stood just beyond Ilona, her large curious eyes watching.

"Lina, go inside and pour water for us," Ilona said. The little girl spun and rushed away.

Ilona turned back to Misa, her warm hands cupping Misa's face.

The touch was gentle, but the new lines of Misa's cheeks felt tender under the gesture nonetheless. "Dear God," Ilona breathed. "It is you. Oh my God, thank you, thank you!"

Arms wrapped around her, crushing her into Ilona's chest. Misa stiffened instinctively, years of imprisonment cloaking her nerves in fear. But the scent of Ilona, the pastry and plum she'd always associated with her friend, found her nose and her body relaxed. Leaning into the embrace, Misa's body began to shake. A sob, lodged for years in the pit of her stomach, tore up from her very core, dislodged by the safety of her friend's closeness. Her legs felt weak and unsteady. Her mind blurring, her consciousness fraying at the edges.

"It is all right. You are safe." The words caressed the border of her understanding. And it was almost enough. Almost. Close but impossibly far.

A small voice called out, breaking through Misa's fog of emotion. "The water is ready." Her eyes shot up over Ilona's shoulder, settling on the little girl who was not Hanna.

"Did you find them?" she asked, pulling from Ilona's tight embrace.

Regret flooded her friend's face, and Misa knew. Darkness descended across her mind faster than a Nazi bullet. She saw it in Ilona's eyes, the look of deepest guilt.

"Come inside. You need to rest."

But Misa didn't want to rest. Her children weren't here. Stephan and Hanna... She'd come all this way, but they weren't here. She had to move on. Had to keep searching. But where? Back to Zagreb? Another round of the orphanages? Another request to the officials?

"I..."

"I know," Ilona said, face drawn. "But you need to be strong for that. Come inside. Eat, talk, rest a little. And we can make a plan."

She drew an arm around Misa's shoulders, urging her towards the house. Misa's body complied, even as her brain screamed in resistance. Her mind could not override her exhaustion. She had to give in, for now.

Half an hour later Misa sat on a soft chair, belly full of krofna and a second glass of cool water in her hand. On the carpeted floor, the little girl, Lina, sat, playing with a doll. An older woman, Ilona's baba, sat in the corner, knitting. It was a picture of domestic bliss. A vision out of Misa's own daydreams of the future she would share with Radič.

Her husband.

Her chest spasmed as she fought down the memory of the day that future was wrenched apart. Radič racing towards her, his eyes wild, the truck churning up the road behind him.

Stephan's wail.

Ilona came into the room, pulling Misa from her panic, moments before it took her under.

"You are comfortable?" she asked.

Forcing away the last tendrils of her dreadful memories, Misa focused on her friend.

"Tell me."

She watched as Ilona's face fell, true sadness blanching her skin. "Baba?" she asked over her shoulder. "Would you take Lina out to pick some daisies? It's such a beautiful afternoon."

Misa watched as the two women regarded each other, unspoken understanding flowing between them. Misa had had that understanding with her family once too. But no longer. She'd found those records: her mama, her Radič, her friends from Petrinja. They were all gone.

"Daisies!" Lina cried out joyfully, bouncing to her feet. Misa couldn't help the smile that curved her lips as the child accepted her baba's hand and, arms swinging happily, hurried from the room. Her smile quickly began to wobble.

Turning back to Ilona, Misa didn't miss the moment of indulgent love that filled her friend's eyes and fought down the surge of bitterness that broke from her soul.

Unaware, Ilona came to sit on the chair beside her, taking her hands.

"It is beyond my dreams that you are here. I prayed every day, but there was no news. How long have you been back in Yugoslavia?"

"A matter of weeks."

"What happened?"

Misa met her friend's gentle gaze and read the sincere love there, and the words flowed. Of the camps and the work. Of the soldiers and the deaths. Of Stephan and Kata's wails. Of Hanna's silent stare. The visions that haunted her nights and her waking hours.

"You didn't find them!" The words ripped from her lips as an accusation, bitter, resentful. And instantly Misa regretted them. Yet her longing still quested, a flame of hope fluttering in her chest that there was a twist coming. That her children had been found. That they were somewhere safe. Just not here.

Even though she knew that could not be true; Ilona would have told her straight away. Hope is a brutal friend.

"I searched," Ilona said, watching Misa's face, brows frowning intently. Misa could feel her desperation to be believed. But her walls were up. Not yet. Not yet.

"I worked with the Red Cross and a woman named Diana Budisavljević. We got the children out of the camps. Took them to orphanages and churches. Lina was one of them..."

She paused, drawing in a deep breath. "Diana let me review

every record. Every. Single. One. I couldn't find them. Not on any list. Not even children who could have matched their descriptions—"

"No," Misa breathed, tremors sparking along her limbs. "No, please, don't say it."

"I don't know." Ilona rushed the words. "There were so many children. And they were traumatised. So many of them did not remember their names or where they came from. Stephan was so young. And what he witnessed... They were strong and healthy. They may live. They just don't know who they are."

Misa latched on to Ilona's words. "This Diana, you say she has records? I need to review them. I know my children. There might be something you missed."

"Da, of course, of course. Diana and I are in regular correspondence. We continue to search, we have never stopped."

"Yet you are here, not in Zagreb!" Misa snapped. She blew out a sharp breath, her fingers raking through her brittle hair in frustration. "I am sorry."

She said the words, but her heart did not feel them. All she felt was want. The want for Radič, for Stephan, Hanna. For her mama and tata. Her whole extended family. For Kata.

The front door squeaked and Ilona stood. "Can you give us a little longer, Baba?"

But it was not the old woman's head that appeared in the doorway. Jovan stepped into the room and Misa's jaw dropped. "He is alive too?"

"Misa? Dear God, it's a miracle."

His long legs strode towards her. He knelt on the floor then an arm pulled her tight. This man she had known her whole life. Radič's closest friend. He lived. Everyone Ilona loved was alive. And everyone Misa loved was dead.

Angry and hurt, she shoved Jovan away roughly. His kind eyes creased momentarily, then softened in pity. Misa didn't want that pity. "Don't," she said, turning away.

Silence fell around them, and Misa felt her strength begin to wane.

Ilona stood and placed a hand on Jovan's shoulder. He rose to his feet. "Will you stay a night or two? I know you wish to return to Zagreb. But a day of rest, or at least a night, will not be the difference."

How could she say that? Misa's mind raged, her thoughts catching against each other, clogging her consciousness. But the heaviness of her limbs. The fog of fatigue. She had fought through that pain so many times on the fields of Germany, pushing her body beyond the point of breaking. Somehow, she knew she could not do it again.

"Come," Ilona said gently. "I will put you in Lina's room. She can sleep in with us for a night or two. Please, Misa, rest."

Misa nodded slowly and accepted the hand Jovan offered to help her to stand. That was when she noticed. He stood differently. His body was lopsided and the right arm lay slackened against his side. Her eyes drifted down the arm, catching on the rolled-up sleeve of his shirt. His elbow and the top of his forearm were smooth and clear, but halfway down as her eyes neared his wrist, his flesh became a mass of scars. Mounds of white scar tissue, speckled with darker patches where the skin had fused in lumps, the bone beneath unknit.

She gasped. "Jovan?" she breathed, hands reaching for his wounded arm, his playing hand. He swivelled slightly, moving from her reach. "Ustaše," he said simply.

They looked at each other. Torment swirled around his irises. Her anger banked, and guilt churned within her. She should have known better. They had all suffered. All of them. Death was not the only way to lose what you love.

"Come," Ilona repeated. "Rest."

Misa followed her to the child's room and fell into a fitful sleep that echoed with her children's cries.

PART SEVEN

FORTY-ONE

Her fingers hold the needles loosely, the clicking of their rhythmic movement soothing as the woollen ball shrinks. "I don't remember much, other than being cold. The kind of cold that becomes a part of you, like you've never felt differently. I am never cold now. I won't accept it. I made sure my children were always warmly dressed. My granddaughter is pregnant. I am knitting the child a winter jumper. My family will never be cold while I live." Her needles continue to clack.

Sara nods. "You are knitting red, is that for a boy?"

Stana shrugs. "Girls can wear red. Red is fierce. It stands out. You don't get lost in red."

Daniel touches her arm gently and Sara turns to face him. He points at the top of the camera. The battery level indicator is low. Sara thinks she has a spare in the van.

"I survived until the end, the Partisans freed me, not the nurses. I was placed in a church orphanage. No one wanted me. My children will always know they are wanted."

She adjusts her needles, loosens more wool and continues. "When the soldiers came, they asked me who I was and where I was from. I knew, of course. But I didn't say. I didn't trust the soldiers. None of us did.

"One of them offered me some bread. I took that. You always take the food."

The battery light blinks red. The battery is out. Daniel's mouth opens to tell Stana to wait, but Sara stops him with a touch and a small shake of her head.

It isn't about her documentary any more, or at least not only. Sara knows that now. These people, their memories, she wants to record them, she wants to share their stories. But more than that, she wants to help them find peace. Peace for all the survivors, peace for her baba.

If she doesn't get all the footage, it doesn't matter. But if Stana stops talking, if they interrupt her as she releases her grief, her story so long held in silence, that does matter.

Later as she and Daniel make their way to the van, he gives her a look.

What?"

"Are you okay?" he asks.

Sara pauses, hand on the van door latch. "Da," she says.

But she's not.

Because it is so big, this thing she has begun, this history she has cracked open. It overflows in waves and surges, and Sara is power-less against it.

Maybe her mama is right. Maybe the past should stay the past.

Sara heaves a breath and sighs. She doesn't believe that, not at her core. Her body feels the truth. That this is important. That she must bear witness.

Maybe.

FORTY-TWO
NADICA

Novska 1991

Nadica rubs her eyes. It had been a late night talking with her mama – there had been so much to share, so much to understand. When her mama disappeared upstairs and returned with a worn and faded cardigan, the very one Baba had wrapped her in all those years ago in an Ustaše camp, the tears had flowed freely.

"You still have it?"

"It was my lifeline."

Over the past few weeks, as Ilona and Misa shared their stories, a heaviness has come over Nadica. But learning of her mama's experience? It made her love her mama, and her baba and deda, even more. She understands her mama's dilemma. How can they leave the only parents Lina has ever known? Especially when they saved her life.

Not for the first time, she wishes her tata were still here.

She doesn't have time for those thoughts, she must focus. She's taken over her mama's shift at the store, allowing Lina time to go and be with her parents and Misa. After everything yesterday, Lina needs her mama and tata.

A blast of cool air hits her face and Nadica looks up, smile at the ready, expecting old Mr Kovacic and Shuma to arrive for the morning paper. Relja streaks into the shop, his face dark like a building storm, tension rolling off him in waves. She tenses instinctively yet a cold kernel of guilt also swims in her stomach. He was always so angry, so ready to fight.

Now she understands why.

His eyes dart around the store, assessing. It's empty but for the two of them. His pace slows, and he comes to the counter. Pausing a few steps back he shoves his hands in his pockets and regards her through lowered lashes. His whole being is on edge, but she can see he is trying to give her space, trying not to scare her.

It's not working.

"Relja? How can I help you?" she asks. The wall she erected between them has not, and will not, come down, even if she can empathise with his view.

She sees it, the moment his hope breaks. His shoulders slump forward, and he takes a subconscious step back. She notes the nervous bob of his throat a second before he speaks. "There will be war," he states. "You and your mama. You have to leave."

Nadica frowns. "People are scared, I know. And the fights are escalating but—"

"The Croatian Military has mobilised. It will be full-scale war."

"We knew it was coming. We can ride it out."

"There has been a massacre."

The air evaporates from the room. Disbelief washes over Nadica and she reaches for the stack of newspapers to confirm his words.

"It's not in the paper yet, I heard from a contact," Relja continues. "A Serb military group have killed Croat civilians in Gospić. It was wrong," he pauses, shaking his head. "But it came from fear."

Nadica's mind is racing. A massacre. The murder of innocent civilians, by a Serb army. How could they? They know what it means to attack civilians. It happened to their relatives. How could they repeat such brutality?

"Relja," Nadica breathes, "you can't justify this."

Anger sparks from his eyes, and his mouth forms into a flattened line. "No, but I must think of our people."

"Relja, we are all one people. My baba is a Croat—"

"And your tata was a Serb."

Nadica blinks. How does Relja know that? She didn't even know that until just last night... He must see the turmoil in her face because his eyes soften. "Our tatas were friends, you know this. They had the same pain." That pain is seared into Relja's soul, Nadica can see it.

Realisation washes over her. Their tatas. Always together at the local tavern. Friends who shared a dangerous secret. Relja's tata knew that Davor was a Serb. Her tata gave away his truth to one person outside their family. So Relja knows. Who else knows from that one indiscretion?

"The Croatian army will see you only one way," he continues. "Just like they see me. You know it's true. Serbia is controlling the Yugoslav Army. They have spread across the country. There are besieged cities across Croatia. This won't be the first mass death."

Her muscles freeze, her limbs locking up as fear traces through her veins.

"What do you mean?"

"The Croatian Army is fighting for independence. Yugoslavia wants to protect the Serb people."

"Relja." She can't believe what she is hearing. "You know it is more than that. The powerful leaders who control the union of Yugoslavia don't want to lose power."

"Our people are in danger."

"Everyone is in danger! Relja, this should not be happening. The nation voted—"

"They will slaughter us!"

Nadica gapes at him, her mouth going dry. She works moisture back with her tongue, ready to speak, but he overrides her.

Stepping boldly forward his hands grip the counter before her, and he stares at her, hard. "Whether you believe me or not, they will come. The Croatian Army will come. The Yugoslavs will resist them. But they cannot stop them. There will be more killings, on both sides. You are part Serb. You are in the middle."

Nadica pauses at that. So, Relja doesn't know it all, doesn't know about her mama's birth family. But she does. The shield her grandparents' lie gave her, it was never real. Nadica is a Serb, through and through.

"So are you."

"No," he shakes his head. "I am exactly where I need to be. I will defend my people."

"Relja," her throat clogs. "This is wrong. They are killing civilians."

"Better theirs than ours."

"You don't mean that."

"This is war."

She is angry with him, frustrated by his intensity and rage. This war has been simmering on the edges of her experience for months, but it is about to overwhelm them all. She hates what Relja believes and hates that he would kill the innocent. But she does not want to see him hurt. "Come with us."

Their eyes meet, and his soften. A smile drifts over his lips. Then his hands slip off the counter and he steps back. "I will stand with my tata. As your tata would have also," he says. The words instantly ignite her ire once more. Relja does not know what her tata would do.

Or does he? The doubt makes her hesitate. After what her tata experienced in Jasenovac, that fear and death, might Davor have chosen to fight? For their family, for the power of Serbia? She gives a small shake of her head. It doesn't matter what Davor might have done, he is gone. Nadica is here in this moment with Relja.

"Relja, this is dangerous. The world as we know it is shifting. We can't stop it. But we can stay in our homes. And we can accept the change."

"They will kill us," he says flatly. "They tried once before. Why would we be foolish enough to trust them now?"

"That was so long ago..." she begins, but the words fall flat. A few months ago she would have believed them, but now, after everything she's come to understand, that history is no longer academic, it is personal. It reaches into the heart of her family. She tries once more. "Then doesn't it make more sense for us to run?"

"This is our home. We deserve to stand on our lands."

It is an eerie echo of her mama's hesitation that Nadica was born and raised here, her tata buried here. That they have a right to stay. But if men are willing to go to war over it, what hope is there of a peaceful transition?

Another gust of air breezes into the store, and old Mr Kovacic shuffles in, Shuma panting on his heels. Relja sinks his hands back into his pockets and gives Nadica one last stare. "Go," he mouths then pivots on his heels and is gone.

She helps Mr Kovacic with his shopping then takes the keys and locks up. It's early, but Nadica doesn't care, she needs to get to her family.

Her bike speeds along the road, eating up the track. All around her is calm and still, the cold a layer of mist surrounds the bare tree branches. There is no sign of Relja's words, no indication of the conflict building in the towns around them. Perhaps it won't arrive at their door? Perhaps they are small enough to be overlooked?

But what if it does? What if they come for her family again?

Nadica doesn't slow as she races down the drive, jumping off her bike and leaving it to crash into the browning grasses of mid-autumn. Up the steps she races, bursting through the doorway into the warmth of her grandparent's home.

Inside is calm and serene. Baba looks up from the fireplace, her knitting in hand, her deda on the chair opposite, sipping coffee.

"Nadica?" her baba says, eyebrows rising. "We weren't expecting you. Is something the matter?"

Across the room her deda instantly snaps to attention. Discarding his cup, he rises slowly and walks to Nadica's side. Taking her shoulder in his good hand he scans her face, his expression falling.

"It is coming?"

"Da."

"Get your mama. She is sitting with Misa."

Nodding, Nadica goes to Misa's room.

The dear old lady is awake, her eyes sharper than usual today as she turns to Nadica. "Ah, my dear one," she says. "It is good to see you."

"It is good to see you too, Misa," Nadica says, gesturing over her shoulder at her mama.

She doesn't want to worry Misa. She doesn't want any of this to be happening.

Slowly Lina stands, hands running down the front of her jeans. It is in the line of her mouth. She knows. Bending, she presses a soft kiss to Misa's forehead. "I will just be a moment," she says, tucking Misa firmly under the blanket.

Misa's eyes slide between them, narrowing slightly. On her good days, she still has all her faculties. Today must be a good day.

She sniffs sharply. "I will not leave my children."

"No one is leaving anyone," Lina says. But her voice is distracted, her body angling towards the door. "Come," she says, taking Nadica's arm and leading her to the door. Nadica feels Misa watching her all the way from the room.

In the lounge, her grandparents stand, clearly arguing. Her baba has crossed her arms over her chest. Her deda is glaring at her.

He isn't getting his way.

As Nadica and her mama come closer she hears her baba hiss, "You left me once before. We should never have parted. We will not part now."

"Ilona, be reasonable," her deda tries. But Nadica can see the words glide over her baba like a mist. "Misa can't and won't travel. But you and our family can."

"I will not leave without you or Misa. We were safe here then, we will be safe here now."

"I am taking Nadica."

Nadica's breath stutters as her eyes slide to her mama. She can feel her mama's apprehension and can feel the conflict within her mind. What a terrible choice she must make. Stay with her mama and saviour, or run with her daughter to a foreign land?

Impossible.

Yet somehow, after months trapped in indecision and doubt, paralysed by her personal trauma and pain, Lina has found a way to make that choice.

Ilona's head whips around to face Lina. Nadica braces, ready for the tirade of reproach and betrayal she expects her baba to feel. But Ilona does not shout, nor does she order her husband to do something. There is no manipulation, no coercion. Slowly, silently she crosses the lounge to her daughter and places one hand on each of her cheeks, drawing their foreheads together.

"Thank you," she breathes.

Nadica's mama tenses and then her body collapses as floods of tears stream from her eyes. Jovan is there, wrapping his good arm around his wife and resting his head against his daughter's. The moment stretches, a world of love and fear and pain and hope twirling around them. Nadica watches on in silence. All this love. It has always been Lina's. Of course Ilona and Jovan understand. Why did Lina ever doubt it? The question burns, because Nadica understands. Trauma runs deep, and its clutches never let go.

The trio breaks apart, all three dashing tears from their eyes. Ilona turns to press her sleeve to Jovan's wet cheeks.

"But, Baba, Deda, come with us. Please," Nadica says, turning to her deda. "You are a Serb."

Her deda lowers his eyes, his mouth curving down. "I won't run. But I won't let you remain in danger."

"Misa?" Nadica says.

"Will understand," her baba says.

They all head to Misa's room. The frail woman has pushed herself up into a sitting position and her hands are gripping the bedhead.

"I will not leave my children," she repeats.

"Of course not," Ilona says, going to her and feathering her fingers over her cheek. "And we will not leave them either."

Misa's head cocks to the side and she squints at Ilona in distrust.

"You gave up on them once before. Why should I believe you that this isn't a trick to make me leave them again?"

The words ravage Nadica's soul as she watches her baba stiffen. Then, inexplicably, Baba's body settles, the tension drifting from her body. The two women, friends from nursing school, sisters of the heart, a Croat and a Serb, stare at each other.

Misa deflates, her grip on the bedhead loosening.

"I forgave you long ago," she says softly.

"I know. It's time to forgive yourself."

Their hands join across the blanket, and Ilona continues. "We will never leave your children. But Lina and Nadica must go."

Misa's eyes find Lina's, their dark depths swimming with sadness and pain. "I wish I'd sent mine away. I wish it every day."

"You could not have known to do so," Ilona soothes.

But Misa ignores her comforting words, continuing to Lina. "You understand why I cannot come with you? You know why I have to stay?"

Lina nods sadly. "Because they are here. All of them. Your Stephen and Hanna. Your Radič."

"I left Kata behind too." Misa's voice breaks on the name, her face morphing into a mask of regret and hopelessness, and Nadica's heart fills with grief. Kata died in Germany, her body disposed of somewhere in the fields of a foreign land. There was nothing Misa could ever have done about that. Misa releases her hold on Ilona's hands and pushes herself up to sit taller on the mattress.

Finally, she faces Nadica. "You will return when it is done. You will visit me."

Nadica tries to be strong. Of course she will return, but who knows if Misa will still be alive? Who knows how long this conflict will continue?

A soft smile flutters over Misa's face, and she gives a tiny nod. "You will visit me, wherever I am."

The words are a goodbye, an acceptance that Nadica will return to visit a grave. Misa's grave. And Nadica can't stop the tears from spilling from her eyes, can't stop the sob that escapes her lips. She crosses the room, throwing her arms around Misa's withered frame, holding her tight as her body gives way to her sadness.

She feels her baba's hand on her back, rubbing in soothing, loving circles.

"I will be with them soon," Misa's voice is a whisper against her ear. "I will hug my Stephan and my Hanna again."

There is a lightness to the words. A sense of release. It is the first time Nadica has ever heard Misa accept that her children did not survive the camps, that they are not still out there somewhere in Croatia, alive and well. It is not said with sadness but with serenity. And Nadica understands. Misa is ready to go. She has made her peace with her God. It won't be long now.

It won't be soon enough either.

She turns to her mama. "Perhaps we can just wait a few more days?"

Lina's face is stricken as she shakes her head. "We will leave in the morning."

How can her mama make this choice? After all her indecision, now she stands firm while Nadica wavers. "But Misa—"

"Your mama is right," Jovan says softly. "War changes quickly. There isn't a few days to wait."

A dry hand touches Nadica's cheek, turning her back to Misa. "You have been my joy in the sorrow," she says. "And you will live free."

The acceptance in her eyes finally settles over Nadica, and she smiles. "I love you, Aunty Misa."

"I love you too, dear one."

. . .

The sun's rays touch the tips of the clouds in streaks of pale yellow. Nadica shoves the last bag into the boot of her mama's Nissan. Cold air whips around her and her breath comes in frosty bursts.

Behind her, Lina pulls the door of their small home shut, locking it for the first time in Nadica's memory. Nadica brushes away fresh tears, the water warm against her morning-cold skin. Her mama comes up beside her, dark circles bruising the tender flesh beneath her eyes. Neither slept much the night before. The knowledge of what daybreak would bring and of the looming war pressing down on their homeland stole the chance of rest. It had been past midnight when Nadica rose from her bed and padded into her mama's room. She'd not done that since her tata's death. Lina's room had been silent and still, but Nadica had known instinctively that her mama was not asleep. Without a word, she'd crossed the space to the bedside and slipped between the sheets. Lina had snuggled her close and pressed a soft kiss to her temple.

"We will be okay," she'd whispered against Nadica's hair.

There had been a few fitful hours of sleep, punctuated with dreams that burned. Arguments for staying, the mental reach to refuse the war, to choose a different path for their nation. The panicked feeling that they were making the wrong choice, or that they were already too late. She'd awoken to the scent of instant coffee and her mama's exhausted face.

Now Nadica allows Lina to hug her, one last moment of support before they climb into the small car and Lina fires the engine. Nadica hopes they have made this decision soon enough, that the roads will not be blockaded, that the soldiers are far away, and that now that they have decided to flee, they can make it.

It will be a long drive to Slovenia. The nation is free, their war already won. It is the safest option for them. They will get there, Nadica resolves to herself, together.

As Lina pulls out onto the rough road of their village, a prickling sensation races along Nadica's spine. It feels as though she is being chased.

Turning in her seat she spies him. His hands are shoved in his pockets, the hood of his jumper up over his hair. Relja. Their eyes meet in the building dawn. He is leaving today, too, Nadica knows. Heading for the towns the Serbian front has already claimed along the border. This parting hurts him, as it does her. The final cut between them, severing the future they once imagined they would share. She does not know what this new war will bring, what will happen to her village, to her friends, to her beloved family. All she can do is trust the choice. Flashing a small, sad smile at Relja, Nadica shifts in her seat, facing forward. Her mama reaches over and grips her hand where it rests in her lap.

"Ready?" she says.

"Da," Nadica replies.

A small squeeze of her hand and Lina lets go and grips the gearstick. She shifts gears, presses the accelerator down, and heads towards the distant mountains.

Nadica didn't know it then but they had joined the single greatest migration in Yugoslavian history. After the fall of Vukovar, over 30,000 Ethnic Serbs fled for neighbouring Slovenia and Serbia, terrified of living through a repeat of the ethnic cleansing that had taken place under Ustaše rule. Many of them were previous victims of the camps of World War Two, now once again forced from their homes. Others remained to fight alongside the Yugoslavian forces. The massacre of Croatian civilians in Gospić was not the only mass killing undertaken by Serb extremists. Whether through ideology or fear, through ethnic belief or to protect what was theirs, the result was the same: a bloody war and a decade of conflict and death as the states of Yugoslavia broke apart and the powerful of the union rained hell down on civilians in a battle for land and control. And people fled and died.

As the sun rose above Nadica and Lina's rattling car, they joined an exodus that changed the demographic and shape of Croatia forever. But all Nadica knew was that her aunty was dying and she would not be there to hold her. That her baba would face that grief without her. That Relja would fight and possibly die. That her village may be destroyed.

And that her mama had chosen Nadica's life above them all.

Neither of them had ever been to Slovenia. They'd never left the borders of Croatia. But they were together. Somehow, they would make it.

She prayed for those they left behind, that the conflict would be short.

That she would return home.

Soon.

FORTY-THREE

NADICA

2003 – Twelve Years Later

The house looks familiar and yet different from what Nadica remembers. The woodwork is in perfect condition, and the paint on the windowsills is fresh. But it's smaller, wonkier, the roof undulating unconvincingly instead of straight. Flowers burst from the small gardens that hug the front wall. Nadica smiles. Ilona didn't let them die.

She flips down the sun visor and checks her face. Tired, lined eyes stare back at her, the fatigue of driving pulling at her skin. She steps from her car and stretches out her lower spine. It was a long drive from Ljubljana. A journey back in time, rewinding from their flight twelve years before.

Nadica was behind the wheel this time. Her mama is in her early sixties, Nadica wasn't going to let her drive this trip alone. Not again. She shuts the door and hears her mama close her door at the same time. Their eyes meet over the roof of the car, and a mix of anticipation and pure joy flashes through Nadica.

She smiles at her mama. This is an emotional moment for her as well. They have had contact, of course. Letters mostly, and recently, phone calls. Nadica sent photos of when she married

Jure, and when her daughter was born, her Ana-Misa. But returning was not possible, not until now.

It has been a long twelve years since she stood on this driveway.

Years in which the Croatian Army forced back the Serbian-controlled Yugoslavian forces, and claimed independence for Croatia, honouring the vote of the people. One independence movement sparked another, and nation by nation Yugoslavia broke apart. The last rattle of gunfire only quieted in 1998. Then came justice. War crime tribunals for the massacres of civilians across the former states of Yugoslavia. Ethnic cleansing on various scales. It would take decades for each death to be avenged.

Nothing can make it right. But now, there is a new peace and a new hope. Now it is time to rebuild.

Despite all that has transpired in the twelve years since her mama drove her away from Novska, the memory of that night – leaving and knowing she would never see her aunty Misa alive again, not knowing what would become of their home – never faded.

Villages only a short walk away from her grandparents' home were destroyed in the bombings that rained down over eastern Croatia. Used as a shelter point by Serb extremists, the houses were blasted apart by the advancing Croatian forces. They have been rebuilt. Her childhood home is no longer there. It is okay. It has been a long time since it was home.

Her grandparent's farm was spared, as were their lives. That is all that matters.

Straightening her shoulders, she crosses to her mama and takes her hand. The front door opens. Ilona and Jovan step into the light of the sun, and time freezes. They are older, greyer, stooped. But to Nadica, it is as though she saw them only yesterday.

Suddenly, she is twenty-one again, the scent of plum krofna filling her nose, her squeaking bike tyres bouncing over rocks beneath her. And her heart swells. Bursting into a run as if she were a child again, Nadica surges into her grandparents' arms.

Soft, warm arms wrap around her as a gasp of joy escapes her lips. She feels her mama arrive and join their family huddle. When they break apart, tears glisten on everyone's cheeks.

Gentle fingers cup her face as her baba presses her lips to her forehead. "My dear one."

Then to her mama, "My child."

The lump in Nadica's throat is a physical thing, pulsing with her heartbeat. "We have missed you," she manages to whisper through the overwhelming emotions.

Her baba sniffs back her tears. "You must be exhausted," she says, her hand coming to rest on Nadica's mama's shoulder, her fingers smoothing over the soft wool of her cardigan. "Come in, I have made refreshments."

"Can we visit her first?" Lina says.

The words are sobering, dousing the unbridled joy of this reunion in a wash of loss.

Nadica watches as mama and daughter's eyes meet.

"Da," her deda says. "This way."

Misa is buried beside Nadica's tata. The grave is simple, a small mound beneath a spruce tree at the back of the cleared acre that surrounds the cottage. A wooden cross, expertly sanded and carved with concave edging, marks the spot, engraved with her name: *Misa Ilić. Loving wife and mother. Rest with your family in Heaven.*

Nadica can see the love in the cuts of the paring knife. Her deda didn't rush this creation. The four of them form a semi-circle before the grave, arms slipping around each other's waists, Nadica bracketed by her mama on one side and her deda on the other. Her baba's hand still clasps Lina's shoulder as if she will never let her child go again.

"It was gentle, in the end," her deda says, his voice low. Nadica already knows, Ilona wrote to them. But it is nice to hear of it in person.

"She slept and didn't wake. Stephan and Hanna came for her," her baba says. "They led her to peace."

The old regret pokes at Nadica. The choice to leave. To run to Ljubljana, leaving her grandparents to ease Aunty Misa's passing. Not being there herself to honour her passage. The years have dampened that regret, but its presence holds a sharp edge, even if Nadica knows it was the right choice.

They stand together, silent, each with their own thoughts and memories of Misa. The woman who survived the camps of the Ustaše and the Nazis. Who lost her husband and her children. Who battled cancer twice before she was done. A force and a heart. A woman who will be remembered by them all, for as long as they live. Eventually, they turn as one, back towards the cottage.

Entering the cottage Nadica is overcome by nostalgia. Everything is as it was twelve years before. The fireplace is lit, and wood is piled in a basket on the side. The kitchen is tidy, the scent of fresh baking drifting across the space. The photos that line the sideboard are the only things that have changed. Nadica feels the pride in her smile as she sees her husband and daughter added to the family frames that sit there.

They gather at the kitchen table, and Ilona makes coffee. It is both comfortingly familiar and awkward. Where once their conversation would flow as smoothly and naturally as a spring creek, a story from their last gathering picking up from where it left off and continuing forward, now there is a stone of time between them. So many years of memories unshared. So many challenges faced separately. The connection of common experience eroded away like the banks of a river and shaped into something new. A dam created by distance has opened between them all. No one knows where to begin to close the gap.

But Nadica does. "Ana, she reminds me of aunty. She is fierce."

Ilona huffs a laugh from across the table. "I knew your daughter would be strong. She may remind you of Aunty Misa, but to me, she sounds like you."

And just like that, the cool sensation of distance warms and melts like morning frost, and the words stream from their hearts.

Deda talks of the long nights of the war, and the sound of

gunfire from their village. His hands tremble against his coffee cup as his eyes find his daughter, the thank you that shines from his face is an unspoken message of love to Lina. *You were right to run,* is written in the lines of his mouth, the sag of his jaw. *You were right.*

Baba details her joy at the announcement of Nadica's engagement and marriage. Tears threatening to spill as she speaks of her love for her grandchild. A child she has yet to meet.

"I will bring her, next time," Nadica promises. It was too far to travel with a two-year-old. And Nadica needed this moment for herself, time to reconnect with her past, with her family. Ana is safe with her tata.

Mama laughs as she recounts Ana's first steps, her pudgy cheeks, the first time she said "No".

Nadica listens as the currents of the memories ebb and flow and eddy around them, a cacophony of time, a stream of moments apart, now shared, knitting them back together into a whole after years cut adrift.

"Many left," her deda says. "They won't return." It is phrased as a statement, but a question lingers on its edges.

Lina clears her throat and Nadica turns to her mama. Lina says, "Actually, I was thinking I might stay a while longer. If that is alright with—"

"This has been your home since you were four," Ilona interrupts. "Your home has never changed."

Lina nods, lips wobbling.

"I will return to Ljubljana alone," Nadica takes up the conversation. "But Jure and I will visit with Ana soon."

Her deda nods, but she sees his disappointment. She understands. He had hoped that they would all return to their lives in Croatia. That they would return to how things were before the Croatian War of Independence. He, of all people, knows that cannot be. War changes everything. Too much time has passed, too much pain and too much new life. Nadica's place is in Slovenia with her husband and child now.

But she will always be tied to Croatia. To these people who loved and raised her.

That warms her heart.

"Relja survived," her deda continues, and Nadica blinks in surprise. She hasn't thought of her ex-boyfriend in years. His dark, haunted eyes. His anger. "He had to flee," Deda continues. "Most of those who fought for Serbia did. A refugee exodus to the west. The fighting was brutal."

Fear dances momentarily in his eyes, and Nadica isn't sure which war her deda is referring to. He has seen so much. More than anyone should ever have to bear.

"That must have been hard. I know he was special to you," Nadica says. She means it. Things may not have worked out between her and Relja, but he was good to her deda.

Jovan shrugs. "I pray he found peace."

A knock sounds on the door and they all look up.

"Oh," Ilona says, standing stiffly. "I didn't realise the time."

"You are expecting someone?" Lina asks, her forehead crinkling.

"Da. There is a young film crew interviewing survivors of the Ustaše. They wanted to talk to me about my work with Diana Budisavljević."

Nadica's mind reels back to Misa's bedside. To the days of stories that revealed Nadica's parentage and past and the bravery of her family.

Ilona is at the door greeting someone warmly. The door conceals the person, but her voice is high and sweet. Ilona steps back, gesturing to Nadica and her family at the table.

"This is my family," she is saying. "My husband Jovan, my daughter Lina and her child, Nadica."

A woman of an age with Nadica stands at Ilona's side. She is small, with short fair hair, her eyes quick and darting. She smiles and gives a little wave. "Hello, everyone. My name is Sara."

FORTY-FOUR
SARA

Sara climbs the stairs to her baba's apartment. A curl of her blonde hair tickles her ear, and she puffs from the corner of her mouth in an attempt to blow the itching strands from her skin. The itch is just a distraction from the churning thoughts in her mind. Sara feels strange; a mix of pride and deepest grief sits in her chest after her interview with Ilona and Nadica. It is the first recording she's done with a nurse who worked directly with Diana Budisavljević. The risk those women took and the horrors they faced are simply incredible to bear witness to.

Throughout the months she has been researching for her documentary, interviewing the survivors of the camps, there was only the horrors and pain, the loss and fear. So many children were torn from their families. So much sadness. But speaking with Ilona, for the first time, Sara has seen the strength and resilience of those who stood up against the Ustaše. Of people like Diana Budisavljević, who did not turn a blind eye and hide away but stepped up, risked their own lives and saved the innocent. It is truly awe-inspiring. It is something to be proud of in a history darkened by the unforgivable. How she wishes she was born twenty years earlier, so she might have interviewed Diana herself. It was her initiative, after all. Without her determination to act, those children might all have died. Diana used her position in society, her intelligence and her language skills and made a difference. A true hero of the war.

Ilona did so much, too. Married to a Serb, her best friend already imprisoned in a labour camp, her parents abandoned her to her fate. And despite it all, she chose to help. She donated what she could, she joined the Red Cross nurses providing food for those being transported to Germany, and she helped move the children from the camps. And when new fear came knocking, she helped to whisk those children into the countryside for safety, adopting one of the orphans and giving Lina a home. Meeting the whole family allowed Sara to see the full cycle. To witness the love and hope that could come out of such tragedy.

It reminds her of her own family.

Her personal reason for making this documentary.

Her baba was in the camps, old enough to be put to work, young enough to survive. When the Croatian War of Independence began in 1991, Sara had left university in Rijeka, and rushed back to Zagreb to be with her baba and mama. They holed up in her home in the lower town of Zagreb and faced the bombings, taping over their windows and praying that common sense would prevail and Croatia could claim its independence without violence. It had been hard for Sara, returning to live under her baba's roof, giving up her studies, but it had been the only choice. A choice that would become life changing.

It was the first time Sara realised the rift between her mama and baba. The silence when they were in the same room. The furtive glances, her mama's angry frown.

Sara didn't know if it was the tension of the time, the fear of the bombs and guns, that had her mama pulling away from her baba. Or if that anger had always bubbled beneath a surface she'd never noticed before. It was something her mama would not speak of, not even now.

They survived, and Croatia won her freedom. But their family issues didn't dissipate with the end of the war. It was like a symbol of the divisions within her nation, and it sparked an idea, a way to further understand the past and her country. She returned to Rijeka and finished her studies, becoming a lecturer. Then her real work began: her documentary of the stories of the children who survived the Ustaše.

At her baba's apartment door, she pulls her keys from her bag, balancing her camera case awkwardly on her hip to ferret around until she hears the tell-tale clang of metal and unlocks the door. The apartment is small and immaculately neat. Her baba moved here after a fall three years ago. The old house was too large, the garden too sprawling for an ageing woman to manage alone. Sara had done most of the work to help her baba move. Her mama was less helpful. The memory still grates, but Sara has learnt not to press on issues between her mama and baba.

Despite that tension, Sara has loved staying here in Zagreb with her baba while she does the interviews for her documentary across central Croatia. It is easy and convenient; she is fed delicious food, and she gets to spend time with her beloved baba.

"Sara? Is that you?" Baba calls from down the hall. She's probably in the kitchen warming potatoes and cabbage for Sara's dinner. She's lived in the city most of her life, but she still cooks like she's in a country kitchen.

"Da, Baba. It's me," Sara calls. It is unnecessary. No one else has a key. But it is a ritual, a part of living between the same walls as another person. Sara likes it. It certainly beats being alone in her apartment in Rijeka. She's missed living in the capital, and being close to family.

She walks down the hallway, passing the bedrooms and coming into the open-plan kitchen and dining area. Her baba looks up. She is small and thin; her tiny bones remind Sara of a bird, her movements slow and cautious. But her face creases in a smile that lights up her eyes and calms Sara's mind. Small lines of concern wrinkle her brow. "Oh, dear one, you look so tired. It was a big day?"

"Da," Sara answers simply, unhooking her satchel and camera bag from her shoulder and setting them on the couch. "A lot of travel." It is true that a round trip to Novska is several hours on a train, but that's not the whole story. Sara hasn't quite found the words for the emotions swirling within her. Not yet. Rolling her neck, she joins her baba in the kitchen, pressing a kiss to her cheek. The potatoes smell amazing.

After a soul-filling shared meal with her baba, Sara settles herself at the computer that sits on a small folding table in the corner of the lounge. She brought the little table and computer with her when she came to stay; she didn't want to take up her baba's dining space. Taking out her camera she plugs the video card into the larger computer screen and begins to review the day's footage. Ilona and Nadica's faces fill her screen, and a wistfulness comes over Sara. The love and bond between everyone in that room moved her to her core. Despite being separated for years, this family never lost their connection. It is beautiful to witness. An opposite to her own family, forced together and driven apart.

Shaking away the thought, she focuses and listens as Ilona begins:

"Diana was so elegant, so beautiful. But when we first arrived at that camp, I had never seen someone so fierce..."

Behind her the domestic sounds of her baba tidying the kitchen echo softly, encasing Sara in the comfort and safety of home as she delves into hell.

"They had hidden the sickest children away. Perhaps to separate them and stop the spread of disease, but it is hard to give them any credit. That is how I found my Lina."

The Ilona on the video looks away across the house, meeting the eyes of her adopted daughter off-screen. It was a tender, beautiful moment. The nurse and the orphan, brought together by tragedy, healed by love. Sara's heart clenches at the memory. She wished she could have recorded it, but Lina didn't want to be videoed. Sara will always respect those wishes.

"My friend Misa was not so lucky. She was separated from her husband and children. When she was transported to a German labour camp, we met briefly on the platform at Zagreb Station. It

was a gift from God to give us that moment together. She asked me to find her children. But I failed."

The word is heavy and full of pain. Sara watches Nadica's hand clasp Ilona's firmly.

"*Misa died twelve years ago, never knowing what became of her babies.*"

Nadica stands at that point, disappearing from the video briefly and returning with a large framed photograph of a middle-aged woman. Dark hair frames a heart-shaped face. She is plain but pleasant of face. Her lips are curved in a smile, but the brown eyes that shine out from the picture are hollow and empty.

"*My aunty Misa,*" video Nadica says, holding up the frame. "*She was strong, right to the end.*"

The soft tread of slippered feet draws Sara's notice, and she looks up at her baba's approach, pausing her recording. "I thought you might like a hot chocolate," baba says, her old eyes soft with kindness. Sara can't help the wry smile that twists her lips. She is not a child any more. But it is so nice to be mothered.

"Thank you, Baba," she says reaching up for the cup.

Her baba's gaze drifts up to the video, paused on the frame of Misa's photograph. She freezes, her lips part in a gasp and her hands begin to shake violently. Then, her spindly fingers go slack, dropping the hot chocolate. The cup spins through the air, a splash of milky chocolate spraying free.

Eyes widening in surprise, Sara reaches to catch the cup, but she's not quick enough. The cup hits the wooden floor with a sharp crack, hot liquid spurting across the surface in a violent brown splatter.

"Baba? Are you okay?" Sara pushes back her chair and grips her baba's shoulders. She is pale with shock. "Don't worry," Sara says. "I will tidy up. You take a seat, Baba." She bends down to collect the fractured pieces of the cup. "I'll get a towel," she says, standing to find a bin and cloth to clean up the sticky liquid. But her baba's hand has clutched her elbow, her fingers pinching into the cotton of her shirt.

"Baba?" Sara pauses, hands holding two large pieces of cup, sticky hot chocolate coating her fingers.

"Who is that?" her baba asks, pointing a trembling finger at the computer screen.

Sara frowns, not understanding. "A friend of the family I interviewed today. She was in the camps, like you. She lost her family too. Now, come, sit down and I'll get this cleaned up."

Her baba doesn't move. "Baba? It's okay, we all drop things." Sara knows her baba worries about getting older, especially since the fall. Now that she is nearing eighty, she doesn't want to lose her independence. Moving into a home would be like returning to a camp to her. Sara would move in with her permanently before she let that happen. "It's honestly all right," she assures her baba, an encouraging smile on her face.

But her baba isn't listening. Her entire being is focused on the screen. Sara watches as her baba swallows, her lips parting. "Was her name Misa?"

The air goes out of the room, and everything seems to slow around her. Sara stares at her baba. "How did you know that?" she asks, her voice a whisper as her heart begins to drum.

Her baba turns slowly to her, her milky eyes suddenly sharp. She wears an expression of wonder. "Because I knew her."

FORTY-FIVE

ILONA

Ilona cannot sit still. Lifting the third tray of krofna dough from the bench and sliding them into the oven, she feels her back stiffen but ignores it. She doesn't want to sit down and rest, her body won't allow it.

She woke with the first dim rays of light through her curtains and had known instantly that she would not return to sleep. Jovan continued to snore quietly beside her. She allowed herself to lay there a while, the warmth of his body seeping into her skin. But the usual comfort of his presence did nothing to still her racing heartbeat. So she got up.

Tray of krofna in the oven, Ilona gathers up a wet cloth and paces into the lounge. One by one, she lifts the photo frames that sit along the sideboard, wiping the frames to clean away the dust, then the surface of the sideboard, and replaces them carefully. There is no dust, though. She did all of this yesterday. Yet she cannot stop herself from checking again. She doesn't want to miss a speck.

A warm arm circles around her waist, the fingers tucking into the edge of her apron. Jovan is old, they both are, the winter years of their life are deepening. But he is still strong, his touch familiar and welcome. Ilona's hands still and she leans back into her husband's embrace.

"I didn't hear you wake," he says quietly by her ear, his voice gentle. "Have you been up long?"

"Not so long," Ilona replies.

"Three batches of krofna?" She feels his amused smile against her cheek.

"Why ask if you know?" she challenges.

A huff, then Jovan turns her around to face him. Her hands rise to smooth over his stubbly cheeks, the lines and wrinkles are dips and markers of time. Time together. She would not trade one of them.

"It will be all right," he says, lowering his forehead to hers. "This is a blessing. A miracle."

"I just wish..."

"I know."

"Oooh, krofna for breakfast. What a treat." Nadica's voice floats through the house. Ilona goes to move, but Jovan holds her firm for one moment longer. One more moment, just of them. "I will be with you."

"Thank you."

They break apart, and Ilona goes to her granddaughter.

"Today is a special day."

Nadica looks at her, a line forming between her brows. It's always been there when she frowns, since she was a small child. The years have deepened it and added fine lines around her eyes. She is still beautiful. Nadica is a wife and a mama now. The facts are there, Ilona has the photos to prove it. But it seems like it was only yesterday that she was sneaking pastries from the pantry on weekends. The world just won't stay still. It never has. Ilona sighs. So many years were lost because of war. The years when her granddaughter became a woman, began her own family...

At least Nadica still loves her baba's krofna.

"How are you feeling?" Nadica asks as Ilona plates up some krofna from the first batch.

"Nervous and excited," Ilona answers honestly. "And grateful you are all here with me."

It is the simple truth. What a blessing that God has brought her family together under her roof for this day. She eyes her grand-daughter. "Are you wearing that?"

Nadica looks down at her blouse and jeans. "Da? Or no... I can change."

"A skirt would be better."

Ilona doesn't miss the amused smile on Nadica's face as she turns away to change.

Later when the knock sounds on the door, Ilona's breath catches. Lina is beside her on the couch, their arms linked together. Nadica stands and heads to the door, the blue of her skirt swishing around her legs. She pauses a moment before opening it, scanning them all as they sit gathered in the lounge. Her gaze pauses on Ilona a moment, a question in her eyes. Ilona nods. Nadica opens the door.

The three women who enter are obviously related, it's in the shape of their brows and the curve of their smiles. Ilona's assessment falls on the older woman, and her heart jumps into a gallop.

She pushes herself up on shaking legs and holds her hand to her chest in a gesture of warmth and says, "Ladies, Sara, you have met us, but for your mama and baba, I am Ilona. Misa was my best friend in all of the world. This is my husband Jovan, my daughter Lina and my granddaughter Nadica. Welcome to our home."

Sara smiles and nods. She is doing a good job of appearing calm, but Ilona can see the nerves. It's in the flush of her skin and the small beads of perspiration on her upper lip. "It is lovely to see you all again. And to learn..." Sara pauses, glancing across at her baba. "I guess the introduction is unnecessary, but for formality, this is my mama, Maja."

The middle-aged woman nods. She is fair-haired like her daughter. She doesn't seem nervous, only deeply tired. Sara continues, pointing to a feather-light older lady of diminutive size. She is younger than Ilona, but appears weaker, more cowed. She is the reason they are all gathered here. "And this is my baba, Kata."

"She protected me like I was her own blood. Fought like a mother to keep me safe. I didn't understand that then, not until I had my own child." Her eyes flick to Maja, but the middle-aged lady isn't looking; her focus is trained on the cup of coffee Nadica placed before her. "I would not be here if it were not for her." They are settled at the kitchen table, a pile of plum-filled krofna on a plate in the centre. Kata holds the large framed photo of Misa before her, staring at the picture. Tenderly, she runs a finger down the frame, her eyes misting with tears.

"I wish I found you sooner..." Her voice hitches and she turns away, sniffing softly. Ilona's arms ache to wrap around her, but Sara is there, pressed close to her baba. As is right.

What a story has unfolded this day. What an unexpected blessing.

Misa spoke often of the young girl she met in Lobor-Grad. Of the bond that developed between them. Misa said that Kata was dead; murdered by Nazis because she became pregnant. And Ilona had no reason to doubt that story. So many lives were lost in those camps. Too many tragic, meaningless deaths. The awful receipt of war.

They never searched for Kata. Never thought to confirm the events in the camp. You didn't search for the dead. It might seem strange to Nadica, Ilona realises. In the modern world, every death is confirmed, funerals are held and burial rites are honoured. But in war? Too many people simply disappeared. And Stephan and Hanna were still unaccounted for. They took up all of Misa's focus.

Now, to learn the girl had lived. That she had given birth to the child she was pregnant with when Misa met her in the camp. Named her Maja, and despite it all somehow they had both survived. It was a miracle.

If only Misa were still with us. Ilona's thought is heavy with sadness.

"She cradled me in Lobor-Grad," Kata continues. "So the men could not come for me again at night. On the trip to Germany, she nursed my sickness and helped me to hide my condition." Ilona notes how Maja stiffens at those words and her chest tightens. What a burden to be born with, to know your life came from violence.

Kata puts down the photo and turns to her daughter and cups her face with her hands. She's so small the touch seems insubstantial, but her words are firm. "She is why I lived and why you lived. I thank her memory every day for that gift. I love you."

Tears of shame are in Maja's eyes. There is a tension across her shoulders that shows a barrier between her and the full truth of those words. Gently releasing her daughter's face, Kata turns back to the photo.

"She protected me every night until the one she could not. I heard her screaming for me. I know how hard she fought. There was nothing she could have done." Kata falls silent.

Ilona's throat is tight. There are so many questions she wants to ask about Misa at the camp, about Kata's life after the war, her family, her joys and sorrows, her reality. But first, she must share what she knows Misa would wish her to say. Misa cannot be here, so Ilona must speak for her. She must honour her oldest and dearest friend.

"Misa loved you like a sister." The words are soft, but their truth is a foundation. "When she returned from the camps, she was destroyed, broken down by the brutality of it all. She needed to stop and heal. So we welcomed her here to stay, and she did. But she never stopped searching for her children. Her Stephan and Hanna. No matter what obstacles came, she pushed through, for them." She pauses, shaking her head. "If she had thought you lived..."

"She could not have known," Kata says sadly. Her lips twist in an ugly grimace. "I barely did."

Ilona feels a rush of sympathy for the woman. How she wishes it could have been different. But it does no good to dwell on what we cannot change. Diana taught her that. It has been one of the most important lessons of Ilona's life.

"Misa found a type of acceptance, eventually," Ilona says. "She always refused to leave the borders of Croatia. She insisted that this is where her children and husband were: alive or..." She leaves the last part unsaid. It isn't needed.

Kata sucks in a breath. "I was in Zagreb. That was where the army took me after my camp was liberated. All this time I was so close."

An opportunity lost. They sit in a shared moment of regret for all that might have been. Had Misa known Kata lived, could she have found her? Could that reunion have brought some solace to her shattered heart? It was not to be, sadly. So beaten down by her time bent under the burden of labour for Germany, how could Misa have had any hope left for a pregnant teenager's fate? Yet finding her would have been something.

It would not have been enough. But it would have been something.

"Did you return to family?" Ilona asks.

Kata shakes her head as her face drops. "Our town was destroyed. My mama and tata didn't survive the round-up. My brothers... I never found any record of them. Perhaps they lived full lives with new families. Or perhaps..." She shrugs. They all understand. "Misa was the last person who was like family to me until my own daughter was born. I found it hard to trust. I never married."

"What happened after you were taken?" Nadica ventures gently. "Aunty Misa was so sure she had lost you."

Kata's eyes drop down to the photo of Misa again and they all wait in silence, watching as she gathers her memories, her mouth working against the pull of fear. Ilona can see it, she knows the look, she remembers it clouding her husband's eyes throughout long, dark nights after he was rescued from the Ustaše prison by her brother. She is desperate to offer Kata comfort but knows there is nothing she can say that will bring Kata from the fog of the past. The only thing that helps is being there, a presence so no one is alone. So she waits in silence. She will listen to what Kata has to say, no matter how it hurts.

"I thought I was lost too," Kata finally begins. "But somehow I was not. At least not permanently. I was taken to a mothers' camp. There were so many of us. Young and old, and pregnant. As the babies were born, one after the other, they were taken squalling from their mama's breast." Her voice wobbles dangerously on the edge of sobbing, and Kata pauses. No one speaks. There is nothing to say.

"The mamas were sent on to continue their work for the Reich. The soldiers gave them no time to heal, just sent them back out into the fields straight from childbirth."

"Why?" the question has slipped from Nadica's lips. Ilona feels pity blanket her body as she turns to her granddaughter. A new mama herself. What an awful fate to imagine. To have your child torn from your side. Ilona can see the understanding that cuts through Nadica. An understanding of her aunty Misa, of all that the parents of Croatia lost in those bloody years.

"They wanted to claim all the children of Germany," Kata answers. "When they realised that my daughter wasn't fathered by a German, they didn't want her. So we were allowed to stay together. They moved us to the labour camp with the other mothers whose babies they'd taken. The barracks smelt of curdled milk from their impacted breasts and pus from their birthing wounds. Many died. I thought I would die..."

She breaks off, turning to her daughter again. This time, she reaches across and takes Maja's hand in hers, her slender fingers are pale against Maja's robust palm. "But you were so strong. You fed well and cried heartily and grew big. You gave me strength, a reason to fight, a reason to open my eyes every morning, a reason to survive every night. Together, we lived long enough for the British soldiers to arrive and free us. Long enough to be returned to Zagreb."

"How did you survive? Was there help for you in Zagreb?" Nadica asks.

Kata meets her eyes. "No. I was a mother, so they classified me as an adult, not a child. My life and my daughter's life were my own responsibility. I found work at a church cleaning the administration offices. The nuns were kind; they often gave me loaves of bread left over from their daily meals. And they allowed me to bring Maja to work. It was low pay, but I made ends meet."

"You were so close. All that time." Ilona can't help but sigh. "Misa would have been so happy to find you." Their conversation lulls, but this time it is a reflective silence. It allows them all some time alone in their thoughts, to find their feet on this shifting ground.

Then Ilona offers. "Would you like to see her now?"

"Da," Kata says. "I want to introduce her to my family. It is hers too, in my heart."

They gather together at the back of the yard, under the spruce. Ilona watches as Kata bends to place a beautiful bouquet of flowers on Misa's grave. She whispers some words that the breeze lifts up and away. For Misa only.

And an unfamiliar feeling washes over Ilona. It has the shape of peace, but its edges are rough and unrefined. It isn't solid and sure, but there is relief in it. A realisation blooms.

It is nearly time.

Misa lost her family, but her kindness and strength live on in Kata, Maja and Sara, who is making a documentary to honour the survivors and victims of the Ustaše. Recording the stories of the children brought to Zagreb, the Serb children stolen from their families and left to die. Through the bravery of Diana Budisavljević and the Red Cross nurses, some survived. Ilona was part of that. For the first time in a long time, she allows a feeling of pride to pass through her. She doesn't let it settle; she is not boastful. But when she stands here with her family and the family Misa saved, she can see the power of taking a stand, of doing something. Her work for the children trapped in the Ustaše camps, Jovan's fight with the Partisans and Misa's protection of an orphaned girl in Germany; they each did what they could with what they had.

And they made a difference.

Now, Sara is taking up that cause, recording an uncomfortable and terrible history so it is not forgotten. It cannot be allowed to be forgotten. It can never be allowed to happen again. She is doing what she can in the eternal fight for freedom. In the fight for what is right.

The breeze is cooling as the sun dips behind the spruce forest.

"Will you stay for supper?" Ilona asks.

"If it is no trouble?" Kata says.

"It is never any trouble to share supper with family."

Kata meets her eyes and the moment stretches. Ilona feels her storm of emotions: grief, sorrow, joy and thanks.

"Come, come," Ilona says. Reaching forward she links her arm with Kata's patting her arm twice. "I have extra proja corn cakes. I hope you like goulash."

"I love it," Kata says.

FORTY-SIX
SARA

Zagreb 2003

The documentary aired two weeks ago. The days since have been a whirlwind for Sara and Daniel. TV and radio interviews, articles in newspapers, and requests from the Croatian government for resources to make a film about Diana Budisavljević. It is everything Sara imagined. And it is too much.

The bleakness that begun to settle over her chest as she met with the survivors and heard their stories in their own words has not lifted. No, it has deepened.

Sara always knew the history: that Serbs were rounded up in camps during World War Two. Her baba was one of them after all. But Diana Budisavljević did not feature in that story. Aktion Diana B was a history Sara discovered all on her own. At first, she'd been fascinated to learn of this Austrian woman who had risked her life for the children in the camps. Her work wasn't perfect of course, nothing is. In her struggle to free the children Diana sent some to a camp run by Red Cross nurses. It did not go well. Just as some children in foster homes and orphanages were mistreated. When she read the camp statistics, she'd been horrified. The number of children affected was far greater than she could ever have imagined. Mistakes were going to be made when fighting against an oppressive, murderous regime. At least Diana had stood up and done something.

Her bravery inspired Sara. She wanted to know more, to capture that piece of history, record it. Make sure it never happens again.

But as the survivors spoke, as she listened to their stories, something within her shifted.

Her original goal was still there, and it remained one she believed in. But it wasn't everything. Not any more.

Feeling restless, Sara pulls on her coat and steps outside, locking her baba's door behind her. It's a Sunday. The streets of Zagreb are quiet. The bells of morning service have fallen silent and people are at home, relaxing with their families, completing domestic tasks, and perhaps starting to prepare dinner. The sun is tracking down the sky, its pale rays tinting the clouds in a gentle yellow. And she strolls.

As her feet pace along the pavement, their stories fill her mind. The lost soul of Jakov, the cheeky smile of Milena, the determination of Stana, the horrors of Jelena, the bravery of Ilona. So many voices, so many accounts. So much pain.

Diana Budisavljević saved over 15,000 children from those camps, but only 12,000 of them survived. Not all those who survived, lived. *Surviving* and *living* are not the same thing. Sara has documented their experiences, made a record that cannot be ignored.

And her work uncovered something so unexpected: the connection between her baba and Misa. The woman who saved her baba's life. The reason Sara exists at all.

She hadn't been searching for her own past, yet it had come for her anyway.

She winds her way through the streets, her mind spiralling outwards into the city of Zagreb. It is a different place now. After decades of war and friction, a hope for a peaceful future has begun to blossom. Sara believes her home can prosper. That the people can come together. All sides of the past must be acknowledged for that to materialise.

The sigh escapes her lips before she can stop it. It is a grand hope. Especially when her own mama struggles to accept that she is wanted and loved. The divide between her mama and baba makes sense now. The truth of Maja's conception cast a pall of shame over her whole life. Sara didn't know that story, not until her baba recognised Misa on the computer screen. She'd always believed her deda died in the war. Discovering he was a brutal Ustaše soldier had turned the world on its head.

Now she sees the reason behind her baba's silence and her mama's quiet anger. They could not talk of the past because it hurt her mama. Maja has never felt she has a place in this world, no matter what Kata says.

Once, Sara might not have understood. Who cares who Maja's tata was? Baba loved her without exception. But now, hearing the history from the mouths of survivors has coloured the reality much darker, and redder, than pages of text in a book. Facts are one thing. Human experience is quite another.

Now she sees her mama's conflict. To know what type of man fathered her. What type of man Sara's own deda was. It hurts. But it does not change how Sara feels about herself, her mama or her baba.

It makes her determined. Because she is not her deda or her past; she is her own person, shaped by her experiences and the stories of her loved ones. Safe in the present, Sara can learn from the cruelty that sits in her ancestry, acknowledge it and choose a different future. One day she hopes her mama can learn to do the same.

She winds past Zagreb Cathedral, its tall white towers glowing in the fading light. She's never been inside. It is a Catholic monument, not the Orthodox of her family. But perhaps she should one day. It is part of her city too. A cold wind whips around the stone walls of the Cathedral, eliciting a ghostly whisper. Sara shrugs deeper into her coat and turns back for her baba's apartment.

The door opens to the soft hum of voices, and Sara's mouth purses in surprise. Her baba never has visitors.

As she hangs her coat on the hook by the door the voices take shape: the familiar wobble of her baba, the deeper tones of her tata and a soft, nervous twitter. Her mama has come to visit. How long since they were last together in her baba's home? Keeping her body calm, Sara enters the open kitchen and dining space. The two women she loves most in the world are sitting face to face at the kitchen table, a pot of coffee between them. Her tata is standing at her mama's side, one hand resting on her shoulder in an unspoken gesture of comfort.

There is an unfamiliar sensation in the air. Sara pauses. Her baba looks up, her eyes red-rimmed from crying. Concern flashes through Sara. Not more discord between them. Please no.

Then her baba smiles the most beautiful smile Sara has ever seen. Her mama and tata turn then, her mama's cheeks are streaked with tears. She stands, breaking from her husband's comforting touch and crossing to where Sara hovers on the edge of the room. Sara is enveloped in a crushing hug. Her arms return her mama's embrace automatically, but her eyes seek her tata over her mama's shoulder, confusion furrowing her brow. He watches on, arms crossed over his chest, lips wobbling as he holds back his own emotions.

"Thank you," Maja says, returning Sara's attention to her mama.

"You are welcome?" The words end on a question, and her mama breathes a laugh.

"Come, sit, and I will explain."

Sara allows herself to be settled at the table, coffee poured and biscuits offered.

Then her mama takes her hands. "I watched it," she says.

"We both did," her tata adds. He has moved to the small

window that overlooks the square. Leaning back on the windowsill he faces Sara. Pride shines on his face.

Sara's eyebrows hit her hairline. Her mama hated Sara's plan to make a documentary. Maja was firmly and vocally against it right from the start. Sara's eyes narrow instinctively on her mama. "What happened to 'let the past alone'?" she asks.

Maja gives a wistful smile, her fingers fidgeting on the tabletop. "Misa."

They haven't really spoken since the meeting with Misa's friends in Novska. It was so much for them all to process, and Sara had been distracted with the documentary release. Clearly her mama has been wrestling with her feelings too.

"Go on," Sara prompts. She doesn't want to assume what her mama is saying. She needs to hear the words from her, she needs that confirmation.

Her mama closes her eyes for a moment, her mouth working as if she is searching her tongue for the words.

"Tell her your heart," Kata says across the table.

Maja opens her eyes. "I wasn't happy when you told me your documentary plan. To me, the past is just that, the past. Why drag it all up? Why relive that pain? I saw it as a waste of time. I saw it as reliving trauma." She pauses, taking a deep breath.

"Then you rang, and said you'd met the friends of the woman who saved mama in the camps... I couldn't believe it."

"Neither could we," Kata says. "When I saw that photo..."

Sara sees the look that passes between her baba and her mama, the open flow of love. A sense of possibility expands within her chest.

"Meeting that family. Meeting Ilona and her adopted daughter, Lina. Hearing of all she did for the children..." She is staring at Kata, water building up in her eyes again. "Those children could have been you if not for a regime's decision to treat teenagers as adults. But you weren't. You were sent to work. And you were brutalised. Became pregnant with me.

"That should have been the end of me. Right then and there.

Misa was a nurse. She knew how to end a pregnancy. She should have hated me, or the potential of me. She should have offered to remove my life and set you free. And you should have agreed."

Kata is shaking her head. "Misa would never have offered that. I could never... I feared for you and for me, da, that is true. But I always loved you."

"So you always said," Maja says softly, eyelids fluttering. "But I could never believe it. Not after I learnt of all the Ustaše did in those camps. That wound, it hasn't healed. Look at the fear that resurfaced just twelve years ago when Croatia voted for independence. A new war, a divide between our people. I am that divide: your daughter and his. People fled, even Ilona's family left, because of the actions men like my father took. How could I align that part of who I am?"

Sara's mouth flies open to protest. Her mama is so, so very wrong. No one sees her as her father's daughter. They have only ever seen her as baba's child. Maja has nothing to answer for. But Sara stills the words as she realises what is happening here, and her breathing slows.

Her mama is being interviewed.

Maja is sharing her story of the trauma of war. She has reached the point in her life where she is ready to look back, ready to share. She has come here to unburden her past. Just as with the survivors in every interview Sara has conducted over the months she spent on her documentary, her role now is to listen. Not to interrupt, reframe, argue or direct. She must be quiet and calm. She must not show judgment. She must let Maja speak her truth. The realisation is weightless in her stomach. Everyone needs to speak freely and unburden their soul. Everyone needs the space to find their past and claim what they want from it. Today it is her mama's turn.

"I thought your documentary would only prove my own belief of myself. The stories of the children that men like my father hurt. But I was wrong."

Sara waits in silence. Longing fills her body. A great aching need for this acceptance, for this moment of healing for all of her family.

Maja continues. "What you have created here, in these interviews... I thought it was just about a record, and as important as that may be, I could not support it. It was too personal, too close. It hurt too much. But now I see your work is so much more. It is the truth. Like an open hand extended from the past into the present. It is understanding and healing."

She searches Sara's face as if looking for something small and fragile.

A sadness dims her eyes. "Your work cannot undo the trauma, the pain and fear. It cannot fix the breaks that are so old they have weathered into separate pieces. But it can bring our people together, even just a little bit. And for me..."

Maja reaches out, palm up, offering her hand to Sara. Sara grips her hand as Maja repeats the gesture to Kata. Sara takes her baba's hand, completing the circle between them.

"Ilona said her own brother was Ustaše. But he saved her husband, Jovan. Misa knew how I came to be. And she helped to keep me alive. Fought for you, Mama. Fought for me.

"It doesn't change the horrors. It doesn't change what happened. But that isn't me."

"It never was," Baba whispers. "Nor was it your daughter."

Maja shakes her head. "I never believed you were anything but perfect," she says to Sara.

Weight sluices from Sara's shoulders. A burden she'd never realised she bore. And suddenly Sara understands the shift within her since finishing the documentary. It wasn't just the history that drove her to record those interviews. It was also her own search for herself. In her mama's confused identity, and the tension between her and baba, Sara's own self-worth had been undermined. She hadn't understood it, but it pressed on her. A weight made of unspoken pain. She'd fought it. Pushed it down. Then made a documentary to try and absolve it.

None of that was the answer. This was. This moment of her mama's acceptance. Now, she could set it free.

"Horrid, unforgivable things happened," Maja continues. "And decades later war came again. But we survived. And now our nation is settled. And we can craft a better future. You, my daughter, are that future."

"Thank you, Mama," Sara says, her breath suddenly lighter. "Together, one step at a time."

"Da," Kata says. "One step at a time."

THE MORNING is crisp and clear, the dew lightly sprinkled over the grasses that spread to the edge of the spruce forest that edges Ilona's home. Her slippered feet move slow and calm, her chest rising and falling with the cadence of peace.

Under her roof, the roof that was once her grandparents', the roof that sheltered her and Ivica, and later Jovan and Lina and now Nadica, her family sleeps. Her heart beats. The world is still.

Still and safe.

She shuffles to her seat on the porch, and rests her hand on the sanded wood. A bird tweets in the eves to her left. She raises her head and smiles. So small, so fragile. But free.

Freedom.

It is the right of every person, yet it tore her country apart. What does it mean, this freedom?

There were times when Ilona thought she knew. Times when she railed against injustice. Days she wavered. Nights she cried.

Because she doesn't know. She doesn't know.

Born under the Austrian-Hungarian Empire. Ethnically Croat and Catholic. She loved and still loves a Serb.

She saved children from Ustaše brutality.

She lived while Serb extremists massacred Croat civilians.

She stands on Croatian land, her family's land, that has been Austrian, Yugoslavian, German, Ustaše, Croatian. But always her family's land.

So what is the answer? What is the meaning?

Decades of hate and death and pain and loss, and what is the meaning?

Now, it seems to be peace. It has been five years since the last government-ordered bullet stole a life in the Balkans. Five years since they re-drew their borders.

For the last time?

Or for now?

Ilona doesn't know, and she is so tired, too tired. It is time to stop wondering about a forever peace. She is alive.

And sleeping in her bed is her Jovan, whose family were born east of here.

In the room downstairs lays her daughter. Her Lina.

A Serb child. Origin unknown.

The memories from the Ustaše camps haunt Ilona's dreams. Lina's skeletal body, her sunken eyes. She can still see the lines of malnourishment on her daughter's face. They aren't real any more, of course, but for Ilona, they will never fade.

Are they why she chose as she did? Why she lied over and over again?

In the days after she brought Jovan to the safety of this farm, Ilona claimed Lina as her own, called her daughter, and allowed Lina to call her and Jovan mama and tata. She would not have revealed that lie. She would never have told Lina the truth. Lina didn't need those memories, didn't need a history in which her own country tried to murder her.

It would have worked too.

Except Misa returned. Something about Misa triggered the child's memory, drawing the cold and fear from where trauma had buried it in her subconscious. Lina's nightmares of the camps intensified. In the end, they had no choice. Lina needed to know the truth; she had to face that trauma. At least she had Ilona and Jovan by her side.

When Nadica was born, Ilona lied again. Despite raising Lina as her own, the girl fell for an Orthodox Serb. A fellow child victim of the camps. Ilona understood. She married for love too, after all. And she'd liked Davor. He was a good husband and a wonderful tata.

But a Serb baby born during an uneasy truce was dangerous. So Ilona decided to make her granddaughter Croat too. They'd all agreed. Nadica didn't need to know the truth of Lina's parentage. And Davor didn't need to worship his religion openly. It was a shield against the past. A way to ensure Nadica's safety in the future.

Did Ilona truly believe it was needed? She doesn't know. Not any more.

But they did it. They kept the truth from Nadica and got on with their lives. War came and blew it all up again anyway.

Two lies, both taken to protect, to shield. Two misdirections to keep those who mattered most to her safe.

But there was a third.

Sliding off her slippers, Ilona takes the steps down the porch one by one. Her legs aren't as steady as they once were. Her bare feet sink into the cool grass, dew from the night still clinging to the blades. It feels good; it feels real. Taking her time, she picks her way across the grasses towards the edge of the spruce forest. The thicket of trees is enough to last her Jovan a lifetime of firewood. An amused smile twists her lips. He likes to take care of them all.

At Misa's grave, she stops. It is nice that she is here beside Davor, that she is not in the ground alone.

"Hello, dear friend," she says. The orange blush of dawn is strengthening, the colours of the farm around her brightening as the rays of the sun build and shine across the fields. Dawn is her favourite time. It always was. Dawn brought Jovan home.

Taking a deep breath Ilona reaches into the pocket of her robe and draws out a letter.

It is Diana's last letter, dictated days before she died.

Ilona smooths the wrinkled pages with her gnarled hands, hands of time. Hands of life.

Diana's words all the way from Austria, scribed by her assistant Oskar, leap from the page.

"I am old and I am tired. I have made my peace with what we did. My time has come. Yours has not.

"Tell her the truth."

A single, glistening tear slips from Ilona's eye as she rereads the words.

They cut her soul.

Because she lied. She lied to Misa.

Ilona's eyes close as her hands gently fold the page.

She told her dearest friend there was hope. That Diana had the records of the children they rescued from the Ustaše, that they were working together to reunite the families. She told her that Stephan and Hanna could be found. That somewhere out there, safely beneath the roof of a loving home, they grew strong and hale and happy. That they were just waiting to be revealed.

But she knew. Because Diana knew.

They would never find them.

In the first months of the new administration of Croatia, a knock sounded on Diana's door. Men in suits, an order from the new Government in hand. They wanted Diana's records of the children they had saved from the camps. Diana tried to argue, tried to explain the importance of those file-cards. But the men would not be swayed. They took the records, every single one.

And the records disappeared.

Even now, fifty-eight long years later, after Tito's decades of rule, multiple new Governments and the fall of Yugoslavia, Diana's cards of the lost children from the camps have never been recovered.

Were they misplaced? Stored in a dark Government cellar and forgotten? Or were they destroyed as part of clearing away a deep national shame?

Ilona doesn't know.

Those records, they were everything. They were the way home for hundreds of children. How many orphans could have been reunited with family? How many lives could have been healed?

Ilona made a choice. She never told Misa that the records were gone. Her friend was weary, pale, barely clinging to life. It was too much. Misa would not have survived it. So Ilona lied. And as Misa's strength returned, she maintained the lie. She pretended that she and Diana were continuing the work. That they were following leads. That they searched. She helped Misa in her own search too, never disclosing the truth.

That the whole time there was no trail to follow.

When the guilt became too much, Ilona confessed to Diana. The woman had been horrified. But she never revealed Ilona's secret.

She accepted her choice.

Ilona never confessed to anyone else. Not even Jovan.

Did she do that for Misa? To spare her friend the pain?

Or for herself? Because the weight of her failure was too much to bear?

Ilona doesn't know, and perhaps it no longer matters.

That time is long past. The war ended, a new war came, Misa passed on back to her children, and Ilona stayed.

Stayed long enough for Lina to return, long enough to hug Nadica again.

And her country is settled. It has the borders it strived for. It has its independence.

She isn't sure she cares about that.

But having her family safe beneath her roof?

That is everything.

Ilona pulls a second envelope from her pocket. This one is from Sara. She'd visited the month before and sat with Ilona for hours, her deft hand scratching charcoal across a sketchbook. And Ilona cast her mind back, back, back and described Misa's children.

Little Stephan with his wide eyes. Tiny Hanna and her determined pout. Radič and Misa reborn in them.

Finger slipping beneath the lip, Ilona coaxes a folded page from within.

It is thick paper, high quality, cream coloured.

An image drawn in black ink fills the page. A circular statue depicting children of various ages staring curiously out into the world. They look like they are playing. They look happy.

Ilona knows two of those faces, the faces of Stephan and Hanna.

It is Sara's petition to the government to erect a statue in memory of the children who suffered in the Ustaše camps. Sara says it will be a symbol of remembrance, honouring the past so they can come together in the future.

And it is beautiful.

Tears run freely as she looks down on the faces of two innocent children she loved like her own. Two sweet lives that deserved to be lived. Her greatest failure. Her deepest regret.

Ilona presses the sketch to her heart. "I hope I remembered them right."

She slips the picture back into her pocket and kneels down. The hard earth presses against her knees. Then her hands are in the soil, digging, digging, digging, handful after handful into Misa's grave. Soon she is deep enough; the natural erosion of the rains and winds won't reach this far. She slips the picture from her pocket and lays it in the dirt. "Back with your mama," she whispers on the winds. "Where you always belonged."

Her tears spot the earth as she slides the soil over the picture, Stephan and Hanna disappearing beneath. Rocking back on her heels, she turns her face to the sky. "Forgive me," she says to the heavens. "Hug each other for me."

A cloud drifts away from the sun, casting a bright beam of warmth down onto her face.

A laugh escapes her lips. "Thank you," she says.

Back in the house, Jovan is up making coffee in the džezva. His soft eyes find hers, a familiar frown of concern forming across his forehead. "Up early. Everything all right?"

"Da, da," Ilona says. "Just felt like a walk."

"Hmmm, and a bit of a dig in the dirt." He glances pointedly at the muddy patches on her nightgown and the dirt on her palms.

He has caught her out, but only love swells in her heart. "I can never get anything by you," she says crossing the room to press a kiss to his stubbly cheek.

"Misa?" he asks, turning to wrap his arm around her waist.

"Da, I had to tell her something."

Jovan's gaze finds hers. "Do you need to talk about it?"

"No. Thank you. It is between Misa and me."

He holds her eyes a moment, his pale irises catch the sun. Then he nods. A swift peck on her cheek and he releases his embrace, turning back to the kitchen.

"I was thinking pancakes—"

A loud scream pierces the still morning and a smile cracks over Ilona's face.

Nadica thumps down the stairs, her arms full of a wailing Ana-Misa. Her hair is awry, her face drawn and harried.

She has never looked more beautiful.

"Sorry, sorry," she says as she comes into the kitchen. "Ana isn't a morning person."

Her husband Jure appears on the stairs behind her, his appearance equally dishevelled and exhausted. It is hard being a parent. Ilona understands.

"Come, come," she says, stepping across the room. "Give me my great-granddaughter."

"You asked for it," Nadica says, palming her squalling toddler into Ilona's waiting arms.

Ilona turns Ana to face her. "Hello, sweetling," she says. Ana's screaming halts, and her large blue eyes stare into Ilona's face. "I have you," Ilona says.

"You can keep her," Nadica quips.

"I second that," Jure adds as he comes into the kitchen. He

already moves like he is at home. It has been so nice to have them visit. They could stay forever if they wanted to.

Lina appears from the room that used to be Misa's. A broad smile on her face she crosses to Ilona. "And how is my granddaughter this morning?"

"Cake!" Ana announces loudly, tears apparently forgotten.

Lina laughs. It warms Ilona's heart.

"Will pancakes do?" Jovan asks.

Ana sways in Ilona's arms, and then her head settles against Ilona's heart, her soft curls tickling her chin.

"Worn out already," Nadica says as her husband draws her close. They lean into each other, tired but happy. And everything falls into place in Ilona's mind.

This. This is all she has ever wanted. Not a career in nursing, not wealth. This.

And now, despite it all, as old as she is, it has come.

"What time are Maja and Kata arriving?" Nadica asks, breaking from Jure's embrace. "Are we making krofna?"

"If you like," Lina says.

"I'll get the flour."

Her family flow into the kitchen. "Wait, I haven't finished the pancakes," Jovan says.

"The krofna won't make itself," Nadica teases.

"There is enough flour for both," Lina chides.

And Ilona smiles.

She hopes that Sara's petition is successful, that the government agrees to commission her statue. That Stephan and Hanna are immortalised in bronze, playing with the other children, happy and smiling. As they should always have been.

It will happen, or it won't. Ilona understands there is nothing she can do either way. But it's all right. Because she is here with her family, and Misa is in heaven with hers. They are all together in this life and the next. And there is peace in that acceptance.

Arms full of the soothing weight of Ana's body, she moves to the kitchen and joins her family.

A LETTER FROM THE AUTHOR

Thank you, from the bottom of my heart, for reading *The Children of Zagreb*. Because of its intense subject matter, this novel is very special to me, and I hope you were drawn into Ilona, Misa and Nadica's journey. If you want to join other readers in hearing all about my new releases and bonus content, you can sign up for my newsletter!

www.stormpublishing.co/lelita-baldock

And for more information about all new releases and bonus content, you can sign up here:

www.lelitabaldock.com/writing-newsletter

If you enjoyed this book and could spare a few moments to leave a review that would be hugely appreciated. Even a short review can make all the difference in encouraging a reader to discover my books for the first time. Thank you so much!

From the moment I learnt of Diana Budisavljević and her work to save the Serb children from camps across Croatia, I knew this was a story that must be told. It took me on a complex and emotional ride through the history of the Balkans. I hope I have gone some way towards sharing this tumultuous but also liberating part of history with you all.

Thank you again for being part of this amazing journey with me, and I hope you'll stay in touch – I have so many more stories and ideas I hope to share with you all.

KEEP IN TOUCH WITH THE AUTHOR

www.lelitabaldock.com

instagram.com/lelitabaldockwrites
facebook.com/lelitabaldockwrites

ACKNOWLEDGMENTS

The history behind *The Children of Zagreb* is complex and challenging. When I first read about Diana Budisavljević and the Red Cross nurses who worked against the odds to save children during World War Two, I knew there was no other story I wanted to write more.

That began the research into a harrowing tale of pain. But in the trauma there can be moments of lightness. Survivor stories portray these glimmers of hope. Through it all what is most important is that we remember – and never allow such events to be repeated.

Thank you to my talented and supportive editor at Storm, Kate Gilby-Smith. You gave me the confidence to pursue this story and helped me to shape this novel into something of which I am especially proud.

To my friends and family, thank you for the distractions, the good times and the hugs.

To my wonderful husband Ryan and our Jazzy-pud, you know I could not do this without your love and support. Thank you for being by my side and for always ensuring that I remember the lightness.

And to everyone who has read this novel, thank you for trusting me with your time and your hearts. I hope the novel proved worthy.

Sincerely,
Lelita